HOMEROOMS & HALL PASSES

By TOM O'DONNELL

Balzer + Bray
An Imprint of HarperCollins*Publishers*

Also by Tom O'Donnell

∽

Homerooms and Hall Passes: Heroes Level Up

THE HAMSTERSAURUS REX SERIES

Hamstersaurus Rex

Hamstersaurus Rex vs. Squirrel Kong

Hamstersaurus Rex Gets Crushed

Hamstersaurus Rex vs. Cutepocalypse

Balzer + Bray is an imprint of HarperCollins Publishers.

Homerooms & Hall Passes
Text copyright © 2019 by Tom O'Donnell
Illustrations copyright © 2019 by Stephen Gilpin
Map art copyright © 2019 by Jordan Saia
All rights reserved. Printed in the United States of America.
No part of this book may be used or reproduced in any manner whatsoever without written permission except in the case of brief quotations embodied in critical articles and reviews. For information address HarperCollins Children's Books, a division of HarperCollins Publishers, 195 Broadway, New York, NY 10007.
www.harpercollinschildrens.com

ISBN 978-0-06-287215-9

Typography by Dana Fritts
20 21 22 23 24   PC/BRR   10 9 8 7 6 5 4 3 2 1
❖
First paperback edition, 2020

For Suzanna and Rudy

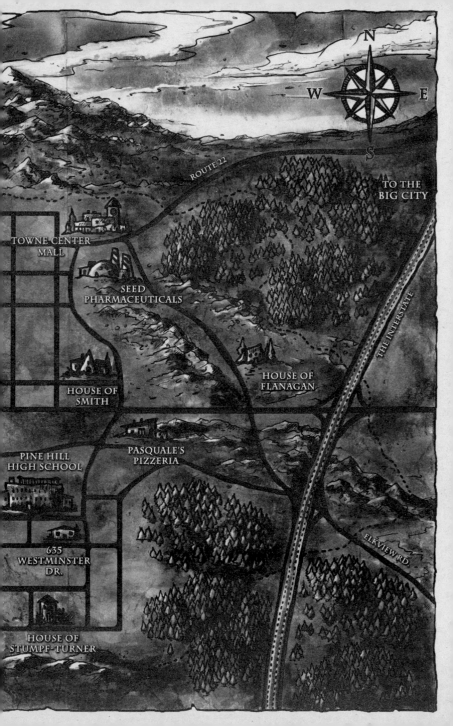

STINKY

LEVEL: 8

PLAYER NAME: Devis

CLASS: Class Clown

ATTRIBUTES: Cunning: 18, Intelligence: 10, Likability: 14, Willpower: 8, Fitness: 12

SKILLS: Apple Polishing –8, Computer +4, Deception +8, Note Passing +9, Stealth +6, Persuasion +7, Practical Jokes +9, Standardized Testing –3, Trivia (British Sketch Comedy) +9

EQUIPMENT: Smartphone, fake vomit, pocket tacos (x4)

CLASS CLOWN

VALERIE STUMPF-TURNER

LEVEL: 8

PLAYER NAME: Vela the Valiant

CLASS: Overachiever

ATTRIBUTES: Cunning: 12, Intelligence: 15, Likability: 16, Willpower: 17, Fitness: 15

SKILLS: Academic Subject (English) +5, Academic Subject (Science) +5, Academic Subject (Social Studies) +5, Academic Subject (Math) +5, Apple Polishing +9, Athletics +5, Computer +5, Musical Instrument (Flute) +5, Standardized Testing +6

EQUIPMENT: Flute, perfect attendance award, spare transcript

OVERACHIEVER

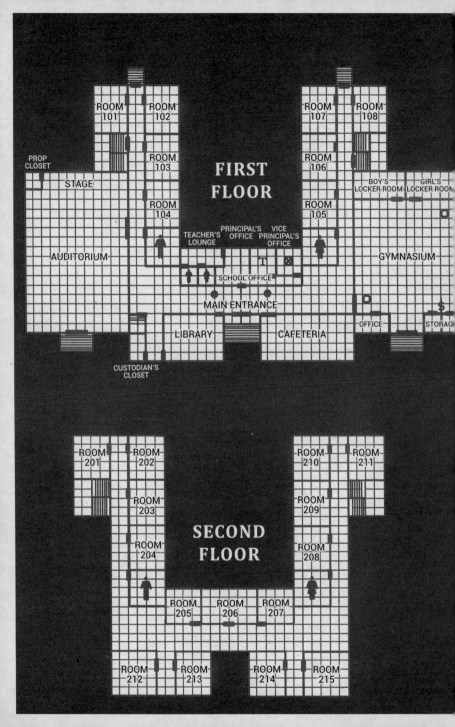

JAMES ALEXANDER DEWAR MIDDLE SCHOOL

LEGEND

▯	DOOR	▦	STAIRS
▯	LOCKED DOOR	⊠	PIT
$	SECRET DOOR	◯	STATUE
●	COLUMN	T	TRAP

□ = 10 FT. X 10 FT.

ROOM B4
ROOM B3
ROOM B2
ROOM B1

BASEMENT

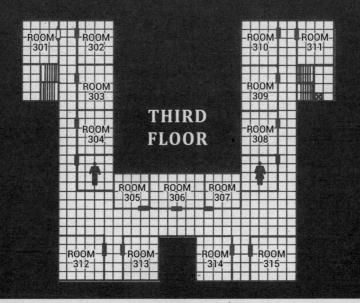

ROOM 301 ROOM 302
ROOM 303
ROOM 304

ROOM 310 ROOM 311
ROOM 309
ROOM 308

THIRD FLOOR

ROOM 305 ROOM 306 ROOM 307

ROOM 312 ROOM 313   ROOM 314 ROOM 315

Chapter 1

Welcome to Homerooms & Hall Passes, the role-playing game of nonadventure! With this book (and a set of dice), you and your friends will unlock a strange new world of routine and boredom set in the fictional Realm of Suburbia. Imagine, if you will, a place without monsters, magic, treasure, elves, quests, or even, to be perfectly honest, much excitement at all. This place is called middle school. . . .

—*Excerpt from* The Hall Master's Guide

FOUR YOUNG ADVENTURERS STOOD at the entrance of an ancient temple, carved into the cliffside. The weathered stone portico resembled the yawning maw of some huge predator. Beyond it, a stairway led down into blackness.

"Gee, I wonder if this is the place," said Devis, the thief.

"Bah! Of course it is, tiny friend!" said Thromdurr, the barbarian, cuffing Devis on the back. "The gate to the Temple of Azathor is known to have the shape of a great and toothy beast! Like so!"

"Yeah, no, this is *obviously* the evil temple. I was being witty," said Devis. "Sometimes I feel like nobody in this adventuring party *gets* me."

"You can explain the joke at length later, and I'm sure we'll all laugh and laugh," said Vela the Valiant, paladin and leader of the band. "But first, the evil that lies beyond that gate must be vanquished!" She drew her longsword and pointed it skyward, perhaps holding the hero pose a moment too long.

"You know, my old party had a bard," said Devis. "That guy loved my one-liners. And he was a professional entertainer, so he knew real talent—"

"Companions, are we prepared?" said Vela, sheathing her blade and cutting him off. "Rope? Rations? Ammunition for ranged weapons? Thromdurr, you were injured in the bandit ambush. You should drink a healing potion."

"'Tis but a scratch," said Thromdurr, indicating the gaping wound across his back.

"Drink one," said Vela.

Thromdurr did. His wound instantly closed.

"Oh, and we must make sure to bring enough extra

torches for this dungeon," said Vela. "Can't ever have too many torches."

Beside her, a shadowy elf in a black cloak seemed to melt out of the underbrush.

"No need," said Sorrowshade, the assassin. "The inky darkness is a gloom elf's home. I have night vision."

"Yes, and that's very well and good for you," said Vela, "but the rest of us are humans. We can't see in the dark."

"Yeah, well, I'm not carrying any torches," said Sorrowshade, crossing her arms.

"Uh, if Sorrowshade doesn't have to carry torches, then I'm not doing it either," said Devis.

"Again," said Vela with a sigh, "we won't be able to see."

"Not my problem that mortals have such *poor eyesight*," said Sorrowshade.

"Our eyesight is normal!" said Vela. "You just happen to have really good eyesight. Do you see the distinction?"

"She's right, though. Torches are lame," said Devis. "Man, if Albiorix was here, he could just cast a light spell. *Zorp!*"

Sorrowshade gave a faraway look. "If only such a spell could brighten the darkness . . . *of my soul.*" She turned away and dramatically threw up the cowl of her cloak.

"Uh-huh," said Vela. "Well, regardless, Albiorix *isn't* here. He's training with the Archmage today. So with regard to subterranean illumination, we'll just have to make do without him."

"Look, Thromdurr is the strongest, right?" said Devis.

"There can be no doubt," said Thromdurr.

"So how about the big guy just carries a bunch of torches in case we need them?" said Devis.

"Bah! I am no simple torch boy!" said Thromdurr. "I am a berserker of Sky Bear clan!"

"Fine, fine," said Vela. "*I'll* carry the extra torches. I swore a sacred oath. It is a paladin's duty to shoulder the burden when the weak falter."

"Weak? *Weak?*" said Thromdurr. "Give me all the torches! Their puny weight is nothing to me! Pile them on my back! Strap them to my meaty haunches! The more torches, the better!"

"Great idea, big guy," said Devis. "Glad you thought of it."

"Into darkness, then?" said Sorrowshade.

And so the four adventurers delved deep into the lost Temple of Azathor, facing abundant perils along the way: They defeated a bloodthirsty band of goblins, disarmed a fiendishly clever poison-dart trap, and discerned the answer to an ancient riddle that opened a magical door (the answer was "Love"). Many extra torches were burned as they made their way to the heart of the vile temple, far beneath the surface world. There they came to a grand hall of fallen columns and piled bones. Sickly green light lit the way ahead. The party doused their flames.

"Look," whispered Sorrowshade.

On a crumbling altar, a skeleton in tattered robes crouched over a glowing sigil and muttered incantations from a large leather-bound tome.

"Unless I am mistaken, that is the warlock Zazirak, back from the dead!" said Vela. "In life they called him the Scourge of Ta'shinn, the Blight of the Shield Coast, and the Slayer of Hotus the Good!"

"And now he's a skeleton guy," said Devis, drawing his dagger, "which is even worse!"

"We need a strategy," said Vela. "Sorrowshade, you hide behind the fourth column to the right and hit him with a barrage of poison arrows, while I approach from the southwest, flanking him as I brandish my Holy Symbol. This should give Devis enough time to creep up from behind for a sneak attack, while Thromdurr—"

"I WILL CRUSH YOU, BONE FACE!" bellowed Thromdurr as he sprang over a pile of rubble and charged at Zazirak, swinging his war hammer.

"Or, yeah . . . we could just do that?" said Sorrowshade.

"Stupid skin bags," hissed Zazirak as he turned. "You dare interrupt the summoning ritual of Azathor the Devourer!"

"We dare indeed, foul wight!" said Vela, drawing her sword.

"Then I am happy to offer four 'heroes' as a blood sacrifice to the great mole-headed demon himself!" said Zazirak. "Arise, my minions! *Alako nav navaavk!*"

With a flash of green light, the piles of bones around the room shuddered and leaped to their feet. They were now animate skeletal warriors, clad in rotting armor, carrying broken weapons.

"Excuse me, did you say '*mole*-headed demon'? As in, lives in the ground and eats earthworms?" said Sorrowshade as she popped out from behind the fifth column to the left and—*thwip!*—deftly lodged an arrow in Zazirak's skull.

Zazirak staggered and gave a hollow laugh. "Ha! Don't you know I am immune to poison damage?" He yanked the arrow out of his head. "And yes, according to the Malonomicon, Azathor the Devourer shall take the form of 'a great and terrible beast with the face of a fearsome mole'!"

"That's kind of dumb, isn't it?" said Devis. He ducked a blow from the rusty axe of a skeletal warrior. "Doesn't sound scary."

"Is too scary!" said Zazirak. He hurled a green bolt of eldritch magic at Vela, who blocked it with her shield. "Your ignorance astounds. How could you not know Azathor has a mole head? What did you *think* the entrance of this temple was carved to look like?"

"I THOUGHT IT WAS A DOG!" screamed Thromdurr as he bashed one of the skeletal warriors to bits with his hammer. "OR PERHAPS A BADGEEERRRR!" With a flying leap, he tackled two more off their bony feet.

"Idiots!" cried Zazirak. "It is the visage of Azathor the Devourer, a demon of untold power who will consume this world at my command!"

"Not if I can help it!" said Vela, holding up a gleaming sun-shaped emblem. "By all that is good and righteous, I call upon the Powers of Light and rebuke you, fiend!"

Zazirak hissed and turned away. His shambling skeletal minions staggered and crumbled back to bones.

"AND I ALSO REBUKE YOU!" said Thromdurr. "WITH MY BIG HAMMER!"

The barbarian leaped forward and smashed the undead warlock. Zazirak flew across the room, hit a wall, and crumpled to the floor.

There was an instant of silence. Then Zazirak cackled. "Fools. Death means nothing to one such as I. With the Malonomicon, I cannot be defeated!"

"Uh, you mean this?" said Devis. He held up the warlock's spellbook. Somehow, in the chaos of the fight, the thief had nabbed it.

"Give the book to me!" said Zazirak, rising. His bony hands began to glow with arcane flame. "OR . . . YOU . . . SHALL—"

"Burn?" said Sorrowshade as she stepped out from behind a scary mole statue and held a lit torch to the edge of Zazirak's robe. With a whoosh, the undead warlock went up like dry kindling.

"Okay, fine. Maybe torches were a good idea," said Sorrowshade.

"Guh," said Devis, burying his face in his sleeve. "That burned-warlock smell is *pungent*."

"Another foe bested! Another dungeon delved! Victory is ours!" said Thromdurr. "Where is the treasure?"

"Rest in peace, Hotus the Good," said Vela, bowing her head. "At long last, your death has been aveng—"

"Aw man, he only had thirty-five gold pieces," said Devis as he rifled through Zazirak's charred remains. "Plus what looks like a Ring of Turtle Speech. Anybody want a Ring of Turtle Speech? Lets you talk to turtles."

The other adventurers shook their heads.

"Man, why did he even have that?" said Devis, who pocketed the ring. "Guess I can try to sell it. Maybe somebody will want it."

"Good luck with that," said Sorrowshade.

"I suppose we should destroy his spellbook too," said

Vela. "It seems pretty evil." With two fingers, she picked up the tome that Zazirak had called the Malonomicon and dropped it into her pack.

"Ugh. I thought this temple was supposed to be stacked with untold riches," said Sorrowshade, looking around. "That troll lied to us. Typical."

"Now that's just prejudiced, Sorrowshade," said Vela. "Besides, we don't do this for treasure. I mean, we *did* stop an undead warlock from summoning an ancient demon to destroy the world."

"Yeah? And what's so great about *the world*?" said Sorrowshade.

"Treasureless dungeons are very frustrating to me!" said Thromdurr. "They intensify the . . . empty feeling I get when a quest is done. Does anyone else have this feeling?"

The other adventurers shook their heads.

"Well, I for one hope we are ambushed by murderous bandits again on the way back to town," said Thromdurr, "to enliven my spirits!"

"Then let us return to Pighaven," said Vela. She started to turn.

"Hang on just a minute, folks," said Devis. "What have we here?"

The thief had been quietly chipping away at the wall behind the altar with his dagger. Long ago, plaster had been cunningly spread over the mortar to conceal a seam. What he had uncovered was a distinctly door-shaped outline.

"It is a secret door!" said Thromdurr. "How can you not see it, tiny friend?"

"My question was rhetorical," said Devis. The thief slipped his fingers into the crack and felt around for a moment. Then he smiled. There was a click and then a low rumble as the door slid aside. Beyond it lay a vault that somehow seemed far older than the rest of the temple. It was piled high with gold, silver, gemstones, and bejeweled weapons of impeccable craftsmanship. The adventurers' eyes grew wide. Some of the heroes may have even started to salivate.

"I want the battle axe!" said Thromdurr.

"That ruby is mine!" said Devis.

"Dibs on that shield!" said Vela.

"I thought we didn't do it for treasure," said Sorrowshade. "And before you go putting your greasy mitts on any of that loot, we might want to figure out what that says first."

She pointed to series of jagged runes that were carved into the doorjamb.

"Hmm. Looks like Old Dragonian," said Vela. "Can anybody read it?"

"I speak Orc," said Thromdurr.

"I've got Elvish and Shadownese," said Sorrowshade.

"It's probably not important," said Devis. "Anyway, I think we're going to need some hirelings to clear this place out. That gilded throne has got to be worth a fortune. Luckily I know a guy who flips thrones."

"Devis, those runes almost certainly describe a terrible curse of some sort," said Vela.

"You don't know that!" said Devis. "It could say 'Great job!' or 'Enjoy the free treasure!'"

"Nobody touch anything inside the vault," said Vela.

Thromdurr shook his head. "The empty feeling grows."

"This dungeon is the worst," said Sorrowshade, pulling up her cowl.

"Can we vote?" said Devis. "How about we vote? I vote in favor of us being rich. And anyway, what's so bad about being cursed? We've all been cursed before. Sorrowshade, remember when that evil shaman turned you into a porcupine? We laugh about that now!"

"I don't laugh about that," said Sorrowshade. "Or anything."

"I tell you what, Devis, I think Albiorix can read Old Dragonian," said Vela. "Perhaps he can translate the runes. If, by some small chance, it turns out *not* to be a curse, we can return to claim the treasure."

She unfurled a blank scroll and made a quick rubbing of the inscription with charcoal.

"By then this whole place will be cleared out by goblins," said Devis. "Can I at least take the ruby? Then it's just me getting cursed. I don't mind."

"No," said Vela.

"There are always more dungeons, tiny friend," said Thromdurr. "Come. Let us away."

And so the four brave adventurers left the lost Temple of Azathor and began their journey home, though Devis the thief did lag behind the others.

Albiorix arrived at the Wyvern's Wrist tavern—the only inn in the tiny hamlet of Pighaven. He was tired and sweaty from carrying a heavy satchel of books for several miles. If Albiorix had been a more powerful wizard, he could have cast a levitation spell on his bag to ease his burden, or perhaps even teleported himself right to the doorstep of the inn, appearing in a puff of impressively colored magical smoke. But the mystical arts take decades to master, and at age thirteen, Albiorix was still a mere apprentice to the Archmage Velaxis. While his friends had gone off to explore the lost Temple of Azathor, Velaxis had made him practice the ward of protection spell over and over again on a sack of grain, until his magicking hand hurt.

As Albiorix stepped inside, he saw the owner of the

Wyvern's Wrist standing behind the bar, polishing flagons.

"Well met . . . er, I mean, hi," said Albiorix with an awkward bow.

She gave him a tight nod. "I cleared out the back room for ye, lad. As always, yer wee friends can stay as long as you're payin' for snacks."

"Excellent!" said Albiorix, perusing the menu. "They should be here any minute, so how about a large bowl of honey-roasted mallorn nuts, two orders of sour cream and onion lembas, and a trencher of cheese dip?"

Albiorix plunked down a few silver pieces, and the inn-keeper pocketed the coins. As he crossed the inn's common room, a mysterious stranger with an eye patch beckoned him over. "Lo there. You have a brave and hardy look about you, lad. Be you an adventurer?"

"Well, that's very flattering about my look," said Albiorix, trying to politely head him off. "Indeed I am an adventurer, but right now I'm actually—"

"Recently I have come into possession of an ancient map," said the one-eyed man, glancing around the tavern for spies. "A map that shows the precise location of the Caves of Thunderbeard. For a cut of the coin I could show you the way. . . ."

"Caves of Thunderbeard. Wow. That sounds very, very

exciting," said Albiorix. "But I really can't take on any quests at the moment. You see, it's Homerooms & Hall Passes night!"

"Hmm," said the one-eyed man with a scowl. "Can I play?"

"Ooh. The group is actually all full at the moment," said Albiorix. "But I can let you know if we ever have an opening."

The one-eyed man spat on the floor.

"Sorry," said Albiorix as he ducked past a dwarven princess hoping to hire a party to restore her to her rightful throne.

"Er, maybe the town guard can help?" he said to a simple farmer who needed help investigating the peculiar exsanguination of several of his pigs.

Just as Albiorix entered the private back room, a travel-worn merchant burst into the tavern.

"My caravan was attacked by ogres!" cried the merchant. "I'd offer a pretty reward to any brave souls who could recover my shipment of rare salves and ointments from the East!"

"Not today," said Albiorix under his breath as he quietly closed the door behind him. He stood in a small room with four chairs and a table. The group had a standing reservation at the Wyvern's Wrist—every Thursday from seven to ten. Albiorix plopped his satchel on a chair and breathed a sigh of relief. Homerooms & Hall Passes night was his favorite night of the week.

Albiorix began to carefully unpack his gaming supplies: an intricately detailed map of J. A. Dewar Middle School, dozens of miniatures lovingly painted to look like students and teachers, a Hall Master's screen that blocked his secret notes from the prying eyes of players, and of course a multi-colored mountain of dice.

Though none knew who had created it, Homerooms & Hall Passes was an enormously popular game in the Realm of Bríandalör. Some played the game to win (though that wasn't *really* the point). Others saw it as a chance to socialize with friends while eating piles of unhealthy snacks. Many enjoyed playing an H&H character who was vastly different from themselves, while just as many opted to play ones who represented themselves exactly. The basic appeal of the game was that it allowed the players to inhabit—if only in their collective imagination—a strange fantasy world that bore only a passing resemblance to reality. Though personally, Albiorix played it to relax.

Quests were great, really they were. And perhaps tomorrow, he and the party would take that one-eyed man up on his map. Or maybe they'd help the dwarven princess? The pig exsanguinations seemed a little beneath them, but they could probably knock that one out in an afternoon, so why not? Thwarting evil. Righting wrongs. Closing infernal gates opened by demented cultists. It was very important work. But it was stressful.

Albiorix sometimes woke up in a cold sweat, thinking he'd been smashed to goo by a hill giant, incinerated by a dragon, or even taken deathly ill from a run-of-the-mill giant rat bite. Despite the fact that he was training to become a wizard, he secretly wondered if he was really cut out for the hero's life. His friends all seemed to thrive on nearly being killed on a daily basis. If Albiorix was being honest, deep down, he craved order, predictability, and safety. That might make him a mediocre adventurer, but it made him a perfect Hall Master.

In Homerooms & Hall Passes, the players embodied "middle-school students," but the Hall Master was in charge of basically everything else. It was Albiorix's job to plan ahead, set the scene, arbitrate the rules, and most import- ant, make sure everyone was having fun. He'd spend hours every week drawing up maps, planning out challenges, and poring over the countless H&H sourcebooks that filled his satchel.

The module he was currently running was called *The Semester of Stultification*. In tonight's game, the play- ers would face a daunting series of challenges: a grueling five-paragraph essay dumped on their characters right at the beginning of JADMS Spirit Week. Not to mention an upcoming earth sciences quiz, a concert band recital, a class election, and a big algebra test. To rise to these challenges would take skill, cunning, impeccable time management, and of course a few lucky rolls of the dice. Albiorix chuckled maniacally to himself.

Just then Vela, Thromdurr, Sorrowshade, and Devis burst through the door, talking loudly among themselves.

". . . and that's why I'll never wear a baldric again," said Devis.

"Makes sense," said Vela.

"Hail, sorcerous friend Albiorix!" said Thromdurr, giving Albiorix a warm and painful hug. "I cannot wait for our game to begin!"

"Glad you're excited," said Albiorix. "How was the dungeon?"

"Ugh. Don't even ask," said Sorrowshade, shaking her head.

"We defeated the evil warlock Zazirak!" said Vela.

"Nice," said Albiorix.

"But the treasure was cursed," said Thromdurr.

"No, it wasn't," said Devis. "How was your day, Magic Man?"

"Oh, you know," said Albiorix. "Just spent it trapped in

a floating tower getting yelled at by a seven-hundred-year-old woman for not being able to bless grain fast enough."

"Take heart, Albiorix," said Vela. "I thought I would be a squire forever, but then, at the age of twelve, I was chosen by the Knights of the Golden Sun to become the youngest paladin in history. And it was all thanks to my extraordinary talent and dedication!"

"Uh-huh," said Albiorix.

"My point is, your apprenticeship will be over before you know it," said Vela.

"Sure. It ends when I'm eighteen. Only five more years," said Albiorix, putting his forehead gently into his palms. "I bet the time will just fly by."

"Wow. The Archmage Velaxis is seven hundred?" said Sorrowshade, grabbing a handful of mallorn nuts. "I can't imagine being that old. If I ever make it to five hundred, somebody shoot me with a crossbow."

"We will all be long dead by then, elf," said Thromdurr, dipping a lembas wafer in cheese.

"Oh, right. Humans," said Sorrowshade. "Sorry."

"So, are you guys ready to begin?" said Albiorix as he passed out the character sheets.

"Douglas, the 8th level Nerd, is ready," said Thromdurr, pounding the table. "Eager to use his superior intellect to crush the subject of earth sciences!"

"Glad to hear it," said Albiorix with a grin.

"Since Valerie is an 8th level Overachiever now, does that mean her intelligence attribute rating goes up?" asked Vela.

"Yeah, it should increase by one," said Albiorix, who didn't even have to consult *The Hall Master's Guide.* "Plus you gain the skill Standardized Testing."

"Excellent," said Vela, making a note on her character sheet.

"I notice you *still* haven't picked a real name for your character yet, Devis," said Albiorix.

"What? Stinky is a fantastic name," said Devis, who was making a little tower out of dice.

"Look, I know it's just a silly game, but I wish you'd take it a little more seriously," said Albiorix. "And could you at least fill in *something* for the background info section?"

"Fine, both of Stinky's parents are *also* called Stinky, and they're, uh, professional soup tasters," said Devis, scribbling it down. "Happy now?"

"Not really," said Albiorix. "And last but not least, we have Melissa the Loner." He handed Sorrowshade her character sheet.

"Uh, thanks," said Sorrowshade quietly. Normally Sorrowshade was always ready with a sarcastic retort, but she was almost shy when playing Homerooms & Hall Passes. Albiorix often wondered if she was having fun at all. But still, she showed up every week, so she must be getting something out of the game.

Albiorix cleared his throat. His companions fell silent. Showtime.

"When last we left off," said Albiorix, projecting his voice, "the students of J. A. Dewar Middle School were preparing for Spirit Week, a traditional festival when the children of Suburbia honor their schools with strange costumes and ritualistic displays of pride. It is a sunny October morning. You're all sitting in first-period English class, taught by Ms. Chapman, who is also your homeroom teacher. She begins to expound upon the subject of persuasive writing."

"Douglas the Nerd pays very close attention to the lesson," said Thromdurr. "He is very eager to master the subject of English and to use this knowledge to conquer his academic rivals!"

Albiorix checked his notes. "Well, Douglas is currently averaging an A-plus in English. The best in the class."

"None can defeat Douglas!" said Thromdurr, pounding the table and knocking over a couple of miniatures.

"Can I ask . . . what is Ms. Chapman wearing?" said Vela.

Albiorix rolled a handful of dice, noted the results, and consulted *The Hall Master's Guide* "Table 44f: Teacher's

Apparel. "Today Ms. Chapman is wearing a . . . tweed blazer and a seasonal turtleneck."

"Valerie would like to wait for an appropriate break in the lesson and compliment Ms. Chapman on her blazer," said Vela.

"Give me an Apple Polishing skill check," said Albiorix.

Vela rolled her dice and consulted her character sheet. "I got a 22!" she said. "Success!"

"Ms. Chapman beams. 'Why, thank you for noticing, Valerie. I bought it at Coat Ranch on Bowman Avenue. They were having a Columbus Day sale,'" said Albiorix, doing his trademark Ms. Chapman voice. "That successful faculty compliment will earn Valerie a +3 bonus on the next English assignment."

"Huzzah!" said Vela.

"Sorrowshade, is there anything you would like Melissa to do?" said Albiorix.

"I dunno," said Sorrowshade. "Just, uh, sit there quietly, I guess."

"Okay," said Albiorix. "Sounds good. No roll needed for that."

"While all this flattery is going on, Stinky is going to pass a note to one of the other kids," said Devis.

"Which one?" said Albiorix, indicating several miniatures placed on the map. "You can easily reach the four adjacent desks: Lucy Bennett, Dave Pittman, Deanna Fernandez, and Sharad Marwah."

"Uh, how about Dave Pittman?" said Devis.

"Sure," said Albiorix. "What does the note say?"

"Hmm. Hadn't thought that far ahead," said Devis. "The note says, uh, 'I think Deanna likes you.'"

"But this is not true!" said Thromdurr. "It is known throughout all of J. A. Dewar Middle School that Deanna Fernandez has a crush on Brent Sydlowski!"

"Yeah, I know that," said Devis.

"Highly dishonorable, Stinky," said Vela, shaking her head.

"Stinky does what Stinky wants," said Devis.

"Roll a Note Passing skill check," said Albiorix.

Devis did. "Oof," he said. "I got a 1."

"The note slips from your fingers and catches Ms. Chapman's eagle eye," said Albiorix. "'Stinky!' she yells. 'You bring that note up to the front of the class right now!'"

And so an amiable game of Homerooms & Hall Passes passed in this way as the brave heroes pretended to be "middle schoolers," and laughed, and ate snacks, and occasionally argued over the rules for longer than was necessary, until a bathroom break was called.

"Whew! That was a great relief!" said Thromdurr as he returned to the table.

"Okay, where were we?" said Albiorix, consulting his notes. "Ah, Douglas, Valerie, Stinky, and Melissa were waiting in the cafeteria line, attempting to decide between tacos and pizza."

"Wait, wait, before we start playing again," said Vela. "Albiorix, can you read Old Dragonian?"

"A little, sure," said Albiorix. "Why?"

"There was a horrid curse inscribed in the hidden treasure vault inside the Temple of Azathor," said Vela, "and I'd like to know what it was."

"Yeah, I'm morbidly curious too," said Sorrowshade.

"You're morbidly everything," said Devis. "I'm telling you: that treasure *wasn't* cursed."

Vela gently set aside Albiorix's miniatures and spread the rubbing she'd made of the runes over the big map of J. A. Dewar Middle School. Albiorix studied it.

"If I'm not mistaken," said Albiorix, "the inscription says something like . . . 'Woe to thee who loots this room. . . . Let thy respite be thy doom.'"

Vela whistled. Sorrowshade shook her head. Devis looked baffled.

"Ha! I was sorely tempted to take that battle axe," said Thromdurr. "Thank you for your caution, Vela. Verily it seems we dodged an arrow."

"Guys, that's not right," said Devis. "Not at all."

"How can you be so sure?" said Vela, squinting at the thief.

"Because!" said Devis. "I stole this!"

He plunked a doorknob-sized ruby onto the table. There was a moment of stunned silence as his companions stared at the jewel in horror.

"If that treasure horde was really cursed," said Devis, "then explain to me why nothing has—"

And in a puff of impressively colored magical smoke, the five young adventurers were gone.

Chapter

2

Unlike some other games you may have played—such as Gryphon Chess or Duck the Broadsword—Homerooms & Hall Passes isn't really about winning or losing. It's about confronting the daily challenges of middle school, exploring the delightfully banal Realm of Suburbia, and, of course, telling great stories with your friends! There are, however, numerous ways to utterly fail and be permanently eliminated from play. In game terms, this is called "Blowing It."

—*Excerpt from* The Hall Master's Guide

❧

". . . HAPPENED?" SAID DEVIS.

The adventurers blinked. They were no longer in the back room of the Wyvern's Wrist tavern in the hamlet of Pighaven. Instead they were somewhere . . . *else.*

"The question," said a woman in a hairnet standing

behind a glass sneeze guard, "was 'Pizza or tacos?'"

"Uhhhhhhh?" said Devis.

"Come on," said a kid behind them. "You're holding up the line."

"WHAT FOUL SORCERY IS THIS?" cried Thromdurr, leaping atop a rolling silverware cart.

"Dude, don't put your feet in the forks," said someone else.

"What's wrong with Schiller?" said another.

"That's Doug the Dork for you," said a third with a snicker.

"Uhhhhhhh," continued Devis.

"Where *are* we?" asked Vela, spinning around.

The party was surrounded, standing in a long line of strangers roughly their own age. These people didn't look hostile, exactly. And they certainly didn't look Bríandalörian. They wore strange, brightly colored clothing. None were armed, and there was nary an elf or dwarf among them. They laughed and chatted among themselves, or stared, quietly transfixed, at glowing handheld rectangles. A few wore bandannas and eye patches that might possibly mark them as pirates.

"Oh, no," said Albiorix. "Oh, no no no no no."

"We're dead and this is one of the Thirteen Hells," hissed Sorrowshade, nocking an arrow. "Just look at the food!"

"Excuse me?" said the woman in the hairnet, crossing her arms.

"Uhhhhhhh," said Devis.

"I AM VERY CONFUSED AND THEREFORE ANGRY!" bellowed Thromdurr.

"Keep your calm, Thromdurr," said Vela. "Our only hope is to—"

"RAAAAAAAAGH!" cried Thromdurr, and he sprang off the cart and charged past the trays of congealing food, nearly knocking over a girl at the salad bar on his way out the door.

"We have to stop him!" said Albiorix.

Vela, Albiorix, and Sorrowshade dashed after the rogue barbarian.

"Uhhhhhhh, how about pizza?" said Devis.

"Pizza," said the woman in the hairnet, and she plunked a slice down on his tray.

Beyond the door there was a cavernous chamber filled with large tables, at which sat hundreds of children, all eating food off trays or out of brown bags. The ambient noise level made it almost too loud to think.

"We can't let Thromdurr hit anyone!" said Albiorix.

"That's the main thing he does," said Sorrowshade.

"BRAAAGHRAAAGH!" roared Thromdurr as he

27

barreled through the room. "GRRRRAAAAAGH!"

People were starting to stare. A severe-looking bald man stepped into Thromdurr's path, stopping the barbarian in his tracks. "Douglas Schiller," said the man, "knock it off. NOW!"

"STAND ASIDE, HAIRLESS ONE," said Thromdurr, "OR FACE MY WRATH!"

"Wrath? Hairless one?" said the bald man. "What on earth has gotten into you, son?"

"THE BATTLE RAGE OF THE GREAT SKY BEAR!" said Thromdurr.

"Uh, what do we do?" said Sorrowshade.

"No idea," said Albiorix.

"Apologies for my companion," said Vela, stepping between Thromdurr and the man. "He means you no harm. His senses are merely . . . overwhelmed by the strange sights and sounds of this realm."

"The cafeteria?" said the bald man. "Look, Douglas, I expect this sort of shenanigans from some of these other knuckleheads." He waved dismissively to the other kids around the room. "A kid like Garrett Palmer is probably going to end up in federal prison. But a straight-A student like you doesn't need to be acting out for attention—running around, screaming about flying bears to get a laugh. That's a road you don't want to start down, son. So consider this a warning."

"From now on, we shall keep the peace," said Vela. "Thank you for your clemency, wise one."

Thromdurr looked at Vela, then at the bald man. The barbarian gave a grunt and a nod. Vela bowed.

"Get up, Valerie. No need for all that," said the bald man. He scowled and shook his head. "It's this idiotic Dress Like a Pirate Day. Every year it encourages rampant mischief and foolishness. It undermines discipline. I'm going to speak to Principal Greene about eliminating it. There are other ways to show school spirit than by wearing a fake parrot on your shoulder and saying 'Arr.' Now finish your lunch and get back to class."

With that, the bald man turned and strode off through the cafeteria, scanning the premises for anything else out of the ordinary. For an instant, his steely gaze fell upon Albiorix, who quickly looked away. The bald man continued on.

"Who was that?" said Sorrowshade. "Some sort of petty tyrant?"

"Close," said Albiorix. "I'm pretty sure that was Vice Principal Myron Flanagan."

Vela, Sorrowshade, and Thromdurr turned to stare at him.

"From our Homerooms & Hall Passes game?" said Vela.

"Afraid so," said Albiorix. "We need to get to a place where we can talk quietly."

He looked around. "Ah, the table over by the flagpole! If I remember correctly, it's always empty because it wobbles."

The four of them sat down and stared at one another in dumbstruck silence. A moment later Devis plopped beside them, his tray piled high with food.

"Guys, this is going to sound crazy," said Devis, "but I'm pretty sure we've been magically transported inside our Homerooms & Hall Passes game." He unsheathed his dagger and started to slice open a pudding cup.

"Yes, Devis. Thanks to you," said Sorrowshade.

"Hey," said Devis. "Nothing happened when I stole the ruby. It wasn't until some *genius* decided it would be a great idea to read the evil curse out loud."

"You can't seriously try to pin this on me!" said Albiorix. "I didn't even go on the stupid quest."

"You're right," said Devis. "I'm thinking this is more Vela's fault."

"How dare you!" said Vela.

"Verily, it seems that I am the only one who bears no part of the blame," said Thromdurr, crossing his arms as he eyed his companions.

"What?" said Sorrowshade. "I was the one who *warned* you that there even was a curse in the first place! Remember?"

"Yeah, but you were so rude about it," said Devis. "Maybe

if you'd had a different tone, we would have taken you a little more seriously."

"Unbelievable!" said Sorrowshade, throwing her hands up. "You humans are so greedy and shortsighted and, I'm sorry, but you guys smell weird. Like bacon."

"See, that is the tone I'm talking about," said Devis, shaking his head. "The bard in my old party always used to say, 'Sometimes *how* you're communicating is just as important as *what* you're communi—'"

"I SMELL NOT LIKE BACON!" snarled Thromdurr.

"Guys, guys. Keep it down," said Albiorix. "We're making a scene. Again."

Indeed, the children at nearby tables were gawking at them. Albiorix gave an awkward thumbs-up and they looked away.

Vela took a deep breath. "Companions, we've been in dire situations before. Remember when we were trapped in the Mines of Ernath as they slowly filled with lava?"

"A fond memory," said Thromdurr, nodding.

"Or when that wicked cryomancer Val'ghul imprisoned our party in the Dimension of Mirrors?" said Vela.

"So many reflections of this handsome face," said Devis with a crooked smile.

"And we must not forget when the mighty Serpent of Transhoon swallowed our entire vessel, whole, as it crossed

31

the Sea of Vosk," said Vela. "We spent three whole days stuck in the beast's gut before we devised a way to make it puke us out."

"It would have happened faster if we'd only had some of that *pizza*," said Sorrowshade, crinkling her nose at the oily slice on Devis's tray.

"Eh, it's not so bad when you add a little of the special yellow sauce," said Devis. He squirted a line of mustard onto the slice and took a bite.

"My point is, it doesn't matter whose fault it is that we're here," said Vela. "Instead of casting blame, we must work together to find a way to get back to Bríandalör, back to the real world."

"I have an idea," said Thromdurr, brightening. "Albiorix can simply cast a spell to magically transport us home!"

They turned toward Albiorix.

"Uh, no, I can't," said Albiorix.

"But . . . you are a wizard," said Thromdurr.

"I'm an *apprentice* wizard," said Albiorix. "Teleportation is a very advanced spell."

The other adventurers frowned.

"Look, my skill set—bending the very fabric of reality by force of will—is maybe a *smidge* tougher to master than waving a sword around or breaking and entering," said Albiorix. "Besides, I, uh . . ." Albiorix quietly mumbled something and trailed off.

"You what?" said Vela.

"He said he forgot his spellbook!" said Sorrowshade.

"Wow, you have good hearing," said Albiorix.

"Albiorix, how could you possibly forget your spell-book?" said Sorrowshade. "That would be like me forgetting my arrows and assortment of deadly poisons."

"Or me forgetting my muscles!" said Thromdurr.

"Look, it was a long walk and I didn't have room in my bag for it with all the Homerooms & Hall Passes stuff, okay?" Albiorix held up his heavy satchel, practically bursting at the straps. "I have to cart around twenty-seven of these books, you know."

The other four adventurers stared at him now in naked disappointment.

"Yes, but Homerooms & Hall Passes is just a game, Albiorix," said Vela. "Perhaps in the future you could choose to carry twenty-six books to leave room for—"

"I know it's just a game! Of course I know that," said Albiorix. "Except now it's not a game, is it? It's real. Look over there."

He pointed to group of girls at another table, chatting conspiratorially among themselves.

"That's Deanna Fernandez, Mary Davis, and Chloe Forte," said Albiorix. "They're probably whispering about how much they love Brent Sydlowski." He nodded toward a handsome boy in a letterman jacket, chomping a taco. "It's all real."

"Bah!" said Thromdurr. "'Tis but a magical illusion devised by some long-dead magician to mock and anger us. This world is no more substantial than faerie fire! See?"

Thromdurr grabbed a fork from Devis's tray and stabbed it into his own arm. There was an instant of silence. Thromdurr gritted his teeth as a trickle of blood dripped down his biceps.

"Hmm. Perhaps a *tad* more substantial than faerie fire," said Thromdurr, as he yanked the fork out and handed it back to Devis.

"Nah, you can keep it," said Devis.

"And please stop doing stuff like that," said Albiorix. "You're acting like a barbarian from Bríandalör. You need to act like your character."

"Douglas, the 8th level Nerd?" said Thromdurr.

"Yes, because that's who everyone here thinks you are," said Albiorix. "Until we figure out a way out of this place, we all have to just be typical eighth graders at J. A. Dewar Middle School."

"Impossible," said Sorrowshade. "It's all good fun to play Homeroom & Hall Passes in the back of a tavern once a week. Note passing and pop quizzes. Very amusing. But the

Realm of Suburbia is a make-believe fantasy land. It bears precisely no resemblance to reality. They don't even have elves here. It's ridiculous."

"That reminds me," said Albiorix. "I'm afraid you need to, ahem, cover up your pointy ears."

Sorrowshade's eyes narrowed. "Albiorix, that is *incredibly* offensive," she said. "I have literally poisoned people for less."

"I'm sorry," said Albiorix. "I know it's not right. But no elves means no elves. You're Melissa the Loner here. You have to pass for human until we get back to Bríandalör."

Sorrowshade glowered. At last she sullenly tucked the tips of her ears into her hair. "I'm not sure how I'm going to achieve the bacon smell," she said.

"The curse said, 'Let thy respite be thy doom,'" said Albiorix. "I think the game itself is our punishment. So I'm guessing the rules of Homerooms & Hall Passes still apply."

"That makes sense," said Vela. "Those who devise ancient curses do seem to have a taste for cruel irony."

"You have to admire that," said Devis.

"No, I most certainly do not," said Vela.

"Well, as you all know," said Albiorix, "in Homerooms & Hall Passes, if you fail any school subject or you have more than three unexcused absences, your character has Blown It and you're eliminated from the game."

"Okay," said Devis. "But what does that mean for us? Do we die or disappear or what?"

"Perhaps our spirits join the Sky Bear in the Great Cave of Clouds?" said Thromdurr.

"Ew. I hope not," said Sorrowshade.

"I don't know what happens if we Blow It," said Albiorix. "But I really don't want to find out."

"The point is moot," said Vela. "Both hazards are easily avoidable. Prioritizing our studies is simply a matter of discipline, which I have in abundance, and truancy is already forbidden by the paladin's sacred code. We shall prevail, comrades."

Albiorix swallowed. "I hope so," he said, "because if anybody in this cafeteria happens to notice the weapons you're carrying are real, you're all going to be immediately expelled."

"Game over?" said Devis.

Albiorix nodded. Thromdurr regarded his war hammer. Vela unstrung her bow. Devis quietly sheathed his dagger as Vela clumsily hid her sword and shield behind her back.

And at that moment the students and teachers eating lunch around them seemed as menacing as any foul creature lurking in the depths of a Bríandalörian dungeon.

Chapter 3

As Hall Master, it is your responsibility to bring the environs of J. A. Dewar Middle School to life! You will describe the sights and sounds of Suburbia—from the dull fluorescent lighting to the interminable ticking of the classroom clock—to your players. It may feel silly at first, but when they encounter the denizens of Suburbia, instead of saying "Hail!" or "Well met, traveler," consider greeting them with a hearty "Yo!" or "Wazzzzup?"

—Excerpt from The Hall Master's Guide

❧

AND SO THE BOLD adventurers managed to sneak out of the JADMS cafeteria without anyone noticing they were violating Article Fourteen, Section K of the student handbook ("No weapons on school grounds"). Though as they made their way down the first-floor hallway, they encountered unforeseen trouble.

"Uh, don't you think you maybe overdid it a little for Dress Like a Pirate Day?" said a boy with a pinched face, leaning against his locker. "If you're too into something it's, like, not cool."

The party stopped.

"We beg safe passage, stranger," said Vela, who stood ahead of the others.

"Pretty sure that's Evan Cunningham," whispered Albiorix. "If I recall correctly, he's got an Intelligence of 6 but a Cunning of 19. Makes fun of people because he's desperate to gain social capital."

"Greetings, Evan Cunningham," said Vela. "We offer you *social capital*." She bowed her head and held both her hands out with palms upturned.

"Huh?" said Evan.

"Seriously, metal armor? Realistic weapons? I bet they all went to the same dumb costume shop," said a shorter boy, who had crept up behind them. "It's sad, is what it is."

"Who's that one and what is he blathering about?" whispered Sorrowshade to Albiorix.

"Hmm, that must to be Derrick Day. He's Evan's lackey. Very insecure, no capacity for independent thought," said Albiorix. "Anyway, I think our Bríandalörian clothing looks strange to them."

"Well, that's rich," said Sorrowshade, "considering everyone in this realm has the fashion sense of a nearsighted tropical bird. I mean, just look at the orange laces on Evan's shoes. Garish."

"What did you say about my shoelaces, Melissa?" said Evan.

Sorrowshade gritted her teeth. "Nothing. They are quite beautiful, Evan Cunningham. It is easy for me to stare directly at them."

"Why are you all even hanging out together?" said Evan. "A nerd, a goody-goody, a freak, and this little goofball?"

"Hi," said Devis.

"It doesn't make sense," said Evan. "And who's the new kid supposed to be?" He pointed to Albiorix.

Before Albiorix could say anything, Derrick piped up again. "Hey, speaking of doesn't make sense . . . what's with the big hammer, Dougie? It's Dress Like a *Pirate* Day, not Dress Like a *Stupid Construction Worker* Day."

The two boys snickered at what might generously be called "the joke." Thromdurr frowned.

"The name of my hammer is Boneshatter," said Thromdurr. "It belonged to my father and his father before him. When the Blood Elk clan ambushed my tribe at the Battle of Zealot's Gorge, Skaek Grimjaw used this very hammer to crush the Blood Elk chieftain's skull to a pulp. He won fame and glory, and his name became legend."

Derrick stared at Thromdurr, who stood a full head taller than him, for a long moment.

"Dude, can you even *believe* this dork?" said Derrick.

Evan burst out laughing. Thromdurr frowned. Albiorix grabbed the barbarian by the elbow, and the party traveled on.

"Well, those guys seemed nice," said Devis.

"This world is terrible," said Sorrowshade. "Unsurprising."

"Albiorix," said Thromdurr, gazing back longingly at the two boys, "at what point may I crush them?"

"Never," said Albiorix. "No crushing anybody here."

"Hmm," said Sorrowshade. "What's the word on discreet poisonings?"

"Sorrowshade!" said Vela.

"Afraid that's no good either," said Albiorix. "Typical eighth graders at J. A. Dewar Middle School definitely do *not* poison people. Aha! I think this is it."

The five of them ducked through a set of double doors and into an empty auditorium. They headed down the aisle and up onto the stage. Behind the curtain there was another door labeled Prop Closet.

"Okay, give me all your weapons," said Albiorix.

None of the other adventurers moved.

"Albiorix," said Vela, "I am aware we're trapped inside the make-believe world of the game and we're not allowed to have swords here, but . . ."

"But what?" said Albiorix.

"But what if we need them?" asked Vela, with a flash of panic in her eyes.

"You won't," said Albiorix. "People don't need weapons here."

"What if a giant monster attacks?" said Thromdurr. "Or even several smaller monsters?"

"They don't have monsters in this world," said Albiorix.

"So what do they kill for gold?" said Devis.

"Nothing," said Albiorix. "That's not really how their economy works. And in fact, youths like us aren't really expected to earn money. The children here are mostly financially dependent upon their parents."

"Pshaw. I left childhood behind the day my entire family was tragically eaten by minotaurs," said Sorrowshade, throwing up the cowl of her cloak.

"So what do the adults do to earn their living?" said Vela.

"You guys have been playing Homerooms & Hall Passes for two years and you don't know *any* of this stuff?" asked Albiorix, who was starting to feel as though he'd failed as Hall Master.

His companions looked back at him blankly.

"The books are, well . . . kind of boring," said Vela.

Albiorix was about to protest, but the reality was, he spent hours every week (frequently neglecting his actual wizarding duties) to prepare for their weekly H&H game. All his players were expected to do was show up.

"To earn money," said Albiorix, "most of the adults either go off and type on a computer all day, or perhaps they work at a chain restaurant."

By now the other adventurers were completely baffled.

"Who would want to eat a chain?" asked Thromdurr.

"I think I'd choose that over the stuff they serve in the cafeteria," said Sorrowshade.

"Ah, that reminds me!" said Devis. The thief pulled two more pizza slices out of his pocket—slices that no one had noticed him obtain—and started to eat.

"Anyway," said Albiorix, holding out his hands. "Your weapons?"

"So you mean for us to hide them inside this 'prop closet'?" said Vela.

Albiorix nodded and threw open the door. Beyond it was a small room filled nearly to the ceiling with mounds of random objects—lamps, fake skulls, and what appeared to be a two-person horse costume. In one corner there was a jumbled pile of stage weapons.

"Occasionally, a school play calls for something like

42

this," said Alboirix. He picked up a plastic Tommy gun. "But there isn't another one of those till the spring, so this should be a safe place to stow them until we can break the curse and get back home."

"Farewell, Boneshatter," said Thromdurr to his hammer, as he glanced around the room. "Rest well among these . . . colorful tights and realistic baby dolls."

With a sigh, Vela set her sword and shield on the pile. Devis removed the dagger on his belt, the dagger in his boot, the dagger he kept up his sleeve, and the other dagger he kept in his boot. Sorrowshade hesitated the longest. At last she dropped her bow and quiver, and she gave a shudder.

"I hope you know what you're doing, wizard," she said.

"I do!" said Albiorix. "I mean, I'm reasonably confident. Let's say eighty percent sure."

"Hey, don't you have anything to add to the weapon pile, Magic Man?" said Devis.

"Nope," said Albiorix, "all I've got is my trusty bag full of—hang on just a second!" Albiorix crouched on the floor and threw open his pack. A stack of twenty-seven Homerooms & Hall Passes sourcebooks practically burst out.

"Carrying that thing around *cannot* be good for your back," said Devis.

"Guys, this is amazing!" said Albiorix, his hands full of books. "*The Hall Master's Guide, The Cyclopedia of Students,*

The Tome of Teachers, The Complete Dictionary of Middle-School Slang! We might be stuck here, but we have all the information we could possibly want about this world. Right here at our fingertips."

"Perhaps next time you could leave *The Fulsome Folio of Foods* at home," said Vela, "which brings me to a somewhat delicate point: Albiorix, without access to your spellbook, are you capable of any magic? Do you have any spells, for lack of a better term, *memorized*?"

"Well, yes, of course. I am a fully trained apprentice wizard, after all," said Albiorix. "I can cast a simple light spell from memory!"

Albiorix's fingers began to trace an arcane pattern through the air. He had parted his lips to speak a mystical word of power when—

Devis flicked the prop closet light switch on. A bulb glowed brightly overhead.

"Eh, this whole world seems pretty well lit," said Devis. "Anything else?"

Albiorix blushed. "Absolutely," he said. "For example, I can do this!"

He reached toward Vela's ear, and suddenly a coin appeared in his fingers. There was a long silence from the other adventurers.

"Hmm," said Vela.

"I pulled this coin from a tiny pocket dimension that *I created with my mind*!" said Albiorix. "I'm also capable of limited acts of clairvoyance. For example, if you were to draw a playing card from a deck without letting me see it, I would likely be able to guess which card you—"

"Okay," said Devis, cutting him off. "So no *useful* magic without a spellbook. Great."

"Hang on," said Sorrowshade. "We *do* have a spellbook."

A musty stench filled the tiny room as Sorrowshade reached into Vela's pack and pulled out the Malonomicon.

"Ha! I had nearly forgotten about the undead warlock's tome!" said Thromdurr. "The answer to our predicament must lie within its yellowing pages. Well done, elf."

"No. *Not* well done, elf," said Vela, snatching the book back. "This thing is pure evil. Just look at the screaming faces on the cover! If Zazirak was using it to summon a world-ending demon, it is undoubtedly filled with forbidden rituals and foul magic. No good can come of dabbling with such dark forces."

"Personally," said Sorrowshade, "I think dark forces sometimes get a bad rap—"

"No," said Vela, in a tone the rest of the party knew meant she wouldn't give an inch. "Albiorix, is there some method by which we can permanently destroy this horrid grimoire?"

"Hmm," said Albiorix as he leafed through the pages of

45

The Manual of Middle-School Maintenance. "Yes! It looks like there's a heavy-duty paper shredder in the school office. We can wait until nobody's around and shove it right in."

"Then do that," said Vela.

She handed him the Malonomicon. Sorrowshade, Devis, and Thromdurr—whose collective morality was perhaps a bit more *flexible* than Vela's—shared a look.

"So if the evil spellbook is off the table, and Albiorix is totally useless—no offense," said Devis, "what's the plan for getting us home?"

Vela stroked her jaw. "Well, if this really is our H&H game, then perhaps if we can achieve the goals of our scenario, the curse will be broken."

"Good thinking!" said Albiorix, digging through his Homerooms & Hall Passes supplements once again. "This is the nonadventure I've been running for you guys."

He held up a thin book. On the cover was a lovingly detailed illustration of several middle-school students in rows of desks, staring back with glazed eyes at an unseen teacher. The title read *The Semester of Stultification: A Homerooms & Hall Passes Nonadventure for Level 8 Characters.*

"So how do we win it, Magicless Man?" said Devis.

Albiorix paused, hesitant to give up any of his precious

Hall Master secrets to his players. His companions stared at him.

"We could all *die*, Albiorix," said Sorrowshade.

"Right, no, I know that," said Albiorix. "Fine. Okay. I'll tell you guys how to win, although that certainly will suck some of the fun out of playing it once we return home and resume our—"

"Spill it, human!" said Sorrowshade.

Albiorix flipped to the final page of the book and read aloud: "'The goal of the scenario is for the players to finish their fall semester of eighth grade at J. A. Dewar Middle School without Blowing It.'"

"That's it?" said Vela.

"Er, not quite," said Albiorix. He continued to read. "'Players earn special distinction if they manage to achieve any of the following: getting elected class president; maintaining a 4.0 grade point average; becoming captain of a sports team; winning the eighth-grade creative writing contest; or making twenty new friends.'"

"These challenges are well within our ability!" said Vela, taking the character sheets from Albiorix's H&H pile and passing them out to the party. "Valerie the Overachiever has been class president the last two years in a row!"

"And Douglas the Nerd only receives A's, because his

mighty brain is without rival!" said Thromdurr, pounding his head as he took his character sheet.

"Twenty new friends will be a breeze," said Devis. "Everybody loves me!"

Only Sorrowshade shook her head. "You all really think it's going to be that simple? There's a reason they call it a *curse*," she said. "Need I remind you of how our last interpersonal interaction went? Our little chat with Evan Cunningham and Derrick Day?"

"Those two are jerks. Not at all representative of everyone in JADMS," said Albiorix. "But I am glad you brought it up. Evan might have an Intelligence of 6, but I think he was onto something. The social groupings of middle schoolers are, uh, kind of specific." He held up a book called *The Codex of Cliques*.

"What do you mean?" said Vela.

"Well, it would be a bit suspicious for us to be hanging out together all the time," said Albiorix. "A Nerd and an Overachiever, maybe. But not with a Class Clown and *especially* not with a Loner."

"So you're saying I should pretend the rest of you aren't my adventuring companions?" said Vela, her eyes narrowing. "That is awfully close to a lie, Albiorix."

A few of the other adventurers may have rolled their eyes

at this. As a noble paladin, Vela was strictly forbidden by her sacred oath from ever lying (even to orcs!). Needless to say, the issue had come up in past quests.

"No, no, it's not a lie," said Albiorix, trying to choose his words carefully, "We just maybe need to keep our interactions a little more discreet, so we don't draw any unwanted attention to ourselves. For the good of the group."

"Socializing is overrated, anyway," said Sorrowshade. "Happy to pretend like I hate all of you."

"Anybody else feel like she was a little too quick with that?" said Devis.

But before anyone could answer, the bell rang, marking the end of lunch.

"The Great Bell of Learning!" said Thromdurr. "Douglas the Nerd's heart leaps at the sound!"

"Okay, that means we have exactly four minutes to get to social studies class," said Albiorix. "That's room 207, Ms. Levy. And just to avoid suspicion, maybe we should . . . leave the auditorium separately." He glanced at Vela, not quite sure where this fell on the lying scale.

"Fine," said Vela, crossing her arms.

"Indeed," said Thromdurr.

"Love it," said Devis, who was now munching a taco he'd been keeping . . . *somewhere*.

49

They turned to Sorrowshade, but the gloom elf was nowhere to be seen. She had already disappeared into the shadows.

So one by one, they waited a suitable interval before exiting the darkened auditorium. Albiorix, the wizard, was last (mainly because it took him so long to get all of his Homerooms & Hall Passes books stuffed back into his pack.)

He exited and blinked for a moment in the bright fluorescent lighting of JADMS. Walking to class was a surreal experience for Albiorix, to say the least. Aside from the strangeness of seeing an impossible fantasy realm come to life, fictional characters he had previously only conceived of in his Hall Master's imagination were now passing him left and right. He saw Mr. Armstrong, the art teacher, frantically trying to blot a stain out of his tie. Nicole Davenport stood by the water fountain, lording over her clique of popular girls. And there was Mr. Driscoll, the custodian, mopping up a mess that was best left unnamed. Albiorix gasped as he walked past the school library: a huge room, full up to the ceiling with books. There were too many to even count. Such a collection would have been the pride of any wizard— any king—back in Bríandalör.

"Hold it right there," said a woman in a blue uniform and badge.

"Ms. Rhee, the school security guard!" Albiorix blurted out.

Ms. Rhee cocked her head. "Yeah . . . the question is: who exactly are you?"

There was a very long pause.

"Huh," said Albiorix at last. And for the first time it dawned on him: unlike his four companions, he had never had a character in their weekly Homerooms & Hall Passes game.

"Um, the Hall Master?" said Albiorix.

"You're going to have to do better than that," said Ms. Rhee. "Come with me."

And so Albiorix, apprentice wizard of Bríandalör, was escorted to the vice principal's office.

LEVY, Irene Joy

OCCUPATION: *Eighth-grade social studies teacher*

ATTRIBUTES: *Cunning: 11, Intelligence: 16, Likability: 13, Willpower: 14, Fitness: 8*

SKILLS: *Academic Subject (Social Studies) +8, Classroom Management +7, Computer +2, Cooking −3, Drive +7, Needlepoint +1, Public Speaking +3, Trivia (80s Hair Metal) +10*

BIOGRAPHY: *Ms. Levy is the longtime social studies teacher at JADMS who is known for her love of both early American history and her fifteen-year-old pug PRINCE WILBERT (see page 296 for game statistics).*

—Excerpt from The Tome of Teachers

O N AN UNCOMFORTABLE GREEN COUCH in the J. A. Dewar Middle School office, beneath a poster of a waterfall with the words "Inspire Leadership," sat Albiorix. Despite the sleepy atmosphere of the office, the wizard was panicking. There was a reason nobody in this world seemed to know who he was. Without a character, he didn't exist. And so he desperately paged through his collection of Homerooms & Hall Passes sourcebooks, attempting to come up with an identity and plausible backstory for himself before his meeting with Vice Principal Flanagan, which, according to the clock, was happening in less than seven minutes. Albiorix consulted Table 11c: Random Student Names. As discreetly as possible, he rolled a handful of dice for his first, then his last name.

"What are you doing?" said a girl sitting across from him, startling Albiorix.

"My name is Armando Boort!" said Albiorix. "And I am a foreign exchange student from Edmonton, Alberta, Canada!"

The girl blinked. ". . . Cool?" she said. "I went to Toronto once when I was eight."

"Toronto is the largest city in Canada, my home country!" said Albiorix.

"Okay," said the girl. "So you're new here too. My mom

got offered a job at Seed Pharmaceuticals. We just moved to Hibbettsfield from the city."

"Well then, er, welcome to our school," said Albiorix. "J. A. Dewar, a Great Place to Learn! Gooooo, Titans!"

The girl cocked her head. "You just said this is your first day."

"Right, yes, good point," said Albiorix, scrambling. "But, the thing is, I've already been filled with school spirit. Because it's Spirit Week. In fact, today is Dress Like a Pirate Day." He indicated his clothing.

"Yeah, I was definitely wondering about the robes. Felt rude to ask," said the girl. "But that *sort of* explains them."

The girl turned back to her phone. Albiorix swallowed. As he replayed their interaction in his mind a few times, it occurred to him that it wasn't exactly *not* suspicious.

"So, what are *you* doing?" said Albiorix.

"Oink Pop," said the girl, not looking up.

Albiorix was at a loss. "I certainly know what both of those words mean, but . . ."

"Oh. It's just a dumb game," said the girl. "You tickle these little pigs until they pop. What, they don't have it in Canada?"

"Exactly!" said Albiorix. "That's exactly it. It's so different there. You wouldn't even believe it."

"Huh," said the girl. "Are your hands greasy?"

Albiorix froze. He didn't know how to answer. Was having greasy hands a good thing here? Had he somehow just missed that detail in the books? At last he spoke. "I believe my hands have the appropriate amount of grease on them."

"Well, I hope that means no," said the girl. She handed Albiorix her phone. "Here. Try it."

"Er, okay," said Albiorix.

On the small glowing screen, a grid of adorable spherical pigs appeared. A timer clock started counting down as peppy, up-tempo music began to play. Albiorix tickled one of the little pigs with the tip of his finger. It started to giggle, then guffaw, then it burst like a balloon.

"I did it!" said Albiorix.

"Yeah, but you want to go for groups of three," said the girl. "That's how you get the Triple Tickle Bonus. Here, like this." The girl grabbed her phone back and expertly began to tickle the pigs. One after another, they laughed and popped. Her fingers danced across the surface of the phone, moving almost too quickly for Albiorix to follow. It occurred to him that if she wasn't fictional, and if people did magic here, then this girl might have made an excellent wizard herself. A friendly chime marked the end of the round.

"Wow, you're really good at that," said Albiorix.

"Ha, yeah, well, 39,730 is an embarrassing score. But that's because I let you play the first half of the round. No offense. I've made top ten on the national leaderboard seven times. I was even number one, twice," said the girl, before she seemed to catch herself. "I mean, it's just a dumb game. I guess being the best at tickling fake pigs until they pop isn't something to be proud of."

"No, it truly is," said Albiorix. "I can do this!" And before he really thought about it, he had reached into a pocket dimension beside her head and pulled out a coin, seemingly from thin air.

"Neat," said the girl. "But please don't lunge toward my ears again. I don't know you."

"Yes, you do," said Albiorix. "I am Armando Boort."

The girl laughed.

"What?" said Albiorix.

"Sorry, I really don't mean to be rude and please don't take this the wrong way," she said. "But that name almost sounds . . . made-up."

"Well, it's a very common name in Canada," said Albiorix, crossing his arms.

"I'll take your word for it," said the girl.

"Wait, what's your name?" said Albiorix, suddenly remembering that he'd forgotten to ask.

But before the girl could answer, Ms. Roland, the receptionist, interrupted. "The vice principal will see you now," she said to Albiorix.

"Okay," said Albiorix. He rose to follow Ms. Roland down a short hallway lined with doors. As he walked, he glanced back at the girl. She was already playing *Oink Pop* again.

Albiorix took a deep breath and tried to steady his nerves. This was a critical hurdle to get over. If he had no Homerooms & Hall Passes character, then he technically wasn't a student at JADMS. If he wasn't a student, then he wasn't allowed on school grounds (see Article Six: Section A of the student handbook). And if he wasn't allowed to come to school, then according to rules, that meant he would Blow It.

Ms. Roland led Albiorix to a sparsely decorated office dominated by a desk and an oversized national flag, topped with a furious-looking eagle. Sitting behind it was the scowling bald man from the cafeteria. He gestured to the chair across from him. Albiorix sat.

"So, who exactly are you?" said Vice Principal Flanagan.

"My name is Armando Boort," said Albiorix. "I am a foreign exchange student from Edmonton, Alberta, Canada."

"Uh-huh," said Flanagan. "Then why doesn't my office have *any* paperwork indicating that?"

"There must have been some sort of administrative mix-up," said Albiorix. "My school back in Edmonton,

Alberta, Canada, submitted everything. Maybe it hasn't arrived yet? Or perhaps the problem is on your end?"

"The problem is *not* on our end!" said Flanagan. "Without the proper documentation, you can't be here. To officially enroll at James Alexander Dewar Middle School, we need to see—"

"A reliable form of identification such as a birth certificate or passport," said Albiorix. In the waiting area, he'd made sure to memorize this section from *The Album of Academic Administration* that he had in his backpack.

"Correct," said Flanagan. "But do *not* interrupt me again, Armando."

"Sorry," said Albiorix. "The good news is that I can definitely get you the paperwork, which I definitely have. And in the meantime, perhaps I can keep going to school here—"

"Absolutely not," said Flanagan. "You enroll first, then you can have the privilege of learning at J. A. Dewar. Those are the rules."

Albiorix sighed heavily and shook his head. "Wow. This will mark an unfortunate break in my education, just because I moved to a new place," he said. "It's too bad. I was so very excited to learn about your country's impressive military history."

Vice Principal Flanagan shifted in his seat. "You know, my father was in the military," he said. "Great man. Heck of a disciplinarian. But his career meant we moved around a lot."

"Really?" said Albiorix. Though in truth, he already knew these biographical facts. He'd read them minutes earlier in the FLANAGAN, Myron James entry in *The Album of Academic Administration*.

"Yes," said Vice Principal Flanagan. "So, believe me, I know how tough these transitions can be on a young person." He drummed his fingers on his desk and looked out the window. "Look, Armando, I'm going to give you the benefit of the doubt and assume there has been a routine mistake somewhere along the line. I'll allow you to enroll in JADMS—"

"Oh, thank you, sir!" said Albiorix, leaping to his feet. "Gooooo, Titans!"

"I said don't interrupt me," said Flanagan. "You can enroll on a *temporary* basis, but unless I get those documents tomorrow, you're gone. Get it?"

Albiorix nodded.

"Don't make me regret this," said Flanagan. "Now get to class."

And so the wizard Albiorix rejoined his brave companions in the midst of their fourth-period social studies class, where the wise Ms. Levy taught them about early colonial history. But when Albiorix arrived, there was nowhere for him to sit. And thus Mr. Driscoll, the doughty custodian, brought another desk, which he managed to sort of wedge in, near the back. And all the while, the rest of the students in the class stared at Albiorix and it was awkward.

"Well, let me be the first to welcome you to our school, Armando," said Ms. Levy.

"Gooooo, Titans," said Albiorix.

"Sure," said Ms. Levy. "So, picking up where we left off . . . can anybody name one of the factors that made North America an attractive location for the European colonial powers?"

Thromdurr's hand shot up. Ms. Levy smiled.

"Yes, Douglas," said Ms. Levy.

"No monsters," said Thromdurr.

At this, the entire class burst out in laughter. Thromdurr looked around, confused.

"Douglas, I never took you for a comedian," said Ms. Levy, with a slight frown. "Perhaps it's best to leave the jokes to Stinky."

She pointed at Devis.

"Excuse me?" said Devis, leaping to his feet, indignant. "How dare you—oh, riiiight. Stinky. My name. That is what I'm called." He slowly sat back down.

"Now," said Ms. Levy, "does anybody have a *serious* answer to my question?"

The rest of the class passed much in this way: a deluge of nonsensical history and fictional place names that they were expected to remember. Occasionally, Thromdurr or Vela would attempt to answer a question posed by Ms. Levy and get it spectacularly wrong. ("No, Roger Williams did *not* found the colony of Rhode Island to honor the brave warrior spirits of his ancestors," "No, the thing Peter Minuit purchased from the Lenape tribe was *not* a magical scepter capable of transforming its bearer into a raven," etc.) Throughout the class Ms. Levy appeared progressively more concerned.

The bell rang, marking the end of fourth period and bringing sweet relief to the confused and beleaguered heroes. Yet the respite was all too brief. (Again, four minutes between classes, which is *barely* enough time to even get there!) And if anything, the next period was worse. At least ancient lore and odd-sounding place names were familiar to them. (Indeed, add an umlaut or two, and "Philadelphia" might well have been some long-forgotten kingdom in Bríandalör.)

But Ms. Snow's earth sciences class was utterly baffling. She seemed to be describing, in excruciating detail, *the process by which rocks were made*. In Bríandalör, rocks were made by the gods (specifically Cragnar, the god of rocks). Here, not so much, apparently. Toward the end of class, they took a quiz that Albiorix was certain they all failed. By the time they made it to their seventh and final period, their brains were nearly too scrambled to make papier-mâché heads for art class. Mr. Armstrong was still fairly encouraging of their middling efforts, and it seemed to the outlanders that in this strange place, success or failure in art might be more subjective.

At last the final bell rang, bringing an end to the school day at JADMS. Kids filed out of their classrooms and filled the halls. They laughed and talked as they headed toward their lockers on their way out the door. The weary party regrouped in a quiet alcove near the library, away from the prying eyes of any peers.

"So . . . *who* makes the rocks?" said Devis.

"I think . . . I think maybe it's other rocks?" said Vela, rubbing her temples.

"That makes no sense," said Devis. "What kind of sick mind dreamed up this place?"

Thromdurr appeared dazed. "Somehow I thought Douglas the Nerd would be . . . smarter?"

"Middle school is *truly* brutal," said Sorrowshade, "and I say this as someone whose entire family was eaten by mino-taurs."

"Our resolve must not flag," said Vela. "Though I admit this was the single *longest* day I can ever remember."

"Er, we actually got here at lunchtime," said Albiorix quietly. "A normal school day would be about four hours longer."

At this, the rest of the party groaned.

"How come playing Homerooms & Hall Passes is fun," said Devis, "but actually living it isn't?"

"Because when we play the game, we're only *pretending* to feel bored," said Sorrowshade. "That's an emotion we rarely have to endure in Bríandalör, thank the gods."

"The scenario ends when the semester is over," said Vela. "How long is that, Albiorix?"

"Two more months," said Albiorix, "give or take."

At this, the party was so demoralized they couldn't even bring themselves to groan. They merely stared at the wizard in shocked silence. At last Thromdurr shook himself all over, like some great, wet beast.

"Bah!" said Thromdurr. "If a task is easy, it is hardly worth doing. The purest joy in life is meeting great challenges head-on and bludgeoning them into submission. Otherwise the empty feeling returns. Mark my words: I will master earth sciences yet!"

"Yes, yes," said Vela. "That's the spirit!"

"Yeah, and the pizza with yellow sauce isn't bad," said Devis. "I can handle Suburbia for a couple of months."

"Glad to hear it, Devis," said Vela.

They all turned to Sorrowshade. The gloom elf shrugged.

"We're all stuck in this miserable place, so we don't really have a choice, do we?" said Sorrowshade. "Besides, happiness is an illusion."

"I'll take it," said Vela, patting the gloom elf on the back. "Albiorix, what say you?"

"Sure, social studies was soporific and earth sciences was utterly impenetrable, but I think my papier-mâché head turned out pretty good!" He held up a soggy, misshapen bust that looked more like a sick goblin than a person. "As far back as I can remember, I've spent all my free time reading *Homerooms & Hall Passes* books, to the detriment of many arguably more important things. If ever there was a place I was *meant* to understand, it is James Alexander Dewar Middle School. Trust me, friends. We can do this. We can break the curse. I'm ninety . . . no, ninety-five percent sure!"

"Huzzah!" said Vela.

"But before we go home," said Albiorix, "I'm afraid it's time for all of us to go home."

"Wait, we're going to split the party midadventure?" said Vela. In Bríandalör, this was only done in the most extreme of circumstances.

"Afraid so. It's two forty p.m. and school is out," said Albiorix. "See you all tomorrow. First bell is at seven thirty. Don't be tardy."

And so the brave Bríandalörian heroes went their separate ways, some on foot, others by bus, across the town of Hibbettsfield in the Realm of Suburbia to return to the most important people in their lives and meet them for the first time: their families.

Chapter 5

Though the school day should obviously remain the focus of play, it is important to remember that in Suburbia, school isn't everything. Optometrist appointments, long waits in grocery-store parking lots, flossing before bed—a creative Hall Master can turn such experiences into miniature nonadventures all their own!

—Excerpt from The Hall Master's Guide

❧

"WHAT ARE YOU *DOING* HERE?" cried the woman at 17 South Euclid Street.

"I have returned from J. A. Dewar Middle School," said Vela the Valiant, who was quite confused—this was the home address listed on her character sheet. Vela stopped herself from bowing. Nervous habit.

"Yes, I *know* that, Valerie," said the woman. "But *why*?"

"Because this is my home? And it is after two forty p.m.

on a weekday?" said Vela. "And you are, presumably, my . . . mother?"

"Is she sick?" said a man—Vela's father—who nudged past his wife in the doorjamb. "Are you sick, honey?"

"Not to my knowledge," said Vela. "Though I did come perilously close to a slice of cafeteria pizza today." She shuddered.

"We sent a lunch for you," said the woman, throwing up her hands. "You didn't eat your lunch?"

Before Vela could answer, the man pressed the back of his hand against Vela's forehead. "She feels hot, Marie!"

"Stop babying her, Andy," said the woman. She turned back to Vela. "Anything less than a fever of a hundred and four degrees, and you should be at band practice, Valerie. First-chair flute is a responsibility you *must take seriously*! There is a recital on Thursday."

"There is? I mean, I will," said Vela, suddenly ashamed she wasn't doing a thing she didn't know she was supposed to do. She quickly glanced at her character sheet. Sure enough, *Monday 3 to 4:40 p.m.—band practice* was scrawled on the back.

"Is this some sort of teenage rebellion?" said Marie to no one. "Where did I go wrong?"

"Perhaps," said Vela, "if I return to school now, I can—"

"No!" said Marie. "By the time you make it all the way

back, you will have missed twenty-five minutes of practice. It's a wash. We need contingency here. . . . Think, Marie, think!"

"Here's a cold compress, honey," said Andy, handing a bag of ice to Vela. "Put it on your face."

"Uh, okay?" said Vela, smooshing her head right into the frosty bag.

"I've got it!" said Marie. "You can use the rest of the hour to study for the PSAT before your father drives you back to debate club practice at five. Then tomorrow you can offer a *written* apology to Ms. Peco, the band director, for missing practice."

"It—it would be an honor to study for the PSAT before proceeding to debate club practice. Tomorrow I shall make my remorse known to Ms. Peco," said Valerie, whose training as a young squire had inured her to a life of order and strict discipline. "I shall not fail again!"

"Thank you for saying that, sweetie," said Marie. "We only want what's best for you. Which is an Ivy League college followed by a top-tier medical school."

She hugged Vela close. "We don't want you to end up a *dentist*."

Andy joined the family hug. "Do you think you have strep throat?" he said.

❧

And at this very moment, not far away, Thromdurr the mighty barbarian entered the modest ranch house at 45 Crescent Drive, which he found to be quiet and empty. And so, Thromdurr sat upon the great recliner and watched television until his father returned from his job at Bowers Heating and Cooling around six thirty p.m.

"Oh, hey, Doug," said a plump, pleasant-looking man as he walked in the door and set a pile of mail on the counter.

"Greetings, Ron, my father," said Thromdurr. "I have been watching the television and have learned much about the Spinco Roastmeister home rotisserie. It can cook one six-pound chicken or two three-pound chickens, side by side, using less than one quarter the energy of a conventional oven. It is available for $89.99. An amazing price, if this tan fellow speaks the truth."

"Ha ha, sounds good, buddy," said Ron, who didn't always understand his son, but who always tried. "So how was school today?"

Thromdurr flinched. "I . . . answered all of the questions correctly, humbling my academic opponents," said the barbarian quietly. "On the field of educational battle, Douglas the Nerd has no equal."

Ron frowned. "Aw, c'mon, son. You're not a *nerd*," he said. "You're just . . . you know, into stuff most other people aren't. Speaking of which, this came for you."

69

He tossed Thromdurr a package. On the box were the words "eStar T6-010 Electronic Minicar Model Kit," and it bore the picture of a small, peculiar wheeled vehicle. Thromdurr cocked his head.

"I am very excited to receive this box," said Thromdurr. "Because I know perfectly well what it is!"

"You're telling me," said Ron. "The little dancing robot you made last time was hot stuff. Look, dinner won't be ready for another forty-five minutes, if you want to go up to your room and crack it open. I'm sure you already finished your homework and whatnot. . . ."

"Of course I did," said Thromdurr, remembering, "Douglas the Nerd creates clockwork automata as his hobby. My eagerness for the eStar T6-010 Electronic Minicar Model Kit knows no bounds."

Ron shot him a thumbs-up. Thromdurr retired to Douglas's room—a space cluttered with books, computer parts, and pristine action figures, still in their original packaging. He opened the eStar T6-010 box. Inside were four wheels and countless tiny, fiddly little electronic components. After reading the instruction booklet for a full thirty minutes (which was in the Common Tongue but might as well have been written in Old Dragonian) and then shocking himself eight times in thirty seconds, Thromdurr flew into a berserker rage.

"Doug?" said Ron, as he cracked the door. "What's going on up here, buddy?"

"THE ESTAR T6-010 ELECTRONIC MINICAR MODEL KIT WILL SLEEP IN THE UNDERWORLD TONIGHT!" cried Thromdurr, as he snapped a circuit board in half and crushed one of the wheels in his hand. "I WILL DESTROY IT!"

"Ah, okay," said Ron. "Well, um, the chili is ready. . . ."

Meanwhile, in another home in the Realm of Suburbia— this one a two-story Victorian house at 29 Sierra Avenue— another concerned parent knocked upon the door of another Bríandalörian adventurer's room.

"Melissa?" said Pam McElmurray through the door. "Do you want to join us for family game night?"

"Nope," said Sorrowshade. The gloom elf sat upon the bed of a room decorated in blacks and grays, with the walls adorned in grim-looking band posters.

"Okay, but tonight we're playing Traders of Oogoo," said Pam.

"That sounds horrendous," said Sorrowshade.

"It's not horrendous. You can trade oats for beef or logs," said Pam. "It's fun."

"I don't like fun," said Sorrowshade. "Never have."

"All right, sweetheart, well, I just want you to know that

we all love you very much," said Pam. "And whenever you're ready to join us, your father, your brother and your sister, and I would be delighted to have you."

"Don't hold your breath, Pam," said Sorrowshade.

And Sorrowshade sat on the bed for nearly an hour listening to the sounds of wholesome laughter echoing up to her room from the first floor, until it became unbearable.

"Fine!" she said at last, as she descended the stairs to a warm, inviting dining room. There was Pam, along with Sorrowshade's father, Keith, her brother, Josh, and her little sister, Carter, all sitting around a board covered in colorful game pieces with ear-to-ear smiles on their faces. As Sorrowshade reached the bottom step, they all turned and stared at her.

"I'm here to play the game, Pam," muttered Sorrowshade.

"Hooray!" the whole family said in unison. "Melissa came to family game night!"

"Ugh," said Sorrowshade, as she sat down at the table.

Pam dealt her in. Sorrowshade glanced at her hand. All oats.

Meanwhile, on the opposite side of the town of Hibbettsfield (800 North Pineknoll Avenue, to be exact), another Bríandalörian sat down with another family at another dinner table.

"So . . . what's on the menu, Dad?" said Devis the thief, who was eager to sample all the delicious cuisine this fantastical realm had to offer.

"Well, not to mix business with pleasure, but . . . *we're having soup!*" said his father, who set a heavy pot onto a trivet in the center of the table. "This is a Cullen skink, a traditional Scottish soup made with potatoes and smoked haddock."

"Yum! That sounds delicious, Stinky," said Devis's mother to his father. She began ladling soup into each of their three bowls. "You know, when I became the official soup/stew critic for *Haute* magazine, I was secretly worried I might get tired of soup."

"Are you serious, Stinky?" said Devis's father to his mother. "I thought *exactly* the same thing when I became vice president of quality assurance for the Clemons International Soup Company. I figured there's got to be a thing as too much soup, right?"

"Well, I'm glad we were wrong!" said Mom Stinky.

They both burst out laughing, then began to voraciously spoon Cullen skink into their mouths.

Devis sipped a spoonful. Not bad. "So . . . tell me again how come we're all named Stinky?" he said.

His mother and father looked at each other.

"We've told you this, haven't we?" said Dad Stinky.

"How can you not know this, son?" said Mom Stinky.

"I just want to make sure I get the details straight. It's for a school project," said Devis, who, unlike Vela, had never had many qualms about lying to anyone for any reason. "If I get an A, they said I get a special medal that says 'Number One Guy' on it."

"Wow," said Mom Stinky. "Well, my real name is Christina, which got shortened to Stina by my family. But when your uncle Max was a baby, he just couldn't say it. He called me Stinky! We all thought it was so cute and so funny and somehow it just . . . stuck." Mom Stinky laughed.

"And as for me," said Dad Stinky, "my great-grandmother's surname was Tinkhauser. But somebody made a mistake when she emigrated from Austria and copied it down as Stinkhauser—with an S at the beginning—and that became the family name! When my parents had me, they knew they wanted to honor my mother's side in some way, so that's how they decided that should be my first name."

"Can you believe it?" said Mom Stinky, shaking her head. "Two Stinkys who are both professional soup tasters. It would almost have been crazier if we *didn't* get married!"

Devis's parents laughed again and then gazed affectionately at each other.

"Hmm. Great story. Lots of surprises," said Devis. "But what about me? Why am I Stinky?"

"Well, son, you're named after me, of course," said Dad Stinky.

"Wait, so my whole name is Stinkhauser?" said Devis. "Interesting."

Dad Stinky smiled and took Devis's hand. "It sure is. You know, I like to think Great-Grandma Stinkhauser is somewhere up there, looking down on her beautiful great-great-grandson with pride, knowing that the family name lives on."

"Sure," said Devis. "And just for the record, what's our last name?"

"Smith," said Mom Stinky.

"Whew!" said Devis.

"Anyway," said Dad Stinky, "for dessert I've made a chilled watermelon gazpacho that I'm sure *both* of my Stinkys will love."

And so, as four brave Bríandalörians made the acquaintance of families they had never known and attempted to live strange lives they had only yet imagined, the final member of the adventuring party passed his evening in a very different way.

Albiorix watched from the window as the last of the big yellow buses pulled away from J. A. Dewar Middle School. The halls were virtually empty now, but there were were still a couple of hours of various school programs and team practices on school grounds. He would need to stay put for a while until Ms. Rhee, the security guard, went home for the day. To keep out of sight, the third-floor boys' bathroom was his safest bet. According to his H&H books, it was the least popular bathroom in the whole school (arguably because the locks on all the stalls were broken). According to Table 119e: Lavatory Usage, Albiorix only had a fifteen percent chance of encountering anyone here after regular school hours. And if someone did happen by, he'd already devised a decent cover story: he had just joined the chess club, which was meeting in the library until five, but today's cafeteria pizza didn't agree with his stomach—hence the bathroom. Believable (if a bit embarrassing).

Albiorix didn't have a character in this game world, and so he had no backstory, no address, and no family. That meant he didn't have a home here in Hibbettsfield. Until the party figured out a way back to Bríandalör or he thought of a better idea, he would be sleeping at school. Where, exactly? Now that was a good question.

Albiorix cracked *The Manual of Middle-School Maintenance*. He studied the maps of J. A. Dewar Middle School, searching for a good place to spend the night. After he found a few likely locations, he cross-referenced them with the custodian's cleaning regimen. (Mr. Driscoll mopped east to west, first floor to third, then cleaned all the bathrooms and emptied all the trash cans in the opposite order.)

"Aha!" said Albiorix.

He'd finally found what he was looking for: room B-3. In the basement, there was a little-used storage closet where the school kept its industrial floor polisher—an unwieldy contraption that was brought out once a week on Saturdays to scour gunk that a normal mop couldn't handle. Tomorrow was Tuesday, so nobody would need the device for five more days. There was only a two percent chance of encountering anyone there on a day other than Saturday. Room B-3 was hardly the most desirable place to spend the night, but as an adventurer, Albiorix had slept in far worse places. To be honest, even many of the actual beds in Bríandalör were moldy straw-filled pallets, often infested with fleas or imps.

Around five fifteen, while Mr. Driscoll was mopping the east side of the second floor, Albiorix crept down the staircase on the west side of the building.

He made a brief detour to the vending machines, where he pulled a handful of magical coins out of a pocket dimension—luckily the same size as quarters—and bought himself some peanut-butter crackers, a bag of corn chips, and a grape soda for dinner (all popular choices from *The Fulsome Folio of Foods,* thank you very much, Vela). It may not have been a feast fit for a Bríandalörian king, but it was a far sight better than the blind lizards the party had once subsisted on as they tried to navigate their way out of the Endless Caverns of Cúach.

After obtaining his rations, Albiorix continued downward to the school basement. It was dim and dusty, honestly a bit dungeonlike. Sure enough, B-3 was a small room dominated by the floor polisher, some boxes of outdated textbooks. and a few other assorted odds and ends. Albiorix reached for the light switch and stopped himself.

"Nope," he said. "Wizard." Then he cast a simple light spell from memory. A soft orb of moonglow rose from his fingertips and drifted up toward the ceiling, bathing the closet in silver light. Albiorix smiled.

Then he ripped open the corn chips and got down to work. Problem one had been solved: he'd located a safe haven for the night. It was on to problem two: figuring out how to prove he really was Armando Boort, a foreign exchange student from Edmonton, Alberta, Canada. After carefully reviewing the relevant portions of *The Album of Academic Administration* and then studying *The Sourcebook of School Subjects*, he hatched a plan that he felt sixty-five percent good about. Maybe seventy percent?

He'd finished the peanut-butter crackers by the time he'd proceeded to problem three. This was the big one: transporting the entire adventuring party back to

Bríandalör without having to spend two more months stuck inside the game world (though if he was being honest, this prospect didn't bother him as much as it seemed to bother the others).

Albiorix read and reread every relevant Homerooms & Hall Passes supplement in his pack: *The Hall Master's Guide*, *The Cyclopedia of Students*, *The Tome of Teachers*, and more. As the night wore on, he tossed the books he'd digested in stacks at his feet. And the stacks grew. After many hours—though Albiorix now knew far more about the most popular brands of sneakers at JADMS and all the faculty members' individual salaries—he hadn't come to a better solution than the one Vela had proposed: that they finish the nonadventure module he'd been running, *The Semester of Stultification*, as successfully as they could.

"Hmph," said Albiorix, crossing his arms. Not being able to outthink someone whose main job was, let's face it, to poke things with the pointy end of a sword, didn't sit right with him. Sure, everyone else was braver, or tougher, or their one-liners were better. But he was supposed to be the smart one, right?

Just then a musty tang caught his nose, and Albiorix remembered that there was still one book left. It wasn't an H&H sourcebook, though. He reached into the bottom of his pack and pulled out the Malonomicon.

Bound in age-stained red leather, the tome had splotches on the cover that faintly suggested dozens of souls melting in agony. Surely it was evil. The paper shredder that Albiorix had found in *The Manual of Middle-School Maintenance* was likely unattended. In a few minutes, he could have destroyed the vile book forever.

Instead, Albiorix the wizard began to peruse its crumbling pages.

Chapter 6

In the real world, to learn something or find something or create something, magic is often your best option. But in the fantastical setting of Homerooms & Hall Passes, many of these same functions fall to mysterious devices called "computers." Though few understand the arcane methods by which they work, computers are everywhere—from cars to toys to the phones in nearly everyone's pocket—and various forms of computer worship stretch back for decades. . . .

—Excerpt from The Hall Master's Guide

❧

"*G*AAAH!" SCREAMED MR. DRISCOLL.

"Bah!" said Albiorix, sitting up from the pile of H&H sourcebooks where he'd dozed off the night before.

"What are you *doing* here?" said Mr. Driscoll, evidently

not expecting to find anyone asleep in room B-3.

Albiorix blinked and tried to collect his thoughts. "I, uh, had Pizza Club, but I ate some chess and, uh, . . . am I early for school?"

"It's six twenty-seven a.m.," said Mr. Driscoll.

"Oh, that explains it," said Albiorix. "Where I'm from—Edmonton, Alberta, Canada—this is when class starts."

"How did you even get into the building?" said Mr. Driscoll.

"The door was unlocked," said Albiorix with a shrug he hoped would sell the lie.

Mr. Driscoll's eyes narrowed. "I'm positive I locked all the doors when I left last night," he said. "Why are you down here in the basement?"

"Oh," said Albiorix. "Isn't this my homeroom?"

"It's *obviously* a storage closet!" said Mr. Driscoll.

Albiorix looked around. "Ah, okay," he said. "That explains the floor polisher."

"Look, I don't care if you're new. There's obviously something fishy going on here," said Mr. Driscoll. "You need to report to Vice Principal Flanagan's office. I mean, as soon as he actually gets in."

"Er, please don't make me do that," said Albiorix.

"And why shouldn't I?" said Mr. Driscoll.

A disciplinary action was definitely not what Armando Boort from Edmonton, Alberta, Canada, needed to make the case that he belonged at JADMS. The wizard's mind raced. He'd read Mr. Driscoll's entry in *The Manual of Middle-School Maintenance* the night before. He knew the man loved baked ziti, hockey, abstract expressionism, and puns. How could he convince Driscoll to go easy on him?

"Look," said Albiorix, "if I get something like this on my permanent record, it could ruin my chances to become a . . . professional hockey player."

Mr. Driscoll stared at him for a long moment. His expression slowly softened. "You play hockey?"

"Yep," said Albiorix, who had definitely also read about hockey in one of his less essential H&H sourcebooks at some point, but had completely forgotten what it was.

"What position?" said Mr. Driscoll.

"Er, all of them," said Albiorix.

"Wow," said Mr. Driscoll. "You know, I used to play goalie for Pine Hill High. Broke my ankle senior year. Didn't get a scholarship."

Albiorix shook his head. "It's a shame how a little bad luck can derail the career of a promising young hockeyist."

Mr. Driscoll took a deep breath. "Okay, fine," he said at last. "You're new here, so I'm going to cut you some slack and assume this was an honest mistake."

"Oh, thank you, Mr. Driscoll!" said Albiorix, who stood and started to leave.

"Wait a second," said Mr. Driscoll, placing a hand on the wizard's chest and stopping him. "I've never met you before. How do you know my name?"

"It's . . . on your shirt," said Albiorix. And luckily it was.

"Oh, yeah," said Mr. Driscoll, glancing down at the patch on his chest. He chuckled. "I always forget about that."

"Well, uh, next time, be *shirt* to remember," said Albiorix with a big smile.

Mr. Driscoll's expression hardened again. "You know, normally I really enjoy puns," he said. "But that one was . . ." He shook his head in quiet disgust.

"Sorry," said Albiorix, as he scrambled to collect all his books and stuff them back into his pack. "I'm still trying to understand your culture."

"For future reference," said Mr. Driscoll, "first bell is at seven thirty. No need to arrive an hour early. And stay out of the basement. It's dangerous down here."

"Got it," said Albiorix.

"Oh, and I don't want to hear that you're up to any more funny business," said Mr. Driscoll. "Focus on the sport and keep out of trouble."

"Yes, sir," said Albiorix. "The only thing you're going to

hear about me is how I did some amazing hockey stuff on the hockey court with my hockey bat."

Mr. Driscoll cocked his head. Albiorix could feel the custodian's eyes on his back all the way up the basement stairs. The wizard silently cursed his luck. Now room B-3 was out and he'd have to find another place to sleep while he was stuck in this strange world. Still, it might have gone worse. Albiorix sat down by the eighth-grade lockers to wait for his companions. He pulled out an H&H sourcebook called *The Great Grimoire of Games*, which detailed many of the strange sports people played here, and began to reread the entry for hockey. Turns out it didn't involve horses at all.

When the other adventurers finally arrived, the wizard almost didn't recognize them. Vela, Thromdurr, Sorrow-shade, and Devis had shed their normal clothing, and they were dressed like true Suburbanites now. In their new outfits—hoodies, T-shirts, sneakers, jeans—the Brianda-lörians were virtually indistinguishable from the natives. Again, the five of them discreetly convened in their mostly deserted alcove near the library.

"Ugh, I can't believe I'm wearing this stupid getup," said Sorrowshade. "So embarrassing."

"I think you look nice," said Vela.

"Thank you, Vela," said Sorrowshade. "I wish I could say the same."

85

A passing student, Nicole Davenport, snickered as she overheard this.

"Shhh," said Albiorix as Nicole disappeared around the corner. "You *definitely* don't want her to notice you."

"Sorry," said Sorrowshade.

"Do people here really change clothes every day?" said Devis, picking at his sweater. "What a waste of time."

"Yeah," said Albiorix. "Most middle schoolers are scared of smelling bad."

"Bah!" said Thromdurr. "A powerful stench lets friend and foe alike know that you are not afraid to exert yourself in pursuit of your goals!"

Albiorix shrugged. "That reminds me," he said. "I can't really wear my robes again today. It'll be too suspicious."

Devis and Thromdurr rummaged through their backpacks to offer their gym clothes to Albiorix to borrow for the day. Devis's were too small and Thromdurr's were too big. In the end, Albiorix decided too big was preferable.

"Thanks," said the wizard as he stuffed the T-shirt and shorts into his own pack. "I'll change before homeroom."

"So," said Vela, "how did everyone's evening goooo . . ." The question trailed off into a long yawn.

"Wow, Vela, you look more tired than I do," said Albiorix, "and I slept on a floor polisher."

"I had to do all of Valerie's activities," said Vela, yawning.

"Debate Club, studying for the PSAT, an hour of solo flute practice—an instrument I have no idea how to play, by the way—and some essay contest about fire safety. My H&H character is overcommitted. I wish I hadn't chosen to play an Overachiever. It seems like a Gamer or a Class Clown would be easier."

"Sure is," said Devis. "All Stinky has to do is crack wise and eat soup. . . . I mean, it *was* a little too much soup. We had soup for breakfast too. I think we're having soup for dinner tonight. Next game, I'm going to think through my backstory a little more."

"How about you, Thromdurr?" said Albiorix. "How was your first night as Douglas the Nerd?"

"I could not build the eStar T6-010 Electronic Minicar Model Kit," said Thromdurr, hanging his head. "I have brought shame upon the name of my father, Ron Schiller."

"Yeah, well, at least you weren't tortured," said Sorrowshade.

The other adventurers turned to stare at Sorrowshade in horror.

"Three hours of Traders of Oogoo with Pam, Keith, Josh, and little Carter," said Sorrowshade, "And then I had to *hug* all of them before bed."

"Sorrowshade, that honestly sounds like a warm and loving home life," said Vela.

"I know," said Sorrowshade. "And I'm not sure I can take two more months of it. Albiorix, have you figured out another way home yet?"

"Er, no, I mean—not as such," sputtered Albiorix. He neglected to mention all the time he had searched the Malonomicon for answers. He'd seen a section on bargaining with demons using your soul as collateral, a spell for raising undead minions from the grave, a nasty little hex called "mass paralysis," and even a ritual for turning inanimate objects evil. Most of the dark magic in the book was well beyond his ken. And so far, none of it seemed especially useful.

"Huh," said Sorrowshade. "Don't take this the wrong way, but it's seeming less and less like you're the smart one."

"What is the *right* way to take that?" said Albiorix.

Sorrowshade shrugged. "Do you at least have a plan for convincing Vice Principal Flanagan not to expel you?"

"Yeah," said Devis. "Which long con are you going to run on the guy? The widow's brother? The Ostädian prisoner? The Tom Bombadil? The ol' kobold in a knapsack?"

"I have an idea that I think could work," said Albiorix.

"Know this, Albiorix," said Vela. "I will not lie on your behalf."

"Oh, here we go again," muttered Devis.

Thromdurr sighed.

Sorrowshade shook her head. "These people are just made-up Homerooms & Hall Passes nonplayer characters," she said, waving to the hall around them. "They aren't real. Who cares if we—"

"*I will not lie,*" said Vela again, her tone hardening to steel.

"And I won't ask you to, Vela," said Albiorix. "But I may need a distraction during second-period Computer Applications class."

"Then you're in luck, Magic Man," said Devis, "because I'm basically a walking distraction."

The first bell rang, cutting their conversation short.

"Okay, I'll see you all in room 106, Ms. Chapman's homeroom," said Albiorix, "Except for you, Vela. You're the student body president, so that means you deliver morning announcements with Olivia Gorman from the video lab, room 311."

"Ah yes," said Vela, swallowing. "The announcements that are . . . seen by the whole school?"

"Yep," said Albiorix, patting her on the shoulder. "Don't mess up."

The party broke. Albiorix made a quick detour to the boys' bathroom to change into Thromdurr's oversized gym clothes. The billowing T-shirt and shorts didn't quite go with his travel-worn adventurer's boots, but there was nothing to be done about that now. The wizard made it to Ms. Chapman's homeroom just before the tardy bell. As he ducked through the door, he noticed the *Oink Pop* girl from the day before, sitting in the front row.

"Good morning, everyone," said Ms. Chapman, who was wearing a tweed blazer and a seasonal turtleneck.

"Good morning, Ms. Chapman," said the class in unison.

"First off, I want to remind you that we are electing our class officers next week. So get ready for some democracy in action! Who knows, maybe this time the class president will be someone other than Valerie!" said Ms. Chapman with a laugh, as though the prospect was very, very unlikely. "Secondly, we have two new students with us today. As I understand it, some of you already met Armando Boort yesterday. On behalf of our school, welcome, Armando!"

"Hello," said Albiorix. "Very excited to be here and, uh, learn."

"Hello, Armando," said the class.

"What is he even wearing?" said Evan Cunningham, eliciting a round of snickers from the back of the class.

"Shhh," said Ms. Chapman. "Now I'd also like everyone to give another warm J. A. Dewar Middle School welcome to our other new student, June Westray."

"Hello, June," said the class.

"Hi," said June, who looked mortified.

"June is from the big city," said Ms. Chapman, "so I'm sure she can tell us what all the hip new styles are. June, when I go to the city I like to eat *falafel*. Have you ever had *falafel*?"

The girl, June apparently, looked like she wanted to die. Her "yes" to the falafel question was virtually inaudible.

Unfazed, Ms. Chapman proceeded to call roll. (Jackie Barrera and Tim Fumihiro were absent.) She then turned on the TV at the front of the room. There sat Vela and a girl with glasses.

"Gooooood morning, Titans. I'm Olivia Gorman, and this is the J. A. Dewar Morning Bulletin," said the girl in a slightly forced monotone. "Today is Tuesday, October sixth, the second day of Spirit Week. Polka Dot Day. For lunch we will have hamburger or fish sandwich. And now Valerie Stumpf-Turner will lead us in the Pledge of Allegiance."

Vela stared directly at the camera, wide-eyed. She said nothing. As the long seconds dragged on, visible beads of sweat began to form on her forehead. Somehow she didn't blink. Albiorix found himself gripping the corners of his desk so hard that his fingernails started to hurt. The other Bríandalörians shot each other concerned looks.

"I think she's broken," said Devis.

This elicited a louder round of laughter from the class than Evan's crack about Albiorix's outfit.

"Shhh," said Ms. Chapman.

"Okay, um, I guess I'll do it?" said Olivia Gorman at last. Then she recited a brief loyalty oath to the flag of the nation. After that, she predicted the weather and shared an "inspirational" quote of the day from some sage called Steve Jobs.

Olivia and Vela returned to class a few minutes later. Olivia was beaming. The paladin looked pale and shaken.

"Nice choke job, Valerie," whispered Evan. "Did you, like, forget how to talk?"

"Hey, did *you* forget how to brush your teeth?" said Sorrowshade, turning to Evan. "Because when you talk, it smells like a haunted sewer."

Evan clapped his mouth shut with an audible snap an instant before the rest of the class burst out laughing. As Ms. Chapman shushed the class again, Albiorix thought he caught a strange look in Nicole Davenport's eye. Not good.

"Valerie, honey, you can have a seat now," said Ms. Chapman.

"Huh?" said Vela, who seemed to have forgotten she was standing at the front of the class staring out into the middle distance. "Yes, ma'am."

"And now let's dive back into those essays!" said Ms. Chapman.

Though not as grueling as earth sciences, Ms. Chapman's

English class was a struggle for the adventurers as they tried to shoehorn complex ideas into the rigid, highly traditional format of the five-paragraph essay. The goal was to persuade the reader of their position, but in this case the two available choices—"Cats Are Good Pets" or "Cats Are Not Good Pets"—seemed totally arbitrary. Worse, all the best Bríandalörian arguments (cats are *good* pets because they can see ancient spirits; cats are *bad* pets because they might be an evil wizard in disguise) were totally off the table.

So the outlanders did their best to try to imagine why your average middle schooler might like or dislike the beasts. Devis's point that cats are good pets because they can be taught to steal trinkets was deemed "unrealistic." And Sorrowshade's contention that cats are bad pets because they are affectionate was called "bizarre." Thromdurr, in particular, was criticized many times by Ms. Chapman for using old-fashioned words that "sounded smart" instead of writing in plain language. It was rough going, and as always, it seemed, they were relieved to hear the sound of the bell.

On the way to Computer Applications class, the party quietly conferred among themselves.

"Vela, what happened with the announcements?" said Albiorix. "I've watched you face down an entire ogre war party by yourself, but I've never seen you like that."

"I don't know," said Vela, "I just . . . froze."

"Hey, instead of Vela the Valiant, maybe we should call you Vela the Vacant," said Devis. "You know, because of the dead eyes."

"Yeah, I thought your whole thing was giving big inspirational speeches," said Sorrowshade. "I feel like I've endured quite a lot of them."

"It *is*, but only to adventuring parties. You don't know what it's like talking to hundreds of people at once . . . all of them *strangers*," said Vela. "What if I had misspoken or . . . I had something stuck in my teeth?"

"Oh, you *did*, actually," said Devis.

"Still do," said Sorrowshade.

Vela frantically began trying to locate and dislodge the bit of spinach from her incisors without a mirror.

"Bah. Trouble yourself not, paladin," said Thromdurr. "Fear is a natural part of life, I am told. One day I hope to experience it myself!"

The party stopped. They stood at the threshold of room 215, the school computer lab.

"Here we are," said Albiorix. "Devis, when I give you the sign, I need you to distract the whole class's attention away from that laser printer by Mr. Gulazarian's desk."

"Okay, what are you thinking? Small fire? Large fire?" said Devis, his eyes lighting up. "What size fire?"

"No fires. We can't have you getting suspended over

94

this," said Albiorix. "I need something *subtle*."

"Subtle," said Devis. "Got it." And he scampered off to take his seat.

"There is no way he got it," said Vela with a sigh. "You understand that, right?"

Albiorix shrugged and nodded. The other four adventurers found their seats as well. Each of them sat down before their very own computer: a boxy, folding device, a bit like a book, with a glowing screen and keyboard instead of pages.

Albiorix smiled. He figured that if the conjuration magic inscribed in his spellbook back in Bríandalör was unavailable, he might well use one of the fabled computers of this world to conjure what he needed instead. The class was currently using a design program to create a menu for a fictional restaurant. Albiorix had decided that this was the perfect cover for forging the documentation he needed to enroll at JADMS.

"When working on your menus, it's very important to properly name the layers," said Mr. Gulazarian, as he made the rounds, inspecting everyone's work in progress. "By the time you get to Layer 27 you're going to have no idea what Layer 1 was."

Albiorix waited until Mr. Gulazarian was distracted and . . .

Nothing. He realized he had absolutely no idea how to use a computer. When a Homerooms & Hall Passes character employed one of the devices in the game to, say, search the web for a research paper or play an online game, they merely checked their Computer skill and rolled the appropriate dice to determine success or failure.

But Albiorix didn't even know where to begin. He tentatively punched the letter C on the keyboard. A small c appeared on-screen. Huh? Why wasn't it a big C? He needed a big C for the word Canada. Albiorix glanced at the clock. He had fifty-three minutes to completely understand computers and use them to create a believable birth certificate. Albiorix took a deep breath. He cracked his knuckles and rolled his shoulders and tried not to hyperventillate. He had fifty-two minutes now. . . .

Chapter 7

GULAZARIAN, Khoren Haik

OCCUPATION: *Eighth-grade Computer Applications teacher*

ATTRIBUTES: *Cunning: 15, Intelligence: 14, Likability: 8, Willpower: 15, Fitness: 10*

SKILLS: *Classroom Management −2, Computer +8, Cooking +7, Drive +4, Poetry +9*

BIOGRAPHY: *As far back as he can remember, Khoren Gulazarian dreamed of being the greatest slam poet of all time. Under the moniker Street Truth, Gulazarian won second place in a number of poetry contests, but circumstances eventually forced him to choose a more practical career. This may explain his general frustration at ending up a middle-school computer teacher.*

—Excerpt from The Tome of Teachers

F IFTY-ONE MINUTES LEFT. Albiorix smashed the C key harder, hoping greater force would make the letter larger. Instead, a long snake of little c's poured forth. What in the world?

"What are you doing?" whispered June, startling Albiorix. The wizard didn't realize she was sitting at the station beside him.

"I'm just . . . practicing my typing," he said.

"Seems like you've got the letter C down," said June. She gave him a thumbs-up.

"Actually, I seem to have temporarily forgotten how to make it a big C," said Albiorix.

June cocked her head, raised her eyebrows, and gave the wizard a look that, for the first time since he had arrived, made Albiorix feel like he truly didn't belong in this world. After approximately eight seconds, she said, "You hold down the shift key."

Albiorix did. Then he typed C. Presto! On-screen appeared a capital C. Albiorix's heart leaped.

"June, you're a computer expert!" said the wizard.

"Uh, no. Not really," said June, "What, have you never used a computer before?"

"Nope," said Albiorix. "We don't have them back where I'm from."

June nodded. "Ah. My cousin went to a school like that.

98

No computers, no grades. They played with sand all day and none of the toys had faces."

"Yes, exactly!" said Albiorix. "And you might not be a computer expert, but it looks like you're pretty good." He pointed to June's screen. In the first five minutes of class she had already laid out a very nice menu for a place called Just Churros.

"Well, I do like to draw and do graphic design and stuff," said June. "So I use my computer at home for that."

"Say, do you think you could help me with something?" said Albiorix.

"I guess," said June, leaning over to Albiorix's computer. "What do you want to call your fake restaurant?"

"Oh, no, not the menu," said Albiorix. "I need to very quickly create a fake Canadian birth certificate that will stand up to close scrutiny."

June blinked. "Why?" she said. "Are you some sort of international criminal?"

"Ha! No, no," said Albiorix. "Nothing like that. It's for a . . . game."

"Oh," said June. "Not gonna lie. I was a little bit hoping you *were* an international criminal. But games are cool too. Although this one seems like it *might* be kind of nerdy."

"No, it's actually *not* nerdy," said Albiorix, his voice rising. "It's a great way to socialize and build imagination and weave amazing stories with your friends! You should really give Homerooms & Hall Passes a—actually, on second thought, I'm not sure it would make much sense to you."

"Ouch," said June. "Well, I don't want to play your nerd game anyway. I've got *Oink Pop* on my phone. Anyway, first we need to do an online image search for a picture of a real Canadian birth certificate."

June's fingers flew across her keyboard, and in a matter of seconds the screen showed a document that said Birth Certificate at the top, with an official-looking seal beside it.

"We save that file and open it in our other program," said June, as she did. "Then we blank out the old name, like so, then type in the new, made-up one over it. What do you want it to be?"

"Armando Boort," said Albiorix.

"Ha," said June. "I *knew* it was a fake name."

"What? No, it's very, very real!" said Albiorix. "Putting your real name on a fake birth certificate is, uh, how you score points in the game."

"Relax, I'm joking," said June. "So we'll type Armando Boort, in a font that's close enough to the real one. Next we'll change the date of birth so it doesn't say 1954, and give the parents the same last name. Click save, and voilà: one fake Canadian birth certificate, ready for your game that is apparently beyond my simple comprehension."

Forty-seven minutes left in class, and Albiorix had the documentation he needed to enroll at J. A. Dewar Middle School.

"Thank you so much, June," said Albiorix. "How can I ever repay you?"

"That will be nine thousand dollars," said June. She held out her hand.

Albiorix blinked. Then he slowly reached toward his own ear, pulled a coin out of a pocket dimension, and handed it to her. June stifled a laugh. Mr. Gulazarian shushed her.

June spent the remainder of the class helping Albiorix with the menu assignment too—he decided to call his fictional restaurant the Sorcerer of Snacks as a little inside joke—and by the end, he felt he had acquired the basic fundamentals of how to use a computer. In Homerooms & Hall Passes terms, his Computer skill would have increased by one. All in all, it was a pretty successful period.

Yet there was still the matter of printing the document without anyone noticing. At 9:31, four minutes before the bell, Albiorix gave Devis the sign: licking both thumbs and running them smoothly across his eyebrows. Devis stared at him. Albiorix did it again. Devis shrugged. They probably should have agreed in advance about what the sign would be. Eventually Sorrowshade noticed and punched Devis in the arm and Devis finally got it.

The thief gave Albiorix a little wink and dropped his pencil. He went down to get it and, a few seconds later, *somehow* popped up on the other side of the room.

"Mr. Gulazarian, where's the pencil sharpener?" said Devis.

"This is the computer lab, Stinky," said Mr. Gulazarian. "We don't *have* a pencil sharpener." He gave a sigh and didn't bother to look up from helping Thromdurr with his menu design.

"Oh," said Devis. "Then . . . what did I just jam my pencil into?"

"Huh?" said Mr. Gulazarian. He stood and started toward Devis but immediately wobbled. An instant later, he fell flat on his face with a horrendous crash. Several students gasped. Others jumped to their feet. A few pulled out their phones to film. Vela quickly stooped to help him up, and Albiorix clicked the print button.

"Mr. Gulazarian, somebody tied your shoelaces together!" said Nick Ribat.

"Impossible," said Mr. Gulazarian. "I'm wearing loafers! They tied somebody *else's* shoelaces together around my ankles. Whose shoelaces are these?" He held up a knotted pair of neon-green laces that he'd managed to untangle from his feet.

"What?" said Evan Cunningham. "How is that—"

"How is *what*, Evan?" said Mr. Gulazarian, pulling himself up off the floor.

"Nothing," said Evan.

"Spit it out!" said Mr. Gulazarian.

"Well, those are my shoelaces, okay," said Evan. He held up both of his sneakers, which had been completely de-laced. "But I—"

"Evan Cunningham," yelled Mr. Gulazarian, "go to Vice Principal Flanagan's office right now!"

"But he didn't *do* anything, Mr. G," whined Derrick Day.

"What are you, his lawyer, Derrick?" said Mr. Gulazarian. "You know what, you're going to the office too. If Evan did something, there's no way you didn't help him."

"Aw, c'mon!" said Derrick. "That's, like, *typecasting*, man."

As the whole class watched the three of them argue, Albiorix slipped out of his seat and swiped the freshly printed page sitting in the tray on the opposite side of the room. Devis gave Albiorix another little wink as he deftly twirled his pencil back and forth across his knuckles.

The bell rang and Albiorix practically dashed to the office. After a short wait beneath the Inspire Leadership poster, Ms. Roland, the receptionist, waved him back to see the vice principal. The red-faced, crying boy he passed coming out of Flanagan's office did give the wizard pause, but Albiorix's optimism had mostly returned by the time he took his seat across the big desk from the vice principal.

"Hello, Armando," said Flanagan. "Did you bring the proper identification required to enroll in J. A. Dewar Middle School?"

"I sure did," said Albiorix. "Here's my birth certificate!"

He handed the printout to the Vice Principal, who put on a pair of reading glasses and scanned it. He frowned as he rubbed it between his finger and his thumb.

"Why is it on printer paper?" said Flanagan. "Where's the original?"

Albiorix's heart sank. Somehow he had assumed that the printer, like a duplication spell back in the real world, would produce a perfect copy of the real thing. Apparently it didn't.

"This is, uh, just a *high-resolution JPEG* of my birth certificate," said Albiorix, trying out some of the new computer-y terms he'd just learned from June. "Obviously the original is with my parents, Jeffrey Dwight Boort and Angela Kay Boort, back in Edmonton, Alberta, Canada."

Flanagan gave a noncommittal grunt. "Fine," he said. "I just need to confirm that you currently reside in our school district."

Albiorix was stunned. "You need to—but . . . but the rules don't say anything about—"

"Sometimes the rules don't cover every situation," said Flanagan, as he slowly removed his glasses and stared at Albiorix with cold gray eyes. "Your circumstances are unusual—we don't have any other foreign exchange students at JADMS—and I'm using my own discretion as vice principal of this school. You're not questioning my authority to do that, are you, Armando?"

"Ah . . . no, sir," said Albiorix quietly, as he looked away.

"So who are you living with while you're visiting us here in the states?" said Vice Principal Flanagan.

"Lovely family, they're called the . . . Albiorixes," said Albiorix, who was never very good at coming up with names on the fly, a real weakness as a Hall Master.

Flanagan jotted it down. "Phone number?"

"Oooh," said Albiorix, "Here's the thing with that: actually, they don't *have* a phone number, per se."

Flanagan squinted at him.

"Because the phone is broken!" said Albiorix, who could hear his own voice speeding up and rising in pitch. "They're getting it replaced. Yep. There was a terrible accident. The phone exploded. Thankfully nobody was hurt. Anyway I'll be sure to let you know as soon as they have it all sorted out. The phone."

"Please do," said Flanagan. "Address?"

"It's 347 Elkview Road," said Albiorix, picking a house

number at random and a street name he vaguely remembered from a map he'd once seen in *The Hibbettsfield Handbook*. He had no idea if the address actually existed.

"Elkview Road?" said Flanagan, staring hard at Albiorix.

"Yes," said Albiorix, "though I haven't ever *viewed* any *elks* there. Ha ha."

"My favorite pizzeria is on Elkview Road. It's called Pasquale's," said Flanagan. "You should order a sausage pie from there sometime. Once the family phone gets fixed, of course."

"Of course," said Albiorix.

"All right, then, Armando. I think we're squared away," said Flanagan, extending his hand. "Welcome to our school."

"Thank you, sir!" said Albiorix, shaking it.

On his way out of the office, Albiorix was feeling pretty good. The phone number and the address were complications, to be sure, but he would sort them out. The important thing was, Armando Boort was now a full-fledged student at J. A. Dewar Middle School. At least for now, he wouldn't get expelled and cease to exist/join the Sky Bear in the Great Cave of Clouds. Hooray!

As he passed through the reception area, Albiorix heard a student—a seventh grader named Sam Keller—complaining to Ms. Rhee, the security guard.

". . . Yeah, I definitely left it in my locker yesterday," said

Sam, "and then I get here this morning, and it's just gone. I mean, the lock was on it."

"Okay, can you describe the piece of jewelry to me?" said Ms. Rhee, as she wrote in her notebook.

"It's not jewelry," said Sam, a little self-conscious. "It's, like, a cool pendant. Of a shark's tooth. It cost me thirty bucks."

"So you think somebody broke into your locker overnight and stole it?" said Ms. Rhee.

"Yeah," said Sam. "Or maybe early this morning?"

As Albiorix edged past them out the door, he noticed Mr. Driscoll standing in the corner, by the water cooler, staring him down. Albiorix gave a weak wave and pantomimed swinging a hockey stick. Mr. Driscoll frowned.

Albiorix rejoined his companions in their third-period gym class in the gymnasium. He walked in just as Thromdurr reached the top of a heavy rope that was suspended from the rafters. Ms. Dumas, and most of the rest of the class, looked flabbergasted as she stared at a stopwatch.

"That's three point five three seconds," said Ms. Dumas. The class moaned in disbelief.

"We have a new, *new* school record, beating the one previously set by Valerie four minutes ago, which, of course, beat the one set by Melissa shortly before that."

"Ha!" said Thromdurr, dropping to the ground. "I have

conquered your puny gymnasium rope. All kneel before Douglas!"

"No need to gloat, Doug," said Ms. Dumas. "But I'll admit it's impressive, considering last week you couldn't even do a single push-up."

"Worry not," said Thromdurr. "My rippling muscles are nothing compared to my juicy brain."

"Huh," said Ms. Dumas. "Next up we have . . . Stinky Smith."

Devis stepped forward and cracked his knuckles. "You might want to keep that record book open, lady," he said.

"Don't call me 'lady,'" said Ms. Dumas. "Just climb the rope, Stinky."

Devis nimbly shimmied to the top of the rope.

"Are you *kidding* me?" said Ms. Dumas, staring at her stopwatch. "Three point four nine seconds."

The other students groaned again.

"Yeah. That's a new school record," said Ms. Dumas, shaking her head as she wrote it down.

Devis did a somersault, landed on the floor, and gave a low bow—without ever catching any of Albiorix's increasingly obvious nonverbal cues to perhaps take it down a notch.

The party regrouped by the edge of the mats as the next kid, George Stedman, struggled to climb the rope.

"Devis," whispered Albiorix, "didn't you see me gesturing at you?"

"Oh, yeah," said Devis. "I thought you were choking."

"Well, if you thought I was choking, then it's even worse that you didn't react!" said Albiorix.

Devis shrugged. "Albiorix, I say this as a friend: signs aren't your thing. Now, the bard in my old party? *That* guy had some great signs." Devis flashed a few: wiggling hand antlers; two fingers down the cheeks like walrus tusks; popping his whole fist into his mouth.

"My point was that we probably ought to be a little more subtle," said Albiorix.

"What are you complaining about?" asked Sorrowshade. "This is finally a middle-school class we aren't all terrible at."

"Yeah, but you can't be *too* good," said Albiorix. "It makes people nervous."

"To perform at any level less than my very best would be a betrayal of my paladin's oath," said Vela, placing her hand on her heart, "and perhaps a lie."

"Oh, come on," said Albiorix, throwing his hands up. "You are *really* expanding the definition of a lie here."

"I tried to take my time, sorcerous friend," said Thromdurr. "Yet even my laughably sluggish pace was inadvertently faster than anyone else's. This strange world is severely lacking in upper body strength."

George Stedman's feet were still dangling six inches off the ground as he huffed and puffed and sweat beaded on his forehead. He would never reach the top.

"You have to remember, these kids don't climb down ropes into dungeons all day," said Albiorix. "They do other stuff, like write five-paragraph essays and look at their phones."

"Sure," said Sorrowshade, "and it's made them all as weak as you."

Thromdurr and Devis snickered.

"Ha ha," said Albiorix, who endured a fair bit of good-natured ribbing about being physically pathetic compared to his Bríandalörian companions. "Anyway, Flanagan bought the fake birth certificate. Armando Boort is now officially a student at J. A. Dewar. So I am the smart one, after all."

Devis shook his hand, Thromdurr cuffed him on the back, and Sorrowshade gave him something that was at least approaching a smile.

"I'm glad you will not cease to exist, Albiorix," said Vela. "But I will not—"

"Lie?" said Albiorix, who'd already thought this through. "You won't have to, my friend. If you ever need to talk to me in front of anybody else, you can just call me A. That works as a nickname for Albiorix and Armando. See? Smart one, over here."

"A?" said Vela.

"That's a weird nickname," said Devis.

"You're called *Stinky*!" said Albiorix.

"Short for Stinkhauser," said Devis. "Completely makes sense if you know the context."

"Very well," said Vela, bowing her head. "It is not a lie to call you A."

"Great," said Albiorix.

"Armando Boort?" called out Ms. Dumas, checking her list. "New Kid, you're up."

Albiorix climbed the rope more slowly than the others in his adventuring party, yet still far faster than the average Suburban eighth grader. And he did have to admit: it felt good not to be objectively terrible at something related to school.

Yet that feeling of triumph was destined to be fleeting. As the bell rang, the five brave companions proceeded from the gymnasium toward their most harrowing middle-school challenge yet: math class.

Chapter 8

The cafeteria is the hub of middle-school life. For twenty-five minutes a day, students may speak freely as they enjoy such delicacies as "chicken fingers with French fries" or "quesadilla with French fries." Here, while their teachers are distracted negotiating their own complex social hierarchy, rival student factions compete for the best tables, and those hoping to make a name for themselves attempt various "antics," "shenanigans," and "high jinks" to impress their peers. . . .

—Excerpt from The Codex of Cliques

"WHAT JUST HAPPENED?" WHISPERED Devis, breaking the bleak silence as the party trudged toward the cafeteria for lunch.

"Algebra I," said Albiorix.

"No way. That had to be higher than one," said

Sorrowshade, massaging her temples. "That felt like it was at least a thirty-five."

"It was worse than when we battled the Kraken of Krence," whispered Vela, "and were forced to retreat in disgrace."

"I think you're all exaggerating," said Albiorix. "It was just math class."

"If it was math, why were there letters?" asked Thromdurr, grabbing Albiorix by the shirt. "WHY WERE THERE LETTERS?"

"I think the letters are actually numbers . . . *I think*," said Albiorix. He had understood marginally more of the class than the other Bríandalörians—algebra bore a passing resemblance to the alchemical formulae wizards in the real world used to transmute various substances into gold. Regardless, Albiorix had still failed the quiz Mr. Botello had given, and he had been unable to answer any of the homework questions correctly. Just like the others.

"I don't like to be negative," said Sorrowshade, "but if we have to pass that class, we're all doomed."

The whole party (even Sorrowshade herself) turned to Vela, who usually countered such dire pessimism with some words of encouragement.

The paladin merely shrugged and held up her sun-shaped holy symbol. "I've prayed to the Powers of Light for a ray of hope, but wherever we are . . . the gods of Bríandalör cannot hear me."

"Guys, Vela is making Sorrowshade sound optimistic," said Devis. "That can't be good."

"It is funny," said Thromdurr. "I never thought I would go out like this."

"Trapped inside a fantasy role-playing game, where academic failure effectively means death?" said Sorrowshade.

"I had hoped to be mauled by wild pigs," said Thromdurr, "the traditional death of a berserker of the Sky Bear clan."

"I kind of figured it would be a poison gas trap or, I don't know, maybe a bad case of gout that finally got ol' Devis," said the thief.

"A paladin will gladly give her life in the service of a higher good," said Vela, "but to perish by flunking math seems sort of . . . meh."

"I didn't even get to kill the stupid minotaurs and avenge my stupid family," said Sorrowshade. "So unfair."

"Okay, okay," said Albiorix, "I know we haven't been doing great in school, so far—"

"We've failed every assignment," said Devis.

"Mr. Botello took me aside to ask me if I have suffered a head injury," said Thormdurr. "Indeed I have suffered many, but not enough for Algebra I to make sense!"

"Sure," said Albiorix, "but those five-paragraph essays are really coming along. I think we all made some really good points about cats today. And remember the rope-climbing in gym? Sure you're all moping now, but that was only fifty-five minutes ago!"

"It's not enough," said Vela. "The rules of Homerooms & Hall Passes say we can't flunk a single class."

"Maybe it doesn't even work that way," said Sorrowshade, with a faraway look in her eyes. "Maybe nothing happens if we fail a class and we're just . . . stuck here. Forever. A fate worse than death."

The adventurers once more fell into silence as they entered the cafeteria and took their places in the line, soon to face the grim choice of hamburger or fish sandwich. Keeping up party morale didn't usually fall to Albiorix. He tried to think of other low points in their adventures, times when they had been close to giving up. It seemed that just when a quest felt most hopeless, a friendly gnome or a helpful unicorn would appear to cast a healing spell, or to provide the party some crucial piece of information or perhaps a magic amulet to warn them against the dangers ahead. Maybe they couldn't do it on their own, thought Albiorix. Maybe they needed help.

He cast his eyes across the cafeteria, searching for any

sign of the middle-school equivalent of a friendly gnome or magic amulet. And there—alone at the wobbly table near the flagpole—he saw her.

"June!" said Albiorix, sitting down beside her.

"Armando," said June, who had chosen fish sandwich but looked like she regretted it.

"I need you to tutor me, and four other students you don't yet know, so we don't fail," said Albiorix.

"Wow, and I thought you were just here to ask for the ketchup," said June. "Which subject are you having trouble with?"

"All of them," said Albiorix.

June cocked her head.

"Well, except gym," said Albiorix.

"Armando," said June, "I'm very flattered, really, but full disclosure: I'm not exactly a star student. If school was sports, I'd be what you would call a utility player."

"Are you going to flunk any of your classes?" said Albiorix.

"What? No," said June, insulted.

"Then you're good enough for us!" said Albiorix.

"I don't know, dude. This seems like a big time commitment and I lead a pretty busy life." She held up her phone to show Albiorix the *Oink Pop* loading screen.

"Then perhaps we could offer you something in return,"

said Albiorix. "Would you like to learn how to sword fight, or pick locks, or concoct deadly poisons?"

"Hmm. Well, I think I'll pass on *those three*," said June, "but yeah, maybe there's something. So who are these other four mystery people?"

"Valerie Stumpf-Turner, Melissa McElmurray, Douglas Schiller, and Stinky Smith," said Albiorix, pointing them out in the cafeteria line.

"Well, I guess I don't have any friends here," said June. "Why not four randos who are apparently failing every subject in school? Sure, Armando. I'll do it."

"Thank you, June," said Albiorix. "You may have just saved my life for a second time today."

"Saved your life?" said June. "You're a little dramatic, you know that?"

"We should start as soon as possible," said Albiorix. "Time is of the essence."

"Okay, I'm going out to dinner for my mom's birthday today, so how about tomorrow?" said June. "You and your friends can come over to my house after school, and I guess I'll do my best."

And so the wizard Albiorix returned to his companions and relayed the good news to them: their academic woes were soon to be over. June Westray would teach them. And indeed their spirits were lifted. And they laughed and chatted among themselves until they noticed an emissary standing beside them. Albiorix recognized the girl as Sophie Sorrentino.

"You," said Sophie, pointing her finger at Sorrowshade.

"Me?" said Sorrowshade.

"Nicole says you're sitting with us at lunch," said Sophie.

The Bríandalörians gave each other nervous looks. Vela stared at the floor. Thromdurr shook his head. Devis let out a long whistle. Albiorix frowned. There were many things that Sorrowshade, gloom elf assassin of the Forest of Tears, did not suffer: fools, flattery, minotaurs. But the thing she despised most in the world was taking orders.

"Nicole who?" hissed Sorrowshade, her eyes narrowing.

"Ugh. Like you don't know," said Sophie with an eye roll. "Nicole *Davenport.*"

Sorrowshade started toward Sophie, perhaps to decapitate her with the cafeteria spoon that had suddenly appeared in her grip, but Albiorix put a hand on the elf's sleeve. Sorrowshade turned to stare at him. Albiorix nodded and gave a little shrug that he hoped conveyed the general sentiment "Please don't hurt anyone."

"All right," said Sorrowshade through gritted teeth. "Lead the way. *To Nicole Davenport.*"

And so Sorrowshade took her place at what was widely acknowledged to be the best table in the whole cafeteria:

whichever table Nicole Davenport and her clique were sitting at.

"I like your style," said Nicole, not looking up from her phone.

"My style?" said Sorrowshade.

"I mean, not your style-style," said Nicole, waving dismissively to Sorrowshade's clothes. "But it was *amazing* how you *destroyed* Evan Cunningham when you made fun of his breath in first period."

"I pinpointed his weakness and used it to inflict maximum damage," said Sorrowshade, throwing up the hood of her sweatshirt. "It is what I do."

"Yes, yes!" said Nicole. "Evan is *such* a little twerp."

"Yeah, he's a twerp," said Madison Gray. "We *hate* Evan."

"We *hate* twerps," said Sophie.

"Um, is there an echo in here?" said Nicole.

Madison and Sophie gave simultaneous, joyless laughs.

"Anyway, Melissa," said Nicole, still scrolling through her social media feeds, "I'm going to be besties with you."

Sorrowshade was taken aback. "Friends made are friends buried," said the gloom elf. "I walk through life *alone*."

"That's totally your brand, and I *love* that about you," said Nicole. "But I need somebody around here who will tell it like it is, who's not just, like, some pathetic sycophant who's totally afraid of me."

"We *hate* pathetic sycophants," said Madison.

"Clearly," said Sorrowshade.

"Anyway, no presh or anything," said Nicole, still rapidly hearting photo after photo on her phone. "If you don't want to be my friend, I could just, like, make it my mission to destroy you or whatever."

"Many have tried," hissed Sorrowshade. "They are no longer breathing."

Nicole paused and looked up from her phone. Then she burst out laughing.

"Isn't Melissa *the best*?" said Nicole to Madison and Sophie, who both nodded rapidly, with fear in their eyes.

"Nicole," said Sorrowshade, "what exactly do I have to do to be your . . . *bestie*?" The gloom elf could barely bring herself to spit out the word.

"Anybody who knows me knows I hate fake people. Just be real, Melissa. Be *you*," said Nicole, "But, like, dress better."

"The clothing in this realm is ridiculous," said Sorrowshade.

"OMG, yes!" said Nicole, "Nobody at this school has *any* sense of fashion. I mean, look at what Evelyn Roy is wearing." She pointed to a girl at a nearby table, who sported a bright pink-and-purple jacket.

"Ugh," said Madison.

"Ugh," said Sophie.

"Indeed," said Sorrowshade. "That garment resembles a toxic cave fungus warning you not to eat it."

Nicole burst out laughing again.

Meanwhile, across the noisy cafeteria, the other Bríandalörians—who sat far enough away from one another to deny the appearance of socializing—made a new acquaintance themselves: June Westray.

". . . and *that's* when it accidentally got changed to Stinkhauser," said Devis.

"Stinky," said Albiorix, "I think you might be boring our new friend June."

"No, no," said June, "I could definitely listen to another fifteen or twenty minutes of this. Please, Stinky, tell me your middle name has a whole origin story too."

"Oho," said Devis, blinking, "was that a joke, June? That is honestly *very* refreshing. I'm used to spending all my time around people with no sense of humor at all."

"I have a sense of humor," said Vela.

"And I am notoriously quick to laugh at the weakness of my foes!" said Thromdurr.

"Foes?" said June.

Thromdurr caught himself. "Er, other honor students who . . . seek the math award."

"Speaking of laughter," said Vela, gazing out across the

lunchroom, "what do you suppose they find so funny?"

Nicole and her clique were giggling, apparently at something Sorrowshade had said.

"I don't know," said Albiorix, "but it does make me a tad nervous."

"Eh, you should be happy that Sorro—that *Melissa* has actually made some new friends," said Devis. "I mean, we all know what she's like, right?"

The Bríandalörians were quiet for a moment.

"Her personality is highly abrasive," explained Thromdurr.

"Yeah, no, I definitely got that," said June.

"Anyway, enough about us," said Devis. "What's your deal, June?"

"Yes," said Vela. "Tell us of the great city that lies beyond Suburbia."

"Oh, hmm. Well, it's kind of loud there. But you can get around on public transit, which is cool," said June. "And I guess there are fewer chain restaurants."

"Again I must ask," said Thromdurr, "*why would anyone want to eat a chain?*"

June tactfully chose to breeze right past his question. "Mainly, I just miss all my friends at my old school."

"I see," said Vela, putting a hand on June's shoulder. "You feel as though you are an exile, cut off from your true home."

"Uh, sure?" said June. "I mean, I still text with them a lot—"

"You swore an oath," said Vela, "but sometimes it seems that oath no longer makes sense here. You are highly capable, yet the customs of this strange new land demand things of you that seem impossible. Such as delivering the morning announcements . . ."

"Guys, I think your friend is, uh, going off on her own thing," said June, looking around for help.

"Valerie!" said Albiorix. "No need to frighten June about J. A. Dewar, a great place to learn. Gooooo, Titans."

Vela shook herself. "Sorry," she said. "You're right, A."

"A?" said June, looking at Albiorix. "That's a weird nickname."

"That's what I said!" said Stinky.

"Hang on," said June. "I somehow must have missed the part about how you guys all know each other?"

Yet before anyone was forced into an awkward lie, the bell rang. And so the brave adventurers journeyed forth from the cafeteria to room 207, where they endured another social studies class, with many more names and dates to commit to their already overstuffed memories. Earth sciences came next, and they fared no better than the day before in discerning the mysterious origin of the rocks. In art class they painted their papier-mâché heads whatever color they wanted, which was nice. And so the last bell mercifully rang, and another day of middle school did come to a close. Though they were weary, the heroes' spirits were buoyed by the prospect of their academic underperformance soon coming to an end under the wise tutelage of June Westray.

As the hall filled with departing students, they discreetly reconvened in their secluded alcove.

"Oof. I yearn for the sweet relief of the big recliner at my home," said Thromdurr. "I shall lounge like a king and let the soothing infomercials wash over me. How is doing this more exhausting than fighting monsters?"

"Too much soup," said Devis. "I think I need more solid foods to keep my energy up. That's why I'm sneaking these home." He had apparently filled his pockets with hamburgers and fish sandwiches.

"My day is far from done," said Vela, shaking her head. "I've got French Club and then band practice for the concert band recital tomorrow. Can any of you teach me how to play the flute?"

"I play a little lute," said Devis. "Does that help?"

"Not in the least," said Vela.

"I can't believe I'm a *bestie* now," said Sorrowshade.

"I didn't want you to make a scene in the cafeteria," said Albiorix. "But if Nicole makes you uncomfortable, perhaps you could delicately remove yourself from her social circle."

"You told me to go sit with her," said Sorrowshade. "I thought I was supposed to make friends with all the humans."

"I know, I know," said Albiorix. "Just be careful, okay?"

And so the party once more split up to make their way to their respective homes. Albiorix took up his familiar hiding spot in the third-floor boys' room and began to leaf through his H&H sourcebooks in search of a new sanctuary. Room B-3 was out, but the wizard soon found an even better place to take refuge.

After all the clubs and teams had gone home for the day, while Mr. Driscoll was mopping the east side of the second floor, Albiorix again crept down the opposite staircase. He stealthily made his way to the gymnasium. According to the books, there was an equipment closet full of balls and jump ropes and other commonly used equipment. And then there was what everyone at the school simply called "the other closet."

Albiorix found an old door with painted-over windows, luckily unlocked. He opened it to see piles of dusty athletic equipment that only rarely saw the light of day—a moth-eaten parachute, a stack of old scooter boards, boxing gloves from a time when that was apparently allowed in middle school. This was the other closet.

"Perfect," said Albiorix.

And so the intrepid wizard created a makeshift bed out of gymnastics mats with a partially deflated dodgeball as a pillow. And Albiorix passed a peaceful night dreaming he was a dwarven princess trying to solve a particularly daunting linear equation. He awoke rested, his secret redoubt undiscovered. And after a breakfast of onion rings and fruit chews from the vending machine, Albiorix had made his way toward the eighth-grade lockers, when a bloodcurdling scream shattered the air. . . .

Chapter 9

Table 106b: *Random Middle School Locker Contents*

To determine the contents of a student's locker, roll five times on the following table:

1 to 3: *Social studies textbook*

4 to 5: *Calculator (dead batteries)*

6 to 9: *Notebook, repeatedly inscribed with the name of a crush (roll on Table 290f: Random Student Crush)*

10: *Petrified cheese sandwich*

11 to 12: *Hidden cache of Halloween candy*

13: *Live guinea pig . . .*

                              —*Excerpt from* The Hall Master's Guide

❧

"IT'S GOOOONE!" CRIED REUBEN Huang, looking around in a panic.

"What's gone?" said Albiorix.

"My tablet," said Reuben. "Somebody stole it right out

of my locker. That thing is worth four hundred and fifty dollars. And it's not even mine, it's my brother's." Reuben moaned and buried his face in his palms.

"Hang on, your locker got broken into too?" said Sherri Rios, running up to them, wide-eyed. "Somebody took twenty-three dollars and a new pair of sneakers out of mine."

"Aaaagh! My Agent Helios, Marksman of G.U.N.N. (Limited Edition Gray Battlesuit) action figure is gone," cried Saul Graham. "My Agent Helios, Marksman of G.U.N.N. (Limited Edition Gray Battlesuit) action figure is gone!"

"What about you, New Kid?" said Reuben. "Did your locker get broken into?"

"Hmm. Well, I don't really *have* a locker, as such," said Albiorix. "But it probably would have . . . if I did."

Reuben, Sherri, and Saul now stared him with naked suspicion.

"Who *are* you, anyway?" said Sherri.

But before Albiorix could answer, a powerful hand grabbed him by the elbow and dragged him aside. It was the school custodian, Mr. Driscoll.

"Uh, hi," said Albiorix. "Hello."

"You lied to me," said Mr. Driscoll in a furious whisper. "I checked around online and there's no Armando Boort on *any* middle-school hockey team in the Edmonton metro area!"

Albiorix was dumbfounded. You could find something like that out using a computer? They really were powerful.

"Okay, yes, that's true," sputtered the wizard, "because back home I played on a team that was so elite it was actually kept secret—"

"Stop lying," said Mr. Driscoll. "Ms. Rhee says there's been a rash of locker break-ins. You were here, in the school, when Sam Keller's shark-tooth necklace got stolen."

"Okay, maybe," said Albiorix, "but—wait, you don't think I did it, do you?"

"Lying? Skulking around the school after hours? Of course I do!" said Mr. Driscoll. "That's why I'm turning you in to Vice Principal Flanagan right this minute."

"But—but won't you get in trouble too?" said Albiorix.

Mr. Driscoll paused.

"You know," said Albiorix, "for not saying anything when you found me asleep in the basement yesterday morning?" The wizard knew he was on dangerous ground here, but what choice did he have?

Mr. Driscoll somehow looked even angrier than ever. His voice fell to a whisper. "Are you trying to blackmail me or something?"

"Absolutely not!" said Albiorix. "I'm trying to *help* you."

Mr. Driscoll gritted his teeth, as he apparently considered this. "I'm going to give you one chance," he said,

"Return the stuff you stole and . . . we can forget this ever happened."

"I didn't *steal* anything," said Albiorix. "But I will track down the culprit and all the stolen stuff. Sure, I may have been, ah, *slightly exaggerating* my hockey credentials, but trust me: where I come from, solving problems like this is pretty much all I do."

"You have until end of day Friday," said Mr. Driscoll, "or I'm dragging you straight to Flanagan's office, and he can expel you for all I care."

And with that, Mr. Driscoll turned and walked away.

"Yikes," said Devis. "What was that all about?"

The other Bríandalörians had witnessed the exchange from a little ways down the hall.

"I do not like to see our wizard being intimidated," said Thromdurr, placing an affectionate hand on the top of Albiorix's head. "'Tis far too easy for bullies to prey upon the weak."

"Thanks, I think?" said Albiorix. "Anyway, we might just have a quest on our hands."

"A new adventure?" said Vela, her eyes lighting up. "A problem to solve? A wrong to right? *An evil to confront and vanquish?*"

Albiorix nodded. "If we don't get to the bottom of these

locker break-ins, I'm going to get blamed, and very likely expelled."

"Did we not just save you from such a fate?" said Thromdurr.

"Yeah, you just keep getting into trouble, Magic Man," said Devis, clucking his tongue. "Is it out of some sick need for attention?"

Before Albiorix could protest. Vela put a hand on his shoulder. "Do not fear," she said. "We shall bring this locker villain to justice. I swear it by all that is good and righteous!"

In total, it turned out that thirteen lockers had been burgled, fourteen counting Sam Keller's two nights ago. Each of the victims filled out an official report with Ms. Rhee. Rumor had it that hundreds, maybe thousands of dollars' worth of items had been stolen. Principal Greene took over morning announcements to address the incident (mercifully sparing Vela from the job). Greene urged the culprit to come forward immediately and promised that the school would temporarily be ramping up security until things had been sorted out.

Between classes, the Bríandalörians asked around for clues among various social groups. Thromdurr questioned the Nerds. Vela took the Overachievers and Jocks. Stinky went for the Class Clowns and Gamers. Sorrowshade worked the

Loners and, paradoxically, the Populars, who had recently embraced her thanks to her new affiliation with Nicole Davenport.

For his part, Albiorix discreetly paged through *The Cyclopedia of Students*, searching for likely suspects. He was looking for students with criminal tendencies and a high enough Cunning attribute to have pulled off the thefts. According to his entry, Mitchell Harrington had once stolen a candy bar from a convenience store when he was eight. On the other end of the spectrum, Cassie Bloom regularly shoplifted electronics from big-box stores. Both of them went on the list, along with twenty-nine other suspects that he and his companions had identified. Yet for Albiorix, one name kept jumping out at him: Evan Cunningham.

Evan had received three days of in-school suspension for the shoelace incident in Computer Applications class the day before. Albiorix felt bad about that, since Evan was innocent. (But not too bad because you could only muster so much pity for a guy like that.) Evan had no particular history of stealing, but Albiorix thought that perhaps robbing over a dozen lockers was a grand act of revenge against the school for his unjust punishment? Revenge was a very common motivator back in the real world of Bríandalör, and it explained the grandiose plots of many a villain. Revenge didn't quite account for Sam Keller's missing necklace the night before, but maybe that was unrelated.

At lunch, Sorrowshade was once again summoned by Sophie Sorrentino to serve as a *bestie*. The gloom elf gritted her teeth and took her place at Nicole Davenport's right hand. Meanwhile, the other adventurers decided to do some investigating.

Derrick Day sat at a table of other middle-school ne'er-do-wells, lesser acolytes of Evan Cunningham. In Evan's absence, it looked as though Derrick might be trying on the ringleader role for size. The others laughed at his jokes and hung on his every word.

"Greetings, Derrick Day," said Thromdurr, sitting down heavily beside him.

"Why are you sitting here, dork?" said Derrick.

Derrick's buddies snickered.

"I am told I cannot crush you," said Thromdurr. "So perhaps we can be friends?"

"Crush me?" said Derrick, "Are you out of your mind, Dougie? I eat nerds like you for breakfast every single day. I am a stone-cold—"

"Greetings, Derrick," said Vela, sitting down on the other side of him. "Is the sloppy joe to your liking? I pray it is as flavorful as your daily breakfast of nerds?"

"What is this, quiz bowl?" said Derrick. "Both of you dorks get lost! Now!"

This got a weaker laugh from his cronies. Especially considering neither Vela nor Thromdurr moved an inch.

"Derrick, if I may," said Devis, who had somehow been sitting at the table the whole time. "You already used 'dorks.' A different insult might have gotten a stronger response. You know, sometimes *how* you're communicating is just as important as *what* you're communicating."

At this, there were a few grunts and nods of agreement from the remaining members of Derrick's crew. A few of them stood up to move to another table.

"Where you going?" said Derrick. "Don't listen to this little chucklehead. Look at him, he's a total d—"

Derrick stopped himself from saying "dork" yet again. Devis clucked his tongue. Derrick was losing control of the situation, and he knew it. He was no Evan Cunningham, after all. More of his friends got up and left.

"Ooh, room for one more?" said Albiorix, taking a newly empty spot.

"No!" said Derrick. "Go back to wherever it is you came from, New Kid."

"Believe me, I'm trying, Derrick," said Albiorix.

"So tell us about these locker thefts," said Vela. "And be honest. Lies cannot save you."

"How should I know *anything* at all about that?" said Derrick.

"Your liege, Evan Cunningham, is responsible," said Thromdurr. "You can admit it."

"*Liege?*" said Evan, throwing his hands up. "Dude, nobody talks like that. Why are you such a huge—"

"Don't say dork," said Devis.

"I wasn't going to!" said Derrick.

Derrick stood up to leave, but Thromdurr put a meaty hand on his shoulder and slowly forced him back down into his seat.

"Take heed," said Thromdurr to his companions. "I did not crush him. It was merely a firm smooshing motion."

"I'll allow it," said Albiorix.

"This is so unfair," said Derrick. "Anytime anything bad happens, people blame Evan! Just like the shoelace thing. Nobody *ever* gives him the benefit of the doubt."

"Perhaps he arouses no sympathy because he is a spiteful person who revels in the misery of others?" said Vela.

"Exactly!" said Derrick. "I mean, no, wait, what?"

"Present the evidence that exonerates Evan," said Vela, steepling her fingers, "or face the swift hammer of judgment."

"Evan didn't do this, because *his own locker* got broken into," said Derrick. "They stole a laser pointer and a pair of headphones from him. You can ask Ms. Rhee."

The Bríandalörians all looked at each other.

And lo, what Derrick Day, loyal toady of Evan Cunningham, said was true. Ms. Rhee, the lawgiver of the school, confirmed the tale. And Albiorix's list of suspects shrank from thirty-one to thirty. He truly had no idea who it could be, as the rest of the school day passed in a timeless haze of academic failure, save the class of art, where the students began to experiment with the form of collage. And so the final bell rang, bringing their misery to an end, albeit a temporary one. Though school might be over, their studies were not. For this was their first day of private tutelage.

"Hi, guys," said June as she answered the door of the house at 410 North Rush Street. "Welcome to Castle Westray."

"Ha!" said Thromdurr. "This small, indefensible house would quickly fall to any attack. Where is the moat? Where is the boiling oil? You don't even have any arrow slits, June!"

"What Douglas means is, you have a lovely home," said Albiorix, nudging past Thromdurr into the door.

"In exchange for your tutelage, we have brought you a gift," said Vela, bowing. "Though we may never truly be able to repay you, please accept this humble gesture of gratitude." Vela handed June thirty-five dollars' (in magic coins) worth of snacks from the school vending machine.

"Wow, that's . . . that's a *lot* of individually wrapped peanut-butter crackers," said June as she accepted the load.

"You know, I do already have food at my house."

"Oh," said Devis. "Well, if you're not going to eat the cheese puffs, I'd be more than happy to take them off your hands."

"Very noble of you, Stinky," said June.

"Yeah," said Devis, ripping into a cheese-puff bag. "I get that a lot."

"All right, let's get this over with," said Sorrowshade, stepping inside. "I have places to be."

And so June Westray spent the better part of an afternoon teaching the outlanders all manner of strange and wondrous things: from social studies, to earth sciences, to Computer Applications, to English. And indeed the Bríandalörians learned much. And at last they begged June to help them with their hated algebra. But June Westray was reluctant, for math had always been her weakest subject. Yet after much pleading, she relented. And then she struggled mightily to explain the "quadratic formula" to the five adventurers.

"If we're trying to solve $7x^2 - 9x + 2 = 0$," said June, "we first need to figure out what a, b, and c are. Can anybody tell me what a is?"

Four Bríandalörians looked back at her with blank, slightly fearful expressions on their faces. The fifth, Devis, was staring at his phone.

"Somebody? Anybody? Nobody?" said June. "Here's a hint: it's the number in our equation that rhymes with *eleven*."

"Is it . . . eleven?" said Vela.

June let out a long sigh. "No, Valerie," she said. "Why would I say eleven rhymes with eleven? Besides, there is no eleven in the equation."

"I have it!" said Thromdurr. "The answer is Kevin."

"Kevin isn't a number, it's a person," said June. "And Stinky, I'm dying to know what exactly is so interesting on your phone." June caught herself. "Wow, I just sounded like a real teacher there, didn't I?"

"Huh?" said Devis, looking up. "Oh, right, Stinky is me. Yeah, no, I was just looking at this picture of a baby hedgehog with the words 'I CAN NOM NOM A BURRITO????' over it. It's called a meme. It's funny." He shrugged and showed the others his screen. Indeed his description was accurate.

"And *how* is that funny?" said Sorrowshade.

"Sorry, I should have been more clear," said Devis. "It's funny *if* you're capable of joy."

"It is not funny," said Thromdurr, shaking his head. "It makes less sense than June Westray's algebra lesson!"

"Hey!" said June. "I'm trying my best here. How did you guys make it all the way to eighth grade being this terrible at math?"

"An ancient curse," said Vela.

"Be that as it may," said June, "I really don't know what more I can do. I told you, I barely understand algebra myself."

"No, no. It's not your fault, June," said Albiorix. "We'll try harder to focus and Stinky will put away his— Hey, where did you even get a new phone? How much did that thing cost?"

"That's a rude question," said Devis. "But let's just say that as a senior vice president at a major international foods company and the one of the top soup critics in the country, the Smith family does very well for themselves."

"Bestowed upon you by your parents? Bah! What coddling!" said Thromdurr. "In my tribe, you become a full adult on your ninth birthday—the day you are sent out into the taiga to hunt an ice tiger with no weapons!"

"I think I'm losing the thread here, guys," said June. "Are you saying on your ninth birthday, your parents made you kill a—"

"Nope. He isn't," said Albiorix. "Just a little joke. Right, Douglas?"

"Yes," said Thromdurr through gritted teeth. "That proud and ancient custom is . . . a joke."

"And how is *that* funny?" asked Sorrowshade. "Don't answer. I have to go. I wish I could say it's been fun, but . . . you know."

"Wait, where are you off to?" said Albiorix.

"We still don't know what number rhymes with eleven," said Vela.

"Seven," said June quietly, face buried in her palms. "Obviously, it has to be seven."

"I have to go be a *bestie*," said Sorrowshade. "Nicole is making me go to Sophie Sorrentino's house to watch some TV program called *Las Vegas Fashion Wives*. I'm sure it will be excruciating."

"But after tutoring, we were supposed to investigate the locker thefts together," said Albiorix.

"Wait, why do you guys care about that?" said June. "Did one of your lockers get hit?"

"No," said Albiorix. "But Mr. Driscoll thinks I did it."

"I knew it," said June. "Armando Boort, international criminal."

"I'm innocent!" said Albiorix.

"And the real culprit still eludes justice," said Vela. "But not for long. The first theft is the key to solving the others. If only we knew who took Sam Keller's shark-tooth necklace . . ."

"Hang on," said June, "I saw somebody wearing a necklace like that."

"You did?" said Vela.

"You did?" said Devis.

"Yeah," said June. "My mom and I went out for dinner

for her birthday yesterday. We ate at the Cheesecakery and then went bowling in this run-down old mall. Anyway, the food wasn't very good and the bowling alley smelled weird. But I definitely saw a kid hanging out by the fountain wearing a silver shark tooth around his neck."

"Did you recognize him from school?" said Albiorix.

June shook her head. "Nope," she said, "but then again, I've only been a JADMS student for two days. I don't really know many people around here."

Vela leaped to her feet. "Well, thank you for your wise tutelage, June," she said, "Now we must away. Companions, to the mall!"

The five Bríandalörians burst out the front door and dashed down the street.

"You guys are . . . weird," called June after them.

But none of the intrepid heroes heard her. They were already well on their way toward the old mall, to bring the swift hammer of justice down upon the head of evil.

Chapter 10

Outside of class, middle schoolers often congregate in areas that paradoxically seem to offer nothing of interest. Parking lots, basements, and backyards are natural meeting places. Such dull, semisecluded environs offer a form of independence to an age group granted more responsibility than "little kids" but not yet trusted to operate motor vehicles.

—Excerpt from The Codex of Cliques

❧

"THIS . . . IS A PLACE of great sadness," said Sorrowshade.

The five adventurers looked around the Hibbettsfield Galleria—what the locals called "the Old Mall." What once had been a thriving enclosed bazaar now felt eerily vacant. Practically every other storefront was dark and shuttered, and those that still persisted mostly offered odd, undesired products, such as leather jackets with wolves painted on them or the odd specialty products Thormdurr knew from infomercials.

"If I remember my Hibbettsfield history correctly, the opening of the Towne Center Mall out on Route 22 and the rise of online shopping were kind of the death knell for this place," said Albiorix. "They do have the aforementioned bowling alley and a cart where you can buy soft pretzels, though."

"Look, there's a map," said Vela, as she pointed to a dingy, glowing sign that displayed the complex's floor plan. "The Cheesecakery is located at 2F, so the fountain June described must be that blue circle, there, on the second floor."

"Guys, why are we even wasting our time with this?" asked Devis, still glued to his new phone. "We're a day late. There's no way the kid in the shark-tooth necklace is still going to be here. Who would ever want to come to this mall twice? Honestly, this pretty much sums up my feeling . . ." He held up the phone: another photo, this time a sleeping baby hedgehog, with the words "LESS TRYING MORE NAPPING."

"That hedgehog's shameful apathy aside," said Vela, "we may yet learn something by exploring the Old Mall, even if the culprit is gone."

"Nicole is not going to be happy I skipped out on *Las Vegas Fashion Wives*," said Sorrowshade with a sigh.

"Bah! You are your own master, elf," said Thromdurr. "What do you care?"

"I don't!" said Sorrowshade. "Nicole is deceitful, vain, and cruel. I just . . . don't want to get on her bad side."

Up ahead, Vela had frozen in her tracks.

"By the gods," said the paladin. "What . . . are . . . those?"

Beyond her were what appeared to be two writhing silver dragons: one slithering upward, the other burrowing down into the ground. It took the adventurers a moment to see that they weren't dragons at all, but instead moving staircases. In all their journeys across Bríandalör—through enchanted temples, haunted fortresses, and floating castles—the five of them had never seen anything like this.

"'Tis some sort of living stairwell," said Thromdurr, who made the protective sign of the Sky Bear.

"Actually, I believe they're called 'escalators,'" said Albiorix. The wizard was vaguely familiar with the concept from his books, yet even he was overawed by the actual sight of them.

"How do we get past them?" asked Sorrowshade, looking around for another route up to the second floor.

"Perhaps if we threw a grappling hook onto the railing there," said Vela, looking upward, "we could use that sunglasses kiosk to climb up."

"Guys, I think—I think we can just ride them," said Albiorix.

"Madness," said Thromdurr. "What if we became trapped between the steps and the floor? We would be pinched to death! What if the staircases became angry while we were clinging to their backs? It is too risky, wizard!"

"Pardon me," said an old lady as she stepped past the heroes and onto the escalator.

They watched her slowly glide all the way up to the second floor and disembark at the top. And so, after a few more minutes of cajoling and steeling their nerves, the adventurers nervously stepped on and rode up, expecting every moment that the escalators might turn on them. After what seemed like an eternity, they stepped off again unscathed and proceeded toward the fountain.

"Guys, this is a bad idea," muttered Devis. "And I should know. I'm an expert on bad ideas."

"My spirit too was shaken by the escalator ride, small friend," said Thromdurr. "But we must press onward!"

"The Cheesecakery is up ahead," said Vela.

The fountain was a murky green, and it smelled like a mixture of chlorine and decay. Seven kids stood around it. They laughed and joked and sipped from disposable soda cups, occasionally showing each other something on their phones. Albiorix didn't recognize any of them as fellow J. A. Dewar students.

"Hello, children of the Old Mall," said Vela, approaching them.

"Hi?" said a boy with spiky blue hair.

"We are searching for a pendant," said Vela, "A silvery shark's tooth. Have any of you seen it?"

"Not really my style," said a girl with a ring through her nose. "Maybe try LA Jewelers?"

"I should be clear: we are looking for a particular pendant," said Vela, fixing her steely gaze upon them. "*A stolen pendant.*"

Six of the kids looked confused. The seventh—a boy in a floppy knit cap—bolted.

"COME BACK HERE!" bellowed Thromdurr as the party sprinted after him.

Before they could catch up, the knit-cap kid ducked into a large discount department store called Maximo's—a cavernous place, selling everything from home appliances to winter coats. By the time the Bríandalörians made it to the entrance, the knit-cap boy had vanished somewhere inside.

Sorrowshade sniffed the air and pointed in two directions, indicating they should separate and corner the boy. Vela and Thromdurr started to go right, while Albiorix and Sorrowshade started left.

"Wait," said Albiorix. "I think we lost Devis."

They looked around. Indeed, their fifth companion was nowhere to be seen.

"Then he will just have to catch up to us," said Vela. "We cannot allow this locker thief to slip through our fingers!"

And so the adventurers split up. Vela and Thromdurr snuck off through women's apparel, while Sorrowshade and Albiorix stalked down the greeting-card aisle. Every so often the gloom elf would pause, cock her head, and listen with her superior hearing. The assassin and the wizard followed a circuitous route through the toy aisle, past the welcome mats, around the electronics section, and back to pillows and bedding, as Sorrowshade read signs that were invisible to mere mortals. At last she stopped at a floor-model bed, apparently worth ~~$499.99~~ $399.99. She pointed underneath. Slowly, Albiorix crouched to have a look.

"Aaaaagh!" screamed the knit-cap boy as he leaped out from under the bed and bowled the wizard over.

"Hey, watch it!" cried Albiroix.

As the boy ran, Sorrowshade scanned the shelf. She grabbed a circular cushion and hurled it with deadly accuracy. The flying pillow caught the boy in the back of the knees, taking his legs right out from under him. With a yelp, he crashed into a bin of discount DVDs. A second later, he was up again, but a powerful arm caught him by the hood of his sweatshirt and held him tight.

"Not so fast, little locker thief," said Thromdurr.

"Let me go!" yelled the boy as he struggled in vain. "I didn't steal anything!"

"Then why did you flee when I asked about the pendant?" said Vela.

"I don't know!" said the boy. "You guys seemed super serious, like you do this *professionally* or something. I panicked, that's all. I'm a well-known coward. Ask anyone!"

"I see," said Sorrowshade. "Well, this is very interesting to find on someone who didn't steal anything." She yanked something from the boy's neck and held it up: a silver shark's-tooth pendant glinted under the fluorescent lights of Maximo's.

"Sure, okay, now that I think about it, that does sound a lot like what you were describing," said the boy. "But I didn't know it was stolen when I bought it."

"And who exactly did you buy it from?" asked Albiorix.

"No idea," said the boy. "I saw an ad online, so I went to his house to pick it up. I never asked his name."

"Well, what did he look like?" said Vela.

"Like . . . like that!" said the boy, and he pointed.

The adventurers turned.

"Oh, hi," said Devis, casually stepping out from behind a lawn-furniture display.

"Hey! Hey, tell them, guy!" said the knit-cap boy. "Tell them I paid you ten bucks for the necklace!"

"It's true," said Devis, "and as a courtesy, I want to offer you a full refund." Devis reached into his pocket and pulled out a thick wad of money. He peeled off a ten-dollar bill and handed it to the boy.

"But promise me next time you'll be more careful when you buy things from strangers off the internet," said Devis.

"Huh? But . . . but you're the one who—okay, okay, fine," said the boy.

Thromdurr released his iron grip, and the boy bolted once more. This time they let him go. All eyes were on Devis now.

Devis sighed. "Look, I know you're all probably angry, but I just want you to know I don't think that kid is the real culprit here."

"Gee, really?" said Sorrowshade, crossing her arms. "Who else might possibly have done something wrong?"

"You probably don't want to hear it right now, but I feel I owe it to you to be honest," said Devis. "You all bear some of the blame as well."

At this, all the other adventurers groaned and threw their hands up.

"You strain my patience, thief!" snarled Thromdurr.

"Exactly! *Thief!*" said Devis. "Stealing is right there in

my job title, friends! If you don't want me to do it, it's on you to tell me so!"

"Oh, please," said Vela.

"Sure," said Devis, crossing his arms, "thieving is all well and good when I'm picking locks to get you guys through dungeon doors. Or robbing a bunch of monsters and then splitting the loot five ways."

"But these middle schoolers aren't monsters," said Albiorix.

"Evan Cunningham might be," said Sorrowshade quietly.

"Can you believe there wasn't a single trap to disarm on any of those lockers?" said Devis. "Seriously! No poison gas. No exploding runes. Nothing. The only protection was a bunch of cheap combination locks. It's like everyone *wanted* me to sneak back into school in the dead of the night and take their valuables. In fact, you almost could say I did the school a service by pointing out how weak their security is—"

"Enough of this nonsense," said Vela. "We must return the stolen goods at once to exonerate Albiorix."

"Okay, fine," said Devis, hanging his head. "Except . . ."

"Here it comes," said Sorrowshade.

"Except I can't actually, *technically*, do that," said Devis.

"And why not?" said Vela.

"I already sold everything," said Devis. He held up the wad of cash again. "Anyway, who wants a soft pretzel?"

Chapter 11

FRANKS, Waldo Dean

OCCUPATION: *Owner of Pan-Galactic Comics and Collectibles*

ATTRIBUTES: *Cunning: 16, Intelligence: 14, Likability: 3, Willpower: 17, Fitness: 6*

SKILLS: *Bargaining +8, Computer +9, Cooking −4, Drive −1, Trivia (Comic Books) +10, Trivia (Science Fiction TV) +10, Trivia (Retro Video Games) +10*

BIOGRAPHY: *Waldo Franks is the thirty-nine-year-old owner of Hibbettsfield's only comic book shop. He enjoys maintaining his in-store terrarium, rewatching science fiction TV shows from his youth, fact-checking others on the internet, and very little else.*

—*Excerpt from* The Hibbettsfield Handbook

"Hello?" said the girl at 635 Westminster Drive, through her screen door.

"Lisa Laporte!" said Devis. "Hi! Remember me? From yesterday? You paid me thirty-five dollars for a pair of sneakers and I offered you a cup of my mom's New England clam chowder and you politely declined?"

"Yeah, I remember you," said Lisa. "Why are you at my house?"

"Well, it turns out I shouldn't have sold those sneakers to you after all," said Devis. "Whoopsie."

"How did you even find me?" said Lisa.

Albiorix nudged his way forward. "It was actually pretty neat. We used the name on your email address to search social media until we found a match. Then we combed through your friends list to figure out who your parents were, and from there it was a simple matter to look up your home address. Computers truly are a wonder!"

"That is . . . *incredibly* creepy," said Lisa.

"Yes, I did realize that as I was saying it," said Albiorix. "Sorry."

"Anyway," said Devis, "I'm afraid I'm going to need to refund your cash and retrieve that pair of sneakers."

"What if I don't want to?" said the girl. She pointed to her feet. She was currently wearing the sneakers Devis had sold her. "I like them."

"Then I'm afraid we must appeal to the angels of your better nature, Lisa Laporte," said Vela. "Our dear friend has been wrongfully accused of the theft of those very shoes, and we need them to prove his innocence."

Albiorix nodded solemnly. "She means me."

"So who's the real thief?" said the girl.

"This little scamp, of course!" said Thromdurr, tousling Devis's hair.

"But obviously I have seen the error of my et cetera and learned a valuable et cetera," said Devis. "It will never happen again, probably. Anyway here's your thirty-five bucks back." He waved a handful of money.

"I don't know," said Lisa. "I . . . think I'm going to keep them."

"Why?" asked Sorrowshade. "They are extremely unflattering."

Lisa frowned. "They are?"

"Beauty is in the eye of the beholder," said Sorrowshade, "but those sneakers make you look like you've got two misshapen yams on the ends of your legs."

Lisa stared at the adventurers for several seconds. "If I give you the sneakers back, will all of you just . . . leave?"

"Absolutely," said Devis.

And so she did, in exchange for a thirty-five-dollar refund. And the brave heroes of Bríandalör continued their winding journey across the town of Hibbettsfield, tracking down all the stolen items that Devis the thief had listed and sold online. For some people they used flattery. Others required guilt. A few needed a bit of cajoling.

Though it took them several hours, they had at last recovered the items from twelve of the thirteen lockers. This brought them at last to what would prove to be their greatest challenge yet. They stood at the West End Shopping Center on Cleveland Street. There, between Ronnie's Sporting Goods and an Aeon Wireless mobile phone store, was Pan-Galactic Comics and Collectibles.

"Doesn't much look like a house," said Sorrowshade.

Albiorix shrugged. "This is the only address I could find for Waldo Franks."

Devis peeked through the window. "Yep. That's the guy, all right."

A bell jingled as the adventurers walked through the door. Inside was a dimly lit store filled, wall-to-wall, with action figures, comic books, and games. A faint musty smell hung in the air. Behind the counter, a man fed two turtles in a glass tank. There were no customers.

"Welcome to Pan-Galactic Comics and Collectibles," said Waldo Franks without turning around. "Can I help you? Or are you just here to get your thumbprints on things?"

"Why, hello again, friend," said Devis, leaning on the

counter and flashing his flashiest smile. "I believe you *can* help us."

"You're not getting it back," said Franks as he continued to shake the box of turtle flakes into the terrarium.

"How did you—I mean, I don't even know what you're—I mean you don't know what I'm . . . hmm," said Devis, who rarely found himself caught off guard.

Waldo Franks turned around. "Yesterday you sold me an Agent Helios, Marksman of G.U.N.N. (Limited Edition Gray Battlesuit) action figure for two hundred and fifty dollars," he said, pointing to a high shelf behind the counter. On it was a glass case marked NOT FOR SALE. EVER; inside was the toy he'd purchased from Devis. "For said figure, I substantially underpaid. Your fault for not doing your research." said Franks. "Anyway, I assume you're here because you're upset about the transaction."

"Er," said Devis.

The adventurers looked at each other, unsure of how to proceed.

Vela cleared her throat. "If I may—"

"No. You may *not*," said Franks. "As far as I'm concerned, that sale is final and I won't part for that action figure for any price."

"Friend, is this not a store?" said Thromdurr.

"It is a store, and I am happy to sell you any number of

the lesser action figures I have available," said Franks, waving dismissively at his other toys. "But the Agent Helios, Marksman of G.U.N.N. (Limited Edition Gray Battlesuit) action figure behind the counter happens to be priceless. You see, it has an incredibly rare misprint: the second N on the reverse of the jumpsuit is backward. According to the price guide there are only fifty-seven of these in existence. And as of yesterday, I possess one of them."

The Bríandalörians failed to see how poor craftsmanship ought to increase value of something, which only made the situation more baffling.

"It is but a toy made of plastic," said Thromdurr.

"Perhaps to an uncultured barbarian such as yourself," said Waldo.

Thromdurr blinked. "How in the name of the Sky Bear did you know that I'm—"

"But to me it represents pure, unadulterated bliss," said Waldo, breathing a deep sigh of contentment. "That misprinted Agent Helios, Marksman of G.U.N.N. (Limited Edition Gray Battlesuit) action figure will be my legacy."

"Then I'm afraid we must appeal to the angels of your better nature, Waldo Franks," said Vela.

"Sorry, I don't have any of those in stock," said Franks with a shrug. "Now, if you're not buying anything, skedaddle."

"Please excuse us for a moment," said Vela.

Franks ignored her. He had already turned back around to the tank and was scratching one of the turtles beneath its scaly chin.

The five adventurers regrouped on the sidewalk outside.

"For a man who surrounds himself with whimsical children's toys, he sure is crabby," said Vela.

Sorrowshade shrugged. "I kind of liked his attitude."

"Albiorix," said Vela, "is there anything about him in the Homerooms & Hall Passes books?"

"Good thinking," said Albiorix. "Let's see." The wizard unslung his heavy pack and then began to sift through his books.

"Look, I'm just going to say it. There happens to be a very simple solution here," said Devis. "We wait till Waldo here closes up shop. Then I sneak back in and pinch the action figure and whatever comics or games you guys happen to want—"

"Absolutely not," said Vela. "Your thieving has brought enough trouble. We must persuade him to accept the money you took from him in return for the toy because it is the right thing to do."

"I don't think that's going to happen," said Albiorix, who had *The Hibbettsfield Handbook* open to the entry for Pan-Galactic Comics and Collectibles. "According to his stats, Waldo Franks has a 17 Willpower. We'll never talk him into doing something he doesn't want to do."

"Plus, and I probably should have mentioned this, I don't actually *have* the money he paid me, per se," said Devis. "I used it to buy my fancy new phone." Devis held it up. On-screen was a picture of another hedgehog, this time sitting in a bowl of spaghetti with the words "THAT'S A SPIKY MEATBALL."

Vela sighed. "Well, no money to exchange certainly complicates things. But still, there must be some way to resolve this situation. We finally have a quest, and we must not fail. Albiorix, what else does his entry say?"

"Hmm. He likes TV shows about spaceships and his pet turtles and . . . that's pretty much it," said Albiorix.

"Then we shall kidnap his beloved turtles and offer them in exchange for the toy!" said Thromdurr.

"I will not menace any innocent turtles," said Vela.

"Then let's cut right to the chase and menace him directly," said Sorrowshade, cracking her knuckles.

"Again, no," said Vela. "We can't go around threatening everyone we don't like. It's not right."

"Waldo Franks is a collector by nature," said Albiorix, "So we'd have to offer him something rarer than that lame action figure."

"Hang on!" said Vela. "We do have something rarer.

And quite possibly lamer too!"

The bell jangled again as the five adventurers marched back into the store.

"Welcome to Pan-Galactic Comics and Games," said Waldo Franks, squinting at them over steepled fingers. "Can I help you?"

"Waldo Franks," said Vela. "What if I told you we can give you something more precious than your misprinted Agent Helios, Marksman of G.U.N.N. (Limited Edition Gray Battlesuit) action figure?"

"I would call you a liar, madam," said Franks. "Because there is nothing more precious than my misprinted Agent Helios, Marksman of G.U.N.N. (Limited Edition Gray Battlesuit) action figure."

"Do we all have to keep saying 'Agent Helios, Marksman of G.U.N.N. (Limited Edition Gray Battlesuit) action figure'?" said Devis. "I feel like shortening that would be a real time-saver for this interaction."

Vela ignored him. "Waldo Franks, we have a collectible so rare that it is the only one of its kind in the entire world."

Franks squinted at her. He licked his lips. "I'll admit," he said, "you have piqued my curiosity."

Vela placed a glittering ring on the counter and slid it across.

"A ring?" said Franks. "Big deal. There are millions of

rings out there. Plus I don't go in for jewelry. I like to keep my look clean, elegant." He indicated his T-shirt, which depicted a drawing of a muscular superhero punching through a tank. "Stop wasting my time."

Vela smiled. "This is not just any ring," she said. "This is a Ring of Turtle Speech."

Franks blinked. "That's not even possible."

"Is it not?" said Vela. "Observe." She slipped the ring onto her finger and turned to the tank behind the counter. Then she began to make a series of strange quiet chirps and grunts, deep in her throat. One of the turtles cocked its head. Then it clicked back at her. Vela made another long series of turtle vocalizations. She paused and grunted once more. This time, both turtles gave a continuous modulated hiss. There was no mistaking it: the reptiles were laughing.

By now Waldo Franks's jaw was hanging open.

Vela slipped the ring from her finger and placed it on the counter once more. "Now, I ask again," she said. "Would you like to trade this Ring of Turtle Speech for the Agent Heli—"

"Toy," said Devis. "Let's just call it the toy."

And so the five brave adventurers walked out of Pan-Galactic Comics and Collectibles bearing the object of their quest: a precious item of rare provenance and prohibitively long name. Behind them, they left a man overjoyed. Waldo

Franks was finally able to share his thoughts and feelings with the only living creatures to which he felt any connection: his two eastern box turtles, Millie and Thad.

"Wow, I cannot believe we actually found somebody who wanted that Ring of Turtle Speech," said Sorrowshade.

"I am curious, paladin," said Thromdurr. "What did you say that those turtles found so humorous?"

"I asked them what turtles do when they score a great victory," said Vela.

"Huh," said Albiorix. "Well . . . what *do* turtles do when they score a great victory?"

"They *shell*-ebrate," said Vela.

The other adventurers paused, dumbfounded.

"Vela told a joke," said Devis, clutching his head for fear it might explode.

"But it was only for the turtles," said Albiorix.

"I told you all I have a sense of humor," said Vela. "And you know I never lie."

With a rare grin, the paladin kept on walking.

Chapter 12

In the real world, political authority comes from noble birth, or in rare cases because someone found a magic sword. But in middle school, class presidents are chosen democratically. This process involves homemade posters, wildly unrealistic promises, and capturing a plurality of the votes cast by the class. Though the title of class president is largely meaningless, it is still relentlessly sought by Overachievers, Nerds, Jocks, and Class Clowns alike.

—Excerpt from The Hall Master's Guide

❧

"AAAGH! MY AGENT HELIOS, Marksman of G.U.N.N. (Limited Edition Gray Battlesuit) action figure!" cried Saul Graham. "It's back! I can't believe it. It's finally back." He grabbed the toy out of his locker and hugged it close.

All around, middle schoolers were shouting for joy as

they discovered that items they thought were gone forever had been returned in the night.

"My brother's tablet," said Reuben Huang. "It's here! It even has a full battery."

"My shoes have been returned too," said Sherri Rios. "Although it seems like somebody has been wearing them." She crinkled her nose.

The five heroes watched with satisfaction. A wrong had been righted, and they were victorious. It was a feeling they hadn't known since they'd left Bríandalör.

"What are you guys grinning about?" said June as she walked up to them in the hall.

"Oh, nothing," said Albiorix, who tried and failed to suppress his smile.

"Seriously, what?" said June.

"Let us just say that justice reigns once more throughout the land," said Vela.

"If I'm being honest, I'm probably not going to say that," said June. "So you guys actually caught the locker thief?"

"Yep," said Sorrowshade. "He was a shifty little creep."

"Yet devilishly handsome," said Devis, "with a singing voice like an angel. Many would question whether he was actually a villain at all—"

"Armando!"

Albiorix turned to see Mr. Driscoll standing a little

ways down the hall. The custodian looked around and then waved the wizard over.

"I can see you did . . . what we talked about," said Mr. Driscoll. He kept his voice low in case someone might be listening.

"Again, I was not responsible, Mr. Driscoll," said Albiorix, "but I and my companions brought the matter to a swift and fair conclusion. Quest closed."

"Quest?" said Mr. Driscoll.

"Never mind. Forget I said that," said Albiorix. "Go, hockey!"

Mr. Driscoll sighed and gave a tight nod, which the wizard hoped meant that they were square. The custodian then continued on his way.

The party's happy mood persisted through homeroom announcements, once more commandeered by Principal Greene—again sparing Vela the daunting task—to deliver the good news about the locker thefts. In English class, June's tutelage paid off, and Ms. Levy even complimented Thromdurr on one of his pro-cat arguments (cats are good pets because they are unafraid to meet household vermin on the field of battle). In Computer Applications class, the adventurers approached their fake menus with gusto, and Mr. Gulazarian seemed impressed. In gym, the game was "kickball." After learning the simple rules, the Bríandalörians excelled, thanks to their superior strength and coordination. The heroes were flying high, and it seemed like nothing could stop them now.

Then, like a bolt of fire from a soaring dragon, Algebra I struck again. Somehow the class made even less sense than it had on the previous day, and all their attempts to solve the "quadratic formula" were met with humiliating failure. Worse yet, Mr. Botello announced there would be a test the following Tuesday. This test would count for a fifth of their grade for the entire semester.

Once more demoralized, the four adventurers—minus Sorrowshade, who was at the popular girls' table—sat together in the cafeteria, each picking at the tuna sandwich or grilled cheese they had chosen.

"Wow, you guys look glum," said June as she finished up a game of *Oink Pop* and sat down beside them. "Does justice no longer reign throughout the land?"

"It is this accursed algebra," said Thromdurr, pounding the table. "We cannot hope to defeat it!"

"None of the math stuff you tried to teach us helped, June," said Devis. "No offense, but . . . you really screwed up."

"What?" said June. "I never said I was good at algebra! I hate algebra! I wish we could do art class all day! Or lunch!"

"Stinky, don't be rude," said Albiorix, elbowing Devis.

"June, your tutelage in every other subject has been invaluable."

"Yet still, we have no choice," said Vela. "We must pass algebra."

"Or what?" said June.

"Or we will cease to exist," said Vela.

"Sounds rough," said June. "I figure I can squeak by with a C, so hopefully that won't happen to me." She took a bite of her grilled cheese and then noticed the others were still staring at her.

"Sorry, guys. I don't know what to tell you," said June. "Maybe find a better math tutor?"

"Like who?" said Vela.

June shrugged. "That girl is always raising her hand in Mr. Botello's class."

At a nearby table sat Olivia Gorman, who was struggling to open a carton of milk.

"Yes!" said Albiorix, brightening. "Olivia Gorman is a Nerd."

"Hey, c'mon," said June. "Be nice."

"No, no, no, it's not an insult," said Albiorix.

"It's her character class, June," said Devis.

"If I recall correctly, Olivia Gorman has a Math skill of +8," said Albiorix. "Second only to Douglas in the entire class."

"Douglas, who's . . . failing?" said June.

"Yes, but not for long," said Albiorix. "Olivia Gorman is the only one who has a shot at getting us to a passing grade. Valerie, you cohost the J. A. Dewar morning bulletin with her. Perhaps you could ask her to help us?"

"I would," said Vela, "but I get the sense that Olivia doesn't like me much."

"Maybe because of how you royally screwed up the announcements and made a fool of yourself in front of the entire school?" said Devis.

Vela sighed.

"Bah! It is because you are an Overachiever, Valerie. You dabble in athletics and theater," said Thromdurr. "You are not a true Nerd—focused solely on pursuits of the mind—like Olivia. And me."

"You guys really love tossing that word around," said June.

"Perhaps a member of her own tribe can persuade her," said Thromdurr. "Wish me luck, friends!"

And with that, Thromdurr stood and went to join Olivia at her table.

"Greetings, Olivia Gorman," said the barbarian.

"Hi, Doug," said Olivia.

"Though I am widely regarded to be the wisest student in all of eighth grade, I now require math tutelage," said

Thromdurr, pounding his chest. "I prevail upon the sacred bond we share as Nerds and humbly ask you to teach me, as well as Valerie, Stinky, Melissa, and Armando, the mysterious ways of the algebra."

Olivia frowned and stared at Thromdurr for several seconds. "No," she said at last.

"No?" said Thromdurr. "But you and I are of one people!"

"Doug, if you're failing math, that means I get the math award at the end of the year," said Olivia. "I would say 'Do the math,' but apparently you can't."

Thromdurr sighed and shook his head. "Though it pains me to concede any contest, you may have this year's math award. I offer it to you freely and will not battle you for it."

"Okay," said Olivia.

"So will you help us now?" said Thromdurr.

"What's in it for me?" said Olivia.

"The math award!" said Thromdurr, who felt his berserker blood rising.

"Again, we've established that you're already failing math," said Olivia. "I'm getting that award anyway. Try harder, Doug."

"Well, what is it that you want?" said Thromdurr. "Perhaps a Spinco Roastmeister home rotisserie?"

"What? No," said Olivia. "I want to be class president."

"If I am not mistaken," said Thromdurr, "Valerie has held that particular office for years."

"Yeah, because it's just a stupid popularity contest," said Olivia. "And I want to win it this time. The election is Monday. If Valerie drops out and you guys make me president, I'll give you people all the free algebra tutoring you can handle."

Thromdurr returned to the table with Olivia's terms.

"Hang on, there's another election?" said Devis. "I thought Valerie was already the president?"

"Valerie is *student body* president, an office elected by all three JADMS grades," said Albiorix. "But class president is the eighth grade only. Even though Valerie usually wins that too."

"Why is everything around here so complicated?" said Devis, shaking his head. "If you guys only knew how many types of soup I'm expected to keep track of at home . . ."

"So what do you say, Valerie?" said Albiorix.

"Hmm," Vela. "Is there no one else who might teach us?"

"After Olivia, you're the third best student in Algebra I, so that's no good," said Albiorix, scanning the cafeteria. "The only other kid who's smart enough is George Stedman, but he'll never agree to help us. He despises Stinky ever since that famous crickets-in-the-gym-bag prank last year."

"I'd forgotten about that," said Devis. "If I'd known we were going to be in this predicament, I would have used, maybe, half as many crickets."

"Then I suppose we have no choice," said Vela. "I will drop out of the race."

"And Olivia Gorman will be victorious," said Thromdurr. "Finally the number-letters of Algebra I will bow before us!"

"Yeah, about that," said Albiorix. "Olivia still probably isn't going to win."

"Why not?" said Vela.

"Last year, you only won by four votes," said Albiorix, "If you're dropping out, then Brent Sydlowski is the favorite."

Albiorix pointed across the cafeteria to an athletic, friendly-looking boy, sitting at a table of fellow Jocks.

June suddenly looked up from the game of *Oink Pop* she had been playing. "Hang on, Armando. How could you possibly know election results from last year? You were in Edmonton, Alberta, Canada."

"I . . . really studied up on this place before I got here," said Albiorix.

June cocked her head. "Valerie, you seem honest. Is he telling the truth?"

Vela sat tight-lipped for several seconds of uncomfortable silence. "Technically, yes," she said.

"Hey, look at this!" said Albiorix. He pulled a coin out of his ear. "Pretty neat, huh? And here's another one!" He pulled a second coin from his other ear.

June frowned. "Wow, I've never seen that one before," she said. "I can't help but feel like you're trying to distract me from—"

"Well, anyway, we should probably tell Olivia that we accept her terms," said Albiorix. "If we are somehow going to win this race for her, we need to start campaigning right now! Later, June."

Thromdurr delivered the group's answer to Olivia, who set a time that afternoon to tutor them all in algebra. And so the brave adventurers began such an endeavor as was heretofore unknown to them: a middle-school political campaign. They split up for the remainder of the lunch period to try to convince their peers to vote for Olivia Gorman for class president. The bell rang, and the entire party regrouped on their way to their lockers. Somehow Sorrowshade already knew that Vela had dropped out of the presidential race (apparently gossip flowed with supernatural speed to the popular girls' table).

"Albiorix was right about Olivia's chances," said Devis. "Everybody I talked to said they were leaning toward Brent. I don't think I changed anybody's mind, despite my charming personality."

"It was the same for me," said Vela. "People seem to like Brent Sydlowski because he is strong and guileless."

"It is a highly appealing combination," said Thromdurr.

"Then it seems we have to knock Brent out of the race too," said Sorrowshade.

"Shall I crush him?" said Thromdurr.

"Nope," said Albiorix. "Still no crushing."

"Aw," said Thromdurr.

"Perhaps if you simply explained to Brent that class president is a ceremonial title conferring no real power, he would lose interest in it," said Vela.

"Yeah. He seems like a nice enough guy," said Albiorix. "Maybe I could just ask him to drop out?"

At that very moment, Brent Sydlowski and his friends walked past the party in the hall, laughing among themselves. Albiorix took a deep breath and approached.

"Hi, Brent," said Albiorix,

"Hey, New Kid!" said Brent.

"You wouldn't consider quitting the presidential race, would you?" said Albiorix. "The whole thing is pretty meaningless, after all."

Brent's friends laughed.

"Nah, I can't quit now," said Brent. "Even if I don't win, my message is too important."

"And what message would that be?" asked Albiorix.

"Homework sucks," said Brent.

"Interesting," said Albiorix, and he couldn't disagree.

"Vote Brent, New Kid!" said Brent.

He gave Albiorix a fist bump and continued on down the hall with his crew. The wizard rejoined his companions.

"He was not persuaded," said Albiorix. "And after speaking with him, I can confirm that he is, in some strange way, very likable. A bit like a large, friendly dog."

"Of course playing nice didn't work," said Sorrowshade. "It rarely does. If Brent Sydlowski will not voluntarily concede, then we must apply pressure—pinpoint his weakness and use it to inflict maximum damage."

"I already told Thromdurr we can't crush him," said Albiorix.

"Not physically," said Sorrowshade with a grin. "Socially."

The other adventurers paused.

"How would we do that?" said Albiorix. "He's one of the most popular kids in the entire school."

"Exactly," said Sorrowshade. "And we know every one of his secrets."

Chapter
13

The game of Homerooms & Hall Passes focuses on the actions of the player characters. But what truly brings the Realm of Suburbia to life are all the nonplayer characters (NPCs) they interact with. Many NPCs can be found in The Cyclopedia of Students, The Tome of Teachers, The Album of Academic Administration, *and various other sourcebooks. But try to remember that these supporting characters are more than just a block of game stats. They have their own goals, fears, and challenges. You may also consider giving them funny voices. . . .*

—*Excerpt from* The Hall Master's Guide

❧

"WHAT? WHAT IS THIS?" said Marie Stumpf-Turner. "Valerie is first-chair flute. Why is she sitting all the way in the back?"

"I can barely see her," said Andy Stumpf-Turner, squinting. "I can't even tell if she looks sick or not."

"Shhh," said another parent in the audience.

Onstage, the James Alexander Dewar Titan Band plodded its way through the first tune of its fall concert. After this week's practices, Vela had been placed on "indefinite leave" from first-chair flute, and Sharad Marwah had been promoted. In addition, Ms. Peco, the band director, had privately told her, "During the concert, just act like you're playing, honey. But don't you *dare* make a noise with that thing."

It was a conundrum for a noble paladin. On the one hand, Vela was honor bound to obey her band director. On the other, pretending to play the flute when she really wasn't felt very close to a lie. As a way of threading the needle, Vela tried to play her flute as quietly as possible. But her musical skill was so poor that she still emitted an occasional shrill squeak. Each time earned her a glare from Ms. Peco, who conducted from the podium.

Out in the audience, Albiorix struggled to stay awake. The lights were down, the Titan Band's performance wasn't exactly electrifying, and he'd been sleeping on gym equipment. Still, the adventurers had done well today. They had held strong in their other classes, and Olivia Gorman's first math lesson had proven invaluable.

Olivia was a tougher tutor than June—she had

confiscated Devis's phone almost immediately—the concepts of algebra were finally starting to sink in. With Olivia's help, Albiorix had been able to simplify his first equation, and it felt almost as good as casting his very first spell ("summon pill bugs"). The other Bríandalörians were making progress too—only Thromdurr still seemed utterly confused, but perhaps with a few more tutoring sessions, the barbarian would be able to catch up.

Onstage, the musicians were bowing now. After what felt like an eternity, the concert had mercifully ended. As the crowd of parents and siblings milled out of the auditorium, the five adventurers converged in the parking lot. They hadn't merely come to support Vela's terrible fluting. They had a plan.

"Are we sure we still want to do this?" said Vela.

"It's clearer than ever that we won't pass math without Olivia's help," said Albiorix. "We have no choice."

"Then I have until my mother finishes berating Ms. Peco for removing me from first-chair flute," said Vela with a sigh. "Truly humiliating, by the way."

"Hey, can't be as bad as freezing up during those announcements, right?" said Devis, punching Vela in the arm.

She groaned. "I just wish we had another quest," said Vela. "All the pressure and practices and prevarication of this realm are starting to wear on me."

"I agree, paladin," said Thromdurr. "But we must press

forward. Our fortunes are looking up. I am on the very cusp of conquering algebra. Today I had an epiphany: perhaps we are always trying to figure out x because it marks the location of some long-buried treasure!"

"Hmm," said Albiorix, not wanting to puncture his companion's fragile confidence. "Anyway, it's six twenty-eight now. In two minutes, Brent Sydlowski should be on his way from lacrosse practice to the school parking lot. As always, he will be surrounded by his friends. We need him alone."

"That is where Devis and I come in," said Thromdurr.

"Right," said Albiorix. "Once Brent is by himself, the rest of us will discreetly approach him, and Sorrowshade will, ah, *persuade* him to drop out of the race."

"Ooh, about that," said Sorrowshade. "I can't."

"What?" said Albiorix. "But this whole thing was your idea!"

"Yes, but I just found out that Madison has a crush on Brent," said Sorrowshade. "She is a fellow bestie of Nicole, so that means I can't be anywhere near this thing; too much drama."

"Seriously?" said Albiorix. "You know, maybe you should worry less about what Nicole—"

But somehow the assassin had already vanished.

"Hey, don't you melt into the shadows while I'm talking to you!" said Albiorix, looking around in vain. "Fine. I guess it's up to me. Let's go."

Not far away, Brent Sydlowski, Kevin Sanchez, C. J. Meier, and Max Cousins exited the field house after a hard lacrosse practice.

"Hey!" called Coach Diggs from inside. "Kevin! C.J.! Max! You three knuckleheads get back in here *right now*! You got some explaining to do!"

Kevin, C.J., and Max looked at each other. They shrugged and jogged back toward the field house, leaving Brent behind. Yet when the boys stepped inside, they didn't see their coach anywhere.

"Hey, Coach?" called Kevin. "Coach? You in here?"

Nor did they notice Devis, who had expertly mimicked Diggs's voice, slipping out the transom window above the back door. They did, however, hear the main door slam shut behind them.

"Huh?" said C.J.

He tried to open the door, but it didn't move.

"Is it locked?" asked Max.

"I . . . don't think so," said C.J., now pushing with all his might.

Yet the door held fast. The three of them tried together to force it open. But it wasn't enough to budge mighty Thromdurr, barbarian of Bríandalör, who held the door shut from the other side.

Meanwhile, Albiorix and Vela hid behind a boxwood bush near the JADMS flagpole. At last the wizard spied Brent Sydlowski making his way toward the school parking lot. He was whistling as he walked.

"You ready?" said Albiorix.

"I do not feel good about this, Albiorix," said Valerie. "It is dishonorable."

"The greater good here is that we don't flunk math and die," said Albiorix. "I can do the talking. I just need you there in case anything unexpected happens."

"As you wish," said Vela.

The wizard and the paladin approached Brent.

"Hello, Brent," said Albiorix.

"Hey, New Kid. Hi, Valerie," said Brent. "Why were you guys in that bush?"

"What? No real reason. Just . . . hanging out in there. Doesn't matter," said Albiorix. "Anyway, I'm, uh, afraid I have to ask you again to drop out of the presidential race."

"No can do, New Kid," said Brent. "My campaign has got Brentmentum! It's crazy, but with Valerie out, I think I might actually win."

"Yes, that's the problem," said Albiorix. "Brent, if you don't drop out of the race, everyone will know that you still sleep with the same plush stuffed bee you've had since you were a baby."

"Huh?" said Brent. "I don't even—I'm not sure what you're—I never . . ."

"Quit now," said Albiorix, "or we will tell the whole school all about Mr. Buzzybottom."

Brent's smile fell away, and his face lost all color. His voice dropped to a whisper. *"How do you know?"*

"Uh . . . ," said Albiorix.

"Who told you?" said Brent.

"Don't, uh, worry about that," sputtered Albiorix.

"Did you break into my house or something?" cried Brent, grabbing Albiorix by the shoulders.

The wizard blinked. Somehow in all their planning, the adventurers had failed to consider that Brent might ask this question. Albiorix's mind was a blank. He had no answer other than to say that all of this was a game and on page 133 of *The Cyclopedia of Students*, there was an entry for SYD-LOWSKI, Brent, that laid out his game statistics and the major details of his life, including the fact that he still slept with his beloved stuffed bee.

"Your sister told us," said Vela.

"Why?" said Brent. "Why would Tina do that to me? Okay, fine, I don't know what I did to make you guys mad, but I'll—I'll drop out of the race. Just *please* don't tell anybody about Mr. Buzzybottom, okay?"

"We won't, Brent," said Albiorix.

Without another word, Brent Sydlowski stared at the ground and continued on his way. He was no longer whistling.

"Whew. Okay, I'll admit that didn't feel great. But we did it, so . . . yay," said Albiorix. "And thanks for the help there. For some reason I couldn't think of—"

"I lied," said Vela.

"Oh. Huh," said Albiorix. "That's funny. Yeah. I guess you did."

"I lied," repeated Vela. Her eyes were wide, her face ashen. She looked even more shell-shocked than Brent had.

"It was just a little white lie," said Albiorix. "If you'd told him the truth, it would have caused more problems for—"

"I have dishonored the vows I took as a paladin," said Vela. "I am . . . an oath breaker."

Vela fell to her knees.

"Um," said Albiorix.

"What happened?" said Sorrowshade, who seemed to melt out of the shadows of a car parked nearby.

"We did it," said Albiorix. "Brent is out."

"I *lied*," said Vela in a strangled whisper.

"Nice!" said Devis, who came running toward them with Thromdurr close behind. "Now that you've broken the seal, you can lie to whoever you want, whenever you want! For example: Thromdurr, you're smart."

181

"Many thanks!" said Thromdurr.

"See?" said Devis.

"I am no longer a paladin," said Vela.

"Well . . . I think that's a bit overdramatic," said Albiorix. "Isn't it?"

Vela gave no answer. The other adventurers all stared at each other, unsure what to do. Albiorix cleared his throat.

"Yes, you lied once," said Albiorix. "But think of all the other times you didn't lie. In the sport of hockey, which I've learned quite a bit about recently, a player is considered really good if they score one out of ten times—"

"Valerie! What are you doing over here?" said Marie Stumpf-Turner as she approached the adventurers with her husband, Andy, close behind. "I've been looking everywhere for you. Get up—you're getting your knees all dirty."

"I'm not feeling well," said Vela.

"I knew it!" said Andy. "I have bandages and cough drops and a neck brace in the car."

Vela let out a quiet sob.

"No need to cry, Valerie," said Marie. "I spoke to Ms. Peco and you're first-chair flute again. Anyway, it's time to go. You've got dance lessons at seven."

The rest of the adventurers watched as Vela silently followed her parents to their maroon hatchback and drove away.

Chapter 14

Veteran players looking for a change of pace may want to consider switching their character class. Perhaps instead of a stressed-out Overachiever, you'd like to play as a laid-back Jock, or a mischievous Class Clown? This decision should not be taken lightly, however, as all skills and abilities associated with your old character class will no longer be available to you. Still, if you are comfortable starting over from scratch, the possibilities are endless (provided you choose from the ten rigidly defined character classes detailed in Chapter Two).

—*Excerpt from* The Hall Master's Guide

"IF VALERIE AND BRENT are out, I don't know who to vote for," said Chloe Forte.

"Have you considered Olivia Gorman?" said Albiorix. The wizard put on his best politics smile and pointed to a posterboard with the words "Gorman for Eighth-Grade President: GO-livia!" written in glitter paint.

"Eh," said Chloe.

Albiorix frowned. The GO-livia! slogan had been his brainchild. Should he have gone with GO-rman! instead?

"You know," said Albiorix, "Olivia is a longtime honor roll student who truly believes in the—"

"If she wins, she's getting rid of earth sciences," said Devis, nudging his way in front of the wizard. "Instead, it'll be a free period when we can all just eat candy and look at our phones."

"Really?" said Chloe. "That sounds amazing. I didn't think class president actually had any power to do stuff like that."

"Oh, yeah. It's all in the student handbook," said Devis. "The hierarchy goes: district superintendent, class president, principal, vice principal, everyone else. Anyway, can Olivia count on your vote on Monday?"

"Hmm," said Chloe. "I still might vote for Dave Pittman. He's my neighbor."

"Oh, really?" said Devis, clucking his tongue. "Even though Dave is the one who did all the horrible locker thefts?"

"That was him?" said Chloe.

"Yep," said Devis. "He has no morals."

"All right," said Chloe. "I guess Olivia it is." She took a lollipop from the bowl they'd set out on their folding table and continued down the hall. The two adventurers watched her go.

"Wow, that was dishonest, even for you, Devis," said Albiorix.

Devis shrugged. "I feel like if even Vela is lying now, then I'm finally off the leash," said the thief. "Anyway, this is all just a game, right?"

"I guess," said Albiorix.

"Hey, guys," said June. "How goes the politicking?"

"Armando stinks at it," said Devis. "But I'm great. Like you'd expect."

"Chloe makes another vote for Olivia," said Albiorix, tallying on his clipboard. "With the field so split between Pittman, Chambers, and Barrera, I think she might actually be within striking distance of victory."

"For what it's worth, I'm probably just going to write in Cheese," said June. "That's my cat's name."

Albiorix and Devis stared at her.

"Kidding!" said June. "This whole thing is meaningless anyway. GO-livia."

At that moment, Thromdurr and Vela arrived. The barbarian carried their clipboard, while the paladin quietly stared out into the middle distance.

"Were you guys able to wrangle any more Gorman support?" said Albiorix.

"A few votes," said Thromdurr. "Though my companion has perhaps been a less than enthusiastic campaigner. I say, 'Vote for Olivia,' and then she says . . ."

"I am an oath breaker," said Vela.

"Not the best pitch," said Albiorix. "Let's hope Melissa has had better luck."

"Psst."

The adventurers turned to see the gloom elf, hiding in a nearby doorway.

"How does she do that?" said June.

Sorrowshade glanced around to make sure no one else had seen her, then beckoned them over.

"Hey," said Albiorix. "Did you get any of the Populars to cosign onto Olivia's campaign? An endorsement like that could really give us the boost we need."

Sorrowshade took a deep breath. "In truth, I did not try."

"What?" said Albiorix. "But this is the last school day before the weekend. The election is on Monday."

"The situation has changed," said Sorrowshade. "With Valerie and Brent out of the way . . . Nicole Davenport has decided to throw her hat into the ring."

"Nicole Davenport!" said Albiorix. "But she's the only kid in school *more* popular than Brent! You have to stop her!"

The gloom elf's eyes narrowed. "I don't *have* to do anything you say, wizard," said Sorrowshade. "Besides, what power have I over Nicole? I came here to warn you—"

"You don't get it," said Albiorix. "Without Olivia's help, there's no way we're passing that algebra test. If we fail that class, we've all Blown It!"

"We're not going to die," said Sorrowshade. "That isn't how the curse works. I know because my soul is closer to the weave of magic than you mortals—"

"Closer to the weave of magic? *Closer to the weave of magic?* I am a wizard!" said Albiorix. "I am the resident magical expert guy, okay?"

"You are an *apprentice* wizard," said Sorrowshade, with a tinge of contempt in her voice.

"Why does everybody keep calling him a wizard?" said June.

The heroes ignored her.

"Even if you're right," said Albiorix, "the best-case scenario is that we end up stuck in Homerooms & Hall Passes forever."

Sorrowshade stared at Albiorix for a long moment. Then she threw up the hood of her sweatshirt. "Yes. So?"

"What do you mean, so?" said Albiorix. "Before, you said it was a fate worse than death!"

"Yeah," said Devis. "Don't you want to get back to the

dungeons and the gold and leave all this make-believe non-sense behind? I mean, look at this." The thief pointed to a nearby water fountain. "A big metal box that shoots water at your face? What even *is* that?"

"He speaks the truth," said Thromdurr. "This is not our world, elf."

"It isn't," said Sorrowshade. "It's better."

The other Bríandalörians were stunned.

"What are you even talking about?" said Albiorix. "Hanging out with Nicole Davenport has changed you. And not for the—"

"All I've ever known is pain and darkness," said Sorrowshade. "Here, I have friends, yes, and a family. For the first time in forever, I don't have to devote my entire life to seeking stupid revenge on stupid mintoaurs!"

"So you really don't want to go back?" said Albiorix.

"No," said Sorrowshade. "And I figured you wouldn't either. After all, you're not *really* an adventurer. Are you, Albiorix?"

"Watch your tongue, elf," said Thromdurr, putting a hand on Albiorix's shoulder. "He has stood beside us, through thick and thin, against all manner of danger!"

"Yeah, he loves the dungeon-delving lifestyle: the loot, the traps, the mortal danger," said Devis. "Don't you, Magic Man?"

"I mean," said Albiorix, "I . . ." The wizard trailed off.

"Hello?" said June. "Am I the only one who's having trouble following all of this? What's an *Al-bee-or-ix*? Valerie, can you please tell me what's happening?"

"I am an oath breaker," said Vela. "I lied."

"Enough of that," snapped Albiorix. "You're not special, Vela. All of us have been lying nonstop since we got to this stupid place. The first thing I had to do was produce a pile of fake paperwork to prove I even exist!"

"Wait," said June. "That's what you did with the birth certificate I helped you make in Computer Applications?"

"Oh," said Albiorix.

"Well, I guess you have been lying nonstop," said June.

"I can explain," said Albiorix.

But he didn't get the chance. Without another word, June turned and left.

"Wow," said Devis. "Nice going, Albiorix. You know, you really should try to be more honest with people."

"Come on!" said Albiorix. "It was Sorrowshade's fault. She's the one who suddenly decided for all of us that we're staying here forever. This discussion isn't over!"

Albiorix turned, but the gloom elf had vanished.

"You know for a seventy-three-year-old," said Albiorix to nobody, "you're really immature."

"Well," said Devis, "the GO-livia! campaign is a bust.

We just lost our only friend. Our leader is catatonic. Our assassin has gone rogue. And for separate reasons, Thromdurr and I probably shouldn't be in charge. What's the plan, smart one?"

"I have no idea," said Albiorix.

"Perfect," said Devis. "Then I guess I'll see you guys in earth sciences class."

The thief turned and started to walk away down the hall, eating a burrito he had picked up somewhere. Thromdurr cocked his head and eyed Albiorix appraisingly.

"You *do* truly want to be an adventurer," said Thromdurr. "Do you not, Albiorix?"

"It's complicated," said Albiorix.

Olivia Gorman approached. She was decked out, head to toe, in GO-livia! campaign gear, carrying a third clipboard.

"So how are things looking, team?" said Olivia. "I'm starting to feel like I might actually—"

"I don't know," said Albiorix. "I've got to go."

The bell rang. Albiorix handed Olivia the clipboard and proceeded to class.

Chapter

15

As with any game, in Homerooms & Hall Passes, interpersonal conflicts will sometimes arise between the players. Perhaps one character has asked another character's secret crush to the school dance, or maybe one was made captain of the basketball team while another lost out, et cetera. As Hall Master, it's your job to make sure that everyone is getting along. When a disagreement occurs, talk to everyone and make sure they feel heard. Do your best to compromise and then rectify the issue moving forward. The point of the game is to have fun! Still, it's best to remember that not every player is a good fit for every group. . . .

—Excerpt from The Hall Master's Guide

☙

I T WAS A BLEAK AFTERNOON for the wizard Albiorix. June wouldn't acknowledge him. Sorrowshade wouldn't talk to him. Vela would only mumble quiet regrets. He couldn't shake the feeling that Devis and Thromdurr were giving him sidelong looks now, questioning his motivations and abilities. Albiorix was tired: tired of eating strange foods, and making mistakes, and struggling to understand everything in this world he thought he knew so well. In short, he was tired of J. A. Dewar Middle School, and he cursed the day he had gotten his first Homerooms & Hall Passes book.

The final bell rang, and the Bríandalörians parted ways without a word to each other. Albiorix sat in the third-floor boys' bathroom and watched the gray, rainy afternoon darken to evening. Avoiding Mr. Driscoll as he mopped, Albiorix made his way to the gym. It was the start of the weekend, so instead of going home to a family or having fun with friends, he would get two whole days to be alone with his thoughts. Wonderful.

"I *am* a wizard," said Albiorix to himself. He cast his light spell, brightening the other closet. "And I *do* want to be an adventurer. Of course I want to be an adventurer. Otherwise I wouldn't be a wizard . . . would I?"

He plopped down on his makeshift bed and idly began to thumb through the first H&H book he happened to see: *The Fulsome Folio of Foods.* He'd spent twenty gold pieces on a two-hundred-forty-page book about the fictional foods that only existed within an imaginary game! Useless. Albiorix tossed the *Folio* across the room, knocking over a bucket of Wiffle balls. He lay back and took a deep breath. A foul, musty tang caught his nose.

Albiorix sat up. There, amid his pile of H&H books, he spotted the dark red binding of the Malonomicon.

"I am a wizard," said Albiorix.

He opened the spellbook to a random page and began to read. It described a ritual called the Returning. Apart from its title in the Common Tongue, the text itself was written in Shadownese, the primordial language of darkness. Gloom elves spoke the language fluently, but Albiorix wasn't about to track Sorrowshade down and beg for her help. The wizard's own shaky grasp of the tongue would have to suffice. He knew enough to read the language phonetically, but his vocabulary was fairly limited. After translating and retranslating for half an hour, he was fairly certain he understood the first two lines of the spell.

Gone from the world to another plane
Who has departed shall return again.

Albiorix gasped. He and his companions were gone from the world to another plane! And indeed they needed to return again. He couldn't believe his luck.

"This is exactly the spell to get us back to Bríandalör!" said Albiorix to no one.

The wizard leaped to his feet and frantically began to gather the ingredients needed listed in the book: a strand of spider's silk, an eyelash, a lump of iron, and an unburned candle. He didn't even have to leave the gymnasium! Once he had everything, Albiorix used a piece of chalk to inscribe the strange mandala, pictured in the Malonomicon, on the floor. He marked key junctures with various Shadownese runes. Then he lit the scented candle he'd snagged from Ms. Dumas's office, filling the old closet with the overpowering smell of butterscotch. He took a deep breath to clear his mind and began to read the incantation from the book.

"*Garu san su zasss sa i'arasus zsi'aru,*" said Albiorix. "*Wa i'ar suzi'assus ri'ass susisr i'aphi'auhr . . .*"

The candle flickered and changed. Instead of warm white light, it had shifted to an eerie green. Something was happening.

"*Canu i'ash sa ir san su ruhru ussr,*" said Albiorix. "*Canu i'ash sa ir san su si'ars a su sui'as . . .*"

A wisp of green smoke floated up from the center point of the mandala as the carefully arranged spider silk, eyelash, and lump of iron started to corrode and crumble. The ritual was working!

Albiorix intoned the final line of the spell: ". . . *Canu i'ash sa ir Zazirak.*"

There was a deafening crack and a blinding flash of green light. It took the wizard a moment to realize he'd been knocked flat on his back. He opened his eyes hoping to see the bright, verdant world of Bríandalör around him.

Instead he saw a ghastly spectral form floating over the chalk circle. It turned to face the wizard—hollow eyes burning with green fire—and cackled. "As I said before, death means nothing to one such as I!"

"Who are you?" whispered Albiorix.

"In life they called me the Scourge of Ta'shinn, Blight of the Shield Coast, Slayer of Hotus the Good," said the spirit. "But you may know me as Zazirak."

"The evil warlock from the Temple of Azathor?"

"In the flesh or . . . lack thereof," said the spirit, as it peered through its translucent hands. "What is this place?"

"That's not—none of your business, mister," sputtered Albiorix. Weak. He'd never been good at snappy retorts.

The ghost paused and almost seemed to sniff the air. Then a horrible grin spread across its face. "Mmm. A realm without magic?" said Zazirak. "It shall burn. Now . . . where is the Malonomicon?"

The tome lay open on the ground at Albiorix's feet.

"Ah," said the specter. It snatched for the book, but its

incorporeal fingers passed through the pages, merely ruffling them like a gentle breeze.

"Curses!" said Zazirak. "This form is useless to me. I require flesh."

Zazirak reached toward the Malonomicon again, but Albiorix threw himself on top of it. If the undead warlock wanted it, he shouldn't have it. Zazirak merely cocked his head and gave another sickening smile.

"Yes . . . ," said Zazirak. "Yours will do." And with that, he flew into Albiorix.

Instantly Albiorix's mind was cold death. He saw good and decent folk brought low and legions of grinning skeletons marching through burning streets and a great mole-headed fiend rising from the flames to eat the entire world.

But the wizard fought. He fought with everything the Archmage had ever taught him about mental focus and resisting enchantment. He bent every atom of his will toward rejecting the vile alien presence that was currently attempting to possess him. And after what felt like an eternity of war, just when he thought his own spirit would give out and his psyche would shatter, the cold death abruptly ceased.

Albiorix blinked. Again he was lying on the ground, and the ghost of Zazirak hovered over him, wearing an irritated expression.

"Why waste the effort? There are plenty of other flesh

puppets here," said Zazirak. "I can smell them."

"Leave . . . them . . . alone," said Albiorix, struggling for breath.

Zazirak cackled again. "Rest now, little wizard. No need to get up," he said. "I'll be right back . . . to destroy you."

And in a flash of green light, the specter floated through the wall and disappeared.

Albiorix grabbed the Malonomicon and struggled to his feet. His mind was still reeling from fighting off the warlock's attempted possession. He burst out into the gymnasium just in time to see a ghostly green trail disappear through the double doors. Albiorix steadied himself and headed after the specter.

The wizard stumbled through empty halls of JADMS searching for the ghost, stopping every so often to let a wave of freezing nausea pass. The place was eerily quiet, and his boots seemed incredibly loud on the linoleum. It started to dawn on him that he didn't even know what he would do if he caught Zazirak. He certainly had no way of fighting the ghost, and he wasn't sure he had it in him to ward off a second attempt at possession. This was bad. This was very bad. At least everyone else had already gone home for the day.

Only . . . they hadn't. Albiorix rounded a corner to see that the lights were on in the office.

"No," said Albiorix to himself.

Someone must have decided to work late. Yet when the wizard peered through the window, he saw no one. As quietly as he could, he eased open the door and crept inside. He snuck past the Inspire Leadership poster toward the short hallway beyond.

There he saw the ghastly, translucent form of Zazirak floating in the air. Albiorix heard the muffled sounds of a phone call coming from inside Vice Principal Flanagan's office.

"Yes, well, the patio furniture rusted almost immediately," said Flanagan. "I understand . . . I understand! But it is still under warranty. . . . How can the warranty not cover rust? Look, I'm going to need to speak with your supervisor. . . ."

The warlock's spirit chuckled, and there was a flash of green light as it flew through the door. An instant later there was a horrible scream.

Albiorix turned and ran as fast as his legs would carry him. He had the presence of mind to make a quick detour before bursting out of the school into the pouring rain outside. He kept running until J. A. Dewar Middle School had disappeared behind him.

What had he done? What had he unleashed? How could he have been so stupid? He was supposed to be the smart one!

At this point, he might have sought out his companions—hardened adventurers of Bríandalör, who would have been ready to meet the danger head-on. But he couldn't bear the shame of facing them after making such a blunder. So instead, the wizard sought another.

Chapter

16

The rules outlined in this book are extensive, but they are not meant to be exhaustive. Situations not expressly covered will arise from time to time. For example, what if a player wants their character to start a new school club, dedicated to ironically watching cheesy movies? Or perhaps they want to buy two dozen hermit crabs and attempt to teach them to play video games? The beauty of Homerooms & Hall Passes is that anything is possible. When the unexpected happens, roll with it! A good Hall Master must be familiar with the rules, but also know how to improvise.

—Excerpt from The Hall Master's Guide

❧

"HONEY, THERE'S A WET KID out here," called Amy Westray. "He says he's your friend."

"What?" yelled June from inside.

"Just come down, sweetie," said Amy.

June descended to the foot of the staircase. Through the front door she saw Albiorix, soaking wet and shivering on the front porch.

"Nope," said June. "Not my friend." She turned and disappeared upstairs again.

Amy looked at Albiorix. She looked back inside. She looked at Albiorix again.

"Well . . . this is awkward," said Amy. "Can I at least call your parents or something?"

"You can't, actually," said Albiorix. "But . . . I'll be fine, Mrs. Westray."

Amy took an umbrella from a holder by the door. "Here," she said. "Keep it."

"Thank you," said Albiorix. "Can you please just tell June that Albiorix says he's sorry?"

"Sure," said Amy. "Stay warm out there."

Amy Westray shut the door and Albiorix opened his umbrella and stepped out into the rain once more. He truly didn't know where he would go, but he started to walk anyway. He had made it to the end of the driveway when someone called out to him.

"Get back in here!" yelled June, who was standing in the front door.

Soon Albiorix was sipping a cup of hot tea in the Westray

kitchen. Cheese, a pudgy orange tabby cat, purred and circled his ankles. Amy Westray stood by the doorway eyeing the wizard warily.

"So . . . this kid *is* your friend now?" said Amy.

"Yeah, Mom," said June. "I just thought he was someone else. That's all."

"Okay, I'm going to assume that whatever's happening is some sort of middle-school drama that moms aren't meant to understand," said Amy. "Please make yourself at home. I'll be in the TV room if you need me." She disappeared down the hallway.

"So you're a huge liar," said June. *"Albiorix."*

"Yes," said Albiorix. "And I am truly sorry. I thought I was doing it for the right reasons, but—"

"You need to just stop at sorry," said June. "That's how apologies work."

"Right," said Albiorix. "Sorry. Full stop."

"Thank you," said June. "Now tell me the truth. Where are you really from?"

And so Albiorix told her. He told June Westray all about the real world—the magical Realm of Bríandalör, with its sorcerers and dragons and mighty empires and forgotten dungeons. And he told her of the game of Homerooms & Hall Passes and the mysterious curse that had brought him and his adventuring companions here. After he was done,

June was silent for a long time.

"That is a *much* worse lie," said June, sipping her tea.

Albiorix shrugged. "Because it isn't one."

"You expect me to believe that I, June Annabelle Westray, am merely a nonplayer character inside a weird game you play in some other world that's full of orcs."

"It's not *full* of orcs," said Albiorix. "There are *some* orcs—"

"Well, first off, I refuse to accept that I'm not real," said June. "So agree to disagree on that one."

"Agree to disagree," said Albiorix.

"Second, if you're a wizard, do some magic and prove it, tough guy," said June. She crossed her arms.

Albiorix sighed and pulled a coin from an area that was generally adjacent, but not too close, to June's ear.

"Nope!" said June. "If I'm going to believe you, you have to turn me into a frog or something."

"It's at least two years before I learn instant frogification," said Albiorix. "You must remember I'm still an apprentice. And I forgot my spellbook when we got trapped here."

"What kind of a wizard forgets his spellbook?" said June.

"A bad one," said Albiorix. "However, if you require a flashier demonstration of mystical power, please turn off the lights."

June did.

Albiorix cleared his throat. Then he traced the outline of an arcane sigil with his fingers as he spoke the secret name of the sun. His fingertips started to glow, and the five points of brightness coalesced into a single beautiful orb of pure light in his palm. The orb began to lazily drift toward the ceiling.

June screamed.

"Shhhh!" said Albiorix.

"What's wrong?" cried Amy Westray from down the hall. "Is everything okay?"

Albiorix flicked the lights back on, and Amy Westray arrived a second later.

June's eyes looked like saucers. "We're . . . we're fine," said June.

"Really?" said Amy.

"Sorry I screamed," said June. "My tea was too hot. Burned my tongue."

"You nearly gave me a heart attack, honey," said Amy. "You don't have to drink it right away. Just let it cool for a minute next time."

"Of course. Lesson learned. Sorry, Mom," said June. "You can go back to the TV room now."

Amy nodded and walked back down the hall. Albiorix took a sip of his own tea.

"Who's the huge liar now?" said Albiorix.

"Shut up," said June.

"Anyway, I came here tonight because I need your help, June," said Albiorix. "And not just with a five-paragraph essay this time."

"For, like, a hero quest?" said June.

"In a manner of speaking," said Albiorix. "I mentioned before that I'm not the best wizard. To that point, I may have, um, unleashed an ancient evil upon the land."

"Do tell," said June.

Albiorix described performing the ritual of the Returning and its catastrophic results.

"And so I am reasonably certain—let's say sixty-five percent sure—that Vice Principal Flanagan has been possessed by the ghost of an evil warlock."

"Sounds like an improvement," said June. "That guy was such a hard case about transferring the credit for my world music studies class from my old school. It's not my fault if J. A. Dewar is too provincial to offer any cool classes!"

"Well, transfer credits aside," said Albiorix, "I'm not exactly sure what to do about this warlock situation."

"Well," said June, "you said your friends beat Zazzmatazz—"

"Zazirak," said Albiorix.

"Right," said June. "They kicked this dude's butt before, yes?"

"They did," said Albiorix.

"And you weren't even there to do any of your spells, some of which I'm assuming are more dangerous than the ear-coin thing." said June. "They didn't need your help."

"Somewhat hurtful," said Albiorix, "but true."

"So it sounds like you guys are more than a match for Zazirak," said June.

"I suppose you're right," said Albiorix. "Perhaps Zazirak isn't so strong after all."

The wizard felt a bit better. He would swallow his pride and enlist the aid of his companions. Together the party would defeat the warlock, just as they had before. His mood lightened, and he was happy to answer June's countless questions about the Realm of Bríandalör.

Were there unicorns? Yes. Were there dinosaurs? No. How many wizards were there? Impossible to say (a lot). How did one become a wizard? Apprentice to an Archmage. Did wizards have their own crazy sports, where they flew around on broomsticks trying to catch a ball with wings? Absolutely not. Were there elves? Of course. Did they make cookies? Occasionally . . .

Eventually they got back around to the subject of Homerooms & Hall Passes.

"I'm sorry, but that game sounds super nerdy," said June.

"Well, we don't have Nerds in Bríandalör, so that's impossible," said Albiorix, a tad defensively.

"You know what I mean," said June.

"Okay, but Thromdurr plays and he's clearly not a Nerd!"

"Thromdurr?" said June.

"Douglas," said Albiorix.

"Dude, Douglas is *constantly* talking about what a nerd he is!"

"I'll admit that was a confusing example," said Albiorix. "He is actually a barbarian."

"Ah. The muscles and the hair make more sense now," said June. "So you know everything about J. A. Dewar Middle School from playing Homerooms & Hall Passes?"

"Not everything," said Albiorix. "But there is a lot of useful information in the sourcebooks."

"Does that mean there's an entry somewhere that's all about me?" said June.

"I haven't checked," said Albiorix. "But probably so."

"Well, that's really weird and I refuse to believe it," said June.

"Suit yourself," said Albiorix. "Anyway, it's getting late, so I should probably go. Thank you for talking this through with me. Please don't tell anyone else that we're secretly adventurers and this world is all a game."

"I can't imagine bringing that up in casual conversation," said June.

"And you're absolutely right," said Albiorix. "You guys

don't have evil warlocks here, but we've faced down plenty back home. Whatever happens with Flanagan and Zazirak, my party and I will be there to handle it." The wizard stood to go.

"Wait," said June. "Where do you even live?"

"In a closet in the school gym," said Albiorix.

"What do you eat?" said June.

"Well, I'm rather fond of the peanut-butter crackers, but the tropical fruit chews are starting to grow on me!" said Albiorix.

"You sleep in an equipment closet and eat vending-machine food for every meal," said June. "In another context, that would be very, very sad."

"It's the life of an adventurer," said Albiorix. "Farewell, June."

"Bye, Albiorix," said June, "I know you're in a weird situation, but you should still try your best to be honest with people."

"I promise I will," said Albiorix. "See you Monday."

The wizard took his free umbrella and headed out into the rainy night.

"Doug, there's a wet kid out here," said Ron Schiller. "He says he's your friend."

Thromdurr bounded toward the front door.

"It is Armando Boort!" said Thromdurr. "My boon companion from middle school. Welcome, Armando, to the House of Schiller."

"Hi, Doug," said Albiorix. "Sorry, I know it's late."

"No worries," said Ron. "If you haven't had dinner yet, there's a bowl of my famous chili with your name on it, Armando!"

"Sure, that'd be great," said Albiorix

Ron headed for the kitchen as Albiorix stepped inside.

"So what brings you to 45 Crescent Drive?" said Thromdurr, lowering his voice so that his father couldn't hear. "Is evil afoot?"

Albiorix paused and debated whether or not he should tell Thromdurr what had happened at school.

"Nah," said Albiorix. "I was just wondering if I could maybe stay here tonight. I'm tired of sleeping on exercise mats."

"Douglas the Nerd's first sleepover!" cried Thromdurr, pounding his chest. "I would be honored to host you, friend. And I have the perfect place for you to sleep. Behold!"

Thromdurr pointed to an overstuffed armchair in front of a gigantic TV.

"Huh," said Albiorix.

"Worry not," said Thromdurr, clapping Albiorix on the back. *"It reclines!"*

Chapter 17

FLANAGAN, Myron James

OCCUPATION: Vice principal

ATTRIBUTES: Cunning: 16, Intelligence: 15, Likability: 4, Willpower: 19, Fitness: 15

SKILLS: Administration +8, Computer +5, Cooking +1, Drive +5, Intimidation +10, Public Speaking +2, Trivia (Military History) +6

BIOGRAPHY: Myron Flanagan is the hard-nosed, eagle-eyed disciplinarian of JADMS. Universally loathed (even among faculty), Flanagan has absolutely no tolerance for any of the following: antics, capers, clowning, goofing, horseplay, mischief, nonsense, pranks, silliness, tomfoolery. . . .

　—Excerpt from The Album of Academic Administration

$\mathcal{T}$ HE WIZARD OF BRÍANDALÖR steeled himself for battle. He took a deep breath, and with a wordless battle cry, Albiorix charged through the door of the vice principal's office, brandishing his umbrella like a club.

"We killed you once, Zazirak," yelled Albiorix, "but somehow you didn't get the message!"

The office was empty. It had taken the wizard quite a while to think up that line, and he was slightly miffed that nobody heard it. Still, an empty office was better than trying to defeat a possessed Vice Principal Flanagan with nothing but an umbrella.

It was Saturday morning, and JADMS was deserted (until Mr. Driscoll showed up to run the floor polisher, at least). With no ghostly warlock to fight, Albiorix decided to poke around Flanagan's office a bit. Everything was disturbingly clean and organized. There didn't seem to be so much as a sheet of paper out of place. Whatever Zazirak had done hadn't made much of a mess. But if Flanagan wasn't at school, then where was he?

In the wastebasket, Albiorix found a piece of junk mail that listed Myron Flanagan's home address.

From the rosebushes, amid a set of slightly rusty patio furniture, the wizard peered through the bay window into

211

the living room of 1120 San Antonio Way. There he saw Flanagan, laughing and eating popcorn as he watched a black-and-white movie.

"Huh?" said Albiorix to himself.

Seeing Myron Flanagan relaxed and cheerful would have been disconcerting even if Albiorix didn't have reason to believe that the dark soul of Zazirak had possessed him. Yet after observing for another forty-five minutes, Albiorix started to wonder if anything had happened to Flanagan at all.

Fighting off the undead warlock's influence was a matter of mental focus, and Flanagan might have done it, just as Albiorix had. According to his H&H stats, the man had a Willpower of 19. Perhaps, thought Albiorix, Zazirak's ghost had tried and failed to inhabit his body, and then moved on to a softer target?

Albiorix stayed to watch the end of the movie. In the meantime, Flanagan didn't cast any spells; his eyes didn't glow; he didn't emit a single menacing cackle. He did, however, tear up when the on-screen monochrome couple got married at the end.

That night Albiorix slept over at Devis's house. Mom Stinky and Dad Stinky were odd, but nice enough. Yet after a dinner of bouillabaisse and a breakfast of bisque, the wizard found himself longing for the solid crunch of some peanut-butter crackers. He had no idea how Devis could possibly consume so much soup.

Olivia Gorman had agreed to meet the entire party at the Hibbettsfield Public Library for more algebra tutoring at three o'clock on Sunday.

"Greetings, Nerd Olivia," said Thromdurr as he arrived. "I have brought a you a gift!"

The barbarian handed her a brand-new Spinco Seven-Tray Jerky Dehydrator.

"You said you didn't want a home rotisserie, so I purchased this instead!" said Thromdurr. "According to the sages, it will revolutionize the way you make jerky at home!"

"I . . . don't eat meat," said Olivia.

"Well, the gods surely smile upon you, Olivia," said Thromdurr, "for you can also use it to make fruit leather!"

Vela was the next to arrive. "Hello," said the paladin, hanging her head. "I am an oath breaker and do not deserve any help in algebra."

"Um," said Olivia. She looked at Albiorix, unsure of how to respond.

"Olivia, will you excuse us for a second?" said Albiorix.

The wizard took Vela to a nearby aisle of books, out of Olivia's earshot. Thromdurr and Devis followed.

"Vela, we have to somehow move past your oath breaking," said Albiorix.

Vela merely sighed and stared at the floor.

"He is right," said Thromdurr. "We cannot define ourselves by our mistakes, friend paladin. Otherwise I would ever be known as the Guy Who Accidentally Broke the Vase of the Gnome Queen."

"Is there any way you can just . . . say you're sorry to Brent or something?" said Albiorix. "I don't even care at this point—you can tell him the truth about the books and everything."

"I might make amends, but . . . it would not be enough," said Vela. "As penance, a fallen paladin must right a greater wrong through great personal sacrifice."

"Okay, let's do that!" said Albiorix.

"Obviously, one so dishonorable as I would be incapable of such a noble act," said Vela.

"But that's circular logic," said Albiorix.

"Yeah," said Devis. "And just for the record, dishonorable people can do some pretty wonderful stuff. Check this out!" The thief began to balance a pencil on the tip of his nose.

"Guys, can we get started already?" said Olivia, interrupting their secret conference. "I don't have all day."

"Perhaps we should just wait a bit longer for Melissa," said Albiorix, glancing at the clock.

"Fine," said Olivia. "But if I don't win the election

tomorrow, this free algebra-tutoring gravy train ends. You got that?"

"Don't worry," said Devis, who had already moved on to scrolling through funny hedgehog pictures on his phone. "You've got the race in the bag."

Olivia brightened. "I do?" she said. "But how can I possibly beat Nicole Davenport? Everyone loves-slash-is terrified of her! Even me!"

"Armando has got it all figured out," said Devis. "Right, Armando?"

Olivia looked at Albiorix.

"Yes, well, the plan is for you to just . . . be yourself," said Albiorix. "I think that authenticity will really carry us through the home stretch."

Olivia frowned again. "It better."

By three fifteen, it was clear that Sorrowshade wasn't going to show, which irritated Albiorix to no end. Olivia confiscated Devis's phone and began the lesson. It was, as the adventurers had come to expect, abrasive but instructive. Albiorix felt himself making rapid algebraic progress. Devis was clearly picking up the material as well, though he was loath to admit he was actually learning anything. Vela, too, when she could be goaded into giving an answer, often had the correct one. Only Thromdurr still seemed lost. Privately Albiorix wondered whether a primitive hunter-gatherer from the Steppes of Ursk could ever comprehend the advanced mathematics of this world. Douglas the Nerd still needed more help.

That evening—after thoroughly searching the entire school for any sign of evil ghosts—Albiorix returned once more to the gym. The threat of Zazirak had moved to the back of his mind. Maybe the warlock had simply given up on this place and returned to the underworld?

The election for class president was the wizard's primary focus now. Albiorix supposed he had no choice but to employ the same tactic that had gotten Brent Sydlowski out of the race. He would use *The Cyclopedia of Students* to learn Nicole Davenport's most embarrassing secret and use it to pressure her to withdraw, clearing the way for a narrow Gorman victory. Dishonorable? Maybe. But what choice did they have?

Yet when the wizard went for his pile of of H&H books to grab the cyclopedia, they were nowhere to be found. He checked again and cursed himself. Then he did a thorough search of the entire closet, and after that the whole gymnasium. While he'd left them unattended, someone had taken all twenty-seven of his Homerooms & Hall Passes sourcebooks.

"Well," said Albiorix. "That's not good."

His theory that Zazirak had decided to leave JADMS

alone now seemed naive. And Albiorix realized he would need to think of some other way for Olivia to win. That night the wizard barricaded the door with a pile of track-and-field hurdles and tried his best to come up with something resembling a plan for the election. Albiorix slept fitfully, his battle umbrella close at hand.

Monday morning before first bell, Albiorix waited on the couch beneath the Inspire Leadership poster until the vice principal could spare a few minutes to see him. Would this be the moment of confrontation? The wizard tried to stay calm, prepared for the worst. At last Ms. Roland called him back.

Sitting behind his desk, with a stern look in his gray eyes, sat Myron Flanagan.

"Good morning, Armando," said Flanagan.

"Good morning," said Albiorix. He studied the man carefully for any sign of ghostly possession: strange movements, odd smells, drooling.

"So, why are you here?" said Flanagan.

"Well, obviously I wanted to wish you a good morning." Albiorix studied him further.

Several more seconds passed. Flanagan cleared his throat. "Okay," he said. "You did that."

"And I just wanted to give you my host family's new phone number," said Albiorix. "As per your request."

Albiorix recited Devis's mobile number. The thief had readily agreed to impersonate Albiorix's host mom on the phone, should the need arise. Honestly, it was the kind of thing Devis lived for.

Flanagan grunted as he jotted the number down. "All right," he said. "Thanks."

Albiorix stared him. "So how was your weekend, sir? Did anything . . . *exciting* happen?"

Flanagan glowered. "Exciting? Armando, I have no idea what you're getting at."

"Can I just do a quick word association with you?" said Albiorix.

"No," said Flanagan.

Still, Albiorix pressed it. "If I said, 'A realm without magic. It shall . . . *blank*.' How would you complete that statement?"

"I would complete it by saying, 'Get out of my office,'" said Flanagan, now visibly irritated. "There's no time for foolishness. I have work to do, and so do you."

"Yes, sir," said Albiorix. And the wizard stood to go.

"Hi, I'm Dave Pittman, and my main deal is, like, the cafeteria food should be better. Or whatever." Dave shrugged and took his seat.

"Okay, very interesting," said Ms. Chapman.

The combined eighth-grade class—meaning Mr. Gutierrez's, Ms. Chan's, and Ms. Chapman's homerooms—sat in the JADMS auditorium as they listened to the closing statements for all their presidential candidates. So far, Albiorix wasn't impressed with the competition.

"Next up, we have Nicole Davenport," said Ms. Chapman.

Nicole took the stage and flashed the assembly a radiant smile.

"Hi, I'm Nicole and I'm not going to waste your time. You *all* know why I should win. But here is my campaign promise to you: If you vote for me, I will personally heart up to three photos you post online. From my main account."

A gasp ran through the crowd, followed by applause.

"Thanks!" said Nicole. "Love you!" She took a quick stage selfie and returned to her seat.

"Hmm," said Ms. Chapman. "And last, but certainly not least, we have Olivia Gorman."

Olivia took the dais and shuffled some notecards. Then she delivered a statement in the practiced monotone of her morning announcements. "Hello, eighth graders. I'm Olivia Gorman, and a vote for me is a vote for responsible leadership. I promise to serve as a levelheaded liaison between

219

Titan students and faculty. I assure you, I will advocate for your interests, within reason, to the best of my ability. Thank you. GO-livia."

Albiorix, Thromdurr, and Devis clapped loudly, while very few others did.

"Well then," said Ms. Chapman. "Without further ado, it is time for the main event."

Mr. Gutierrez wheeled out a green chalkboard, while Ms. Chan placed a cardboard ballot box on the stage.

"Eighth graders," said Ms. Chapman. "It is now time to choose your—"

"Excuse me, Ms. Chapman," said Albiorix, raising his hand.

"Yes, Armando?" said Ms. Chapman.

"May I deliver a statement too?"

"Are you running for class president?" said Ms. Chapman.

"Yes?" said Albiorix.

Ms. Chapman looked at the other eighth-grade homeroom teachers. They shrugged and nodded.

"Okay," said Ms. Chapman. "Let's hear your pitch, Armando."

Albiorix took the stage and cleared his throat. "Not many of you know me. And those who do refer to me as 'New Kid.'"

"They should call you New Haircut," yelled Devis.

"Because that's what you need!"

The entire assembly laughed.

"Can you not heckle me, please?" said Albiorix.

"Is that what your mom said when the doctor handed you to her?" yelled Devis.

Another laugh.

"Stinky, stop!" cried Albiorix.

"Sorry," said Devis.

"Anyway," said Albiorix. "I *am* new here: new to this school; new to this town; new to this land. Where I come from, we don't even choose our leaders by voting!"

"Wait. I thought you came from Canada," said Ms. Chapman.

Albiorix ignored her and pressed on. "Yet as an outsider, I feel that I can judge this race with a clear and objective eye. And I firmly believe the best candidate for eighth-grade class president is Olivia Gorman. So I hereby withdraw my own candidacy, which I just declared, and throw all my support to her!"

The class largely looked confused. June looked like she might burst out laughing. Nicole was glaring at Albiorix as if she might be able to melt him with her eyes. Beside her, Sorrowshade—who had now completely abandoned her dark loner clothes in favor of preppy popular girl attire—was unreadable.

The wizard continued. "Other candidates have offered you unrealistic promises or even bribes for your vote. But only Olivia has articulated a smart, pragmatic vision for the future of this class. And if you vote Olivia, I'll give you a free pack of peanut-butter crackers from the vending machine—"

"All right. Sit down, Armando," said Ms. Chapman.

Armando sighed and took his seat. His speech had not been quite as rousing as he'd hoped. It was up to the gods now.

At this point, the homeroom teachers passed out ballots. Every student wrote the name of his or her preferred candidate. One by one, they walked to the front and dropped their slip into the ballot box. After a few minutes, everyone had cast their vote.

"Okay, time to tally them up and see who wins," said Ms. Chapman. "This is almost too exciting!" She dumped out the ballot box and picked up one of the paper slips.

"One vote for Olivia Gorman," said Ms. Chapman.

Mr. Gutierrez made a tally mark on the chalkboard. Ms. Chapman reached for another ballot.

Chapter 18

Contrary to the spirit of the game, some Homerooms & Hall Passes players may attempt to cheat. Someone who fudges their dice rolls or lies to the Hall Master about abilities can ruin everyone's fun. If you catch a player cheating, don't be afraid to call them out force-fully and tell them to stop. If they persist after such a warning, consider having a wizard cast a mantle of truth on the offending player before the next game session begins.

—Excerpt from The Hall Master's Guide

"TWO VOTES FOR OLIVIA," said Ms. Chapman.

Mr. Gutierrez made another mark on the board. Albiorix was on the edge of his seat. Thromdurr looked hopeful. Devis winked. June played *Oink Pop.*

At sixty-seven votes for Olivia Gorman, the race was called. She had received over fifty percent of the vote and so would be the new eighth-grade class president. Ms. Chapman and the other homeroom teachers congratulated her. Olivia was beside herself with joy. Albiorix was ecstatic too. Perhaps his speech had been rousing after all, just the thing to push her over the edge? GO-livia!

By the time there had been one hundred votes counted for Olivia, the atmosphere of the assembly had darkened considerably. Students whispered among themselves. Teachers gave each other knowing looks. Olivia looked scared. Nicole looked furious. Devis winked.

When the one hundred thirty-second, and final, vote was counted ("Olivia Gorman"), Ms. Chapman addressed the assembly.

"Ahem. It appears that Olivia has received one hundred percent of the votes cast," said Ms. Chapman.

"Yay!" said Devis.

An instant later, the assembled students erupted in disbelief. Olivia burst out crying. Albiorix shook his head.

The assembly was dismissed. As the students made their way back to class, the adventurers (minus Sorrowshade, of course) talked in hushed tones as they walked.

"What happened in there?" hissed Albiorix.

"I thought whoever got the most votes won?" said Devis.

The thief looked baffled. "I don't get what everybody is so hung up about."

"Perhaps getting too many votes is a bad thing," said Thromdurr. "The way eating one mutton shank is delicious, but ten can cause a slight stomachache."

"Getting too many votes is a bad thing *when none of your opponents even voted for themselves*," said Albiorix.

"Wait. They can do that?" said Devis. "That feels a little embarassing, no?"

Albiorix shook his head. "Devis, please tell me you didn't secretly switch out all the ballots?"

"Albiorix," said Devis, "I didn't secretly switch out the ballots."

"Are you lying?" said Albiorix.

"Yes," said Devis. "Of course I switched the ballots. So Olivia would win!"

"Well, the way you did it was highly suspicious," said Albiorix.

"Look, I don't know how democracy is supposed to work!" said Devis. "My deal is sneaking around and stealing stuff and that's what I did, because your plan was a dud!"

"My plan was a dud?" said Albiorix. "My plan was to get Nicole out of the race, but when I checked, all my Home-rooms & Hall Passes books had been stolen. Was that you too?"

"How dare you!" said Devis, stopping in his tracks. "I would *never* steal from a party member."

"You stole seven copper pieces from me when first we met," said Thromdurr.

"As a joke!" said Devis. "You want it back?" The thief reached into his pocket.

"Yes," said Thromdurr.

"Well . . . I spent it. Also as a joke," said Devis. "Bought these." He pulled out a pair of spectacles with googly eyes painted on them. He put them on. "Pretty funny, right?"

"Yes!" said Thromdurr, with a chuckle. "Coin well spent!"

"Guys, focus," said Albiorix. "Books aside, Devis, if anyone finds out you rigged the election, you will be in big trouble."

"How big?" said Devis. "Are we talking warning and a fine or they chop off a hand or—"

"I don't know. Something like this is a violation of the school's code of conduct," said Albiorix. "Why can't we seem to stay out of trouble?"

"Because we live bold lives, my friend," said Devis. "Anyway, nobody is ever going to figure it out. We just sit tight, wait for things to cool off. They can't pin anything on us. There's no proof. Ooh, except these."

Devis pulled a handful of paper slips—the real ballots—out of his pocket.

"Put those back!" hissed Albiorix.

Devis did. "Fine, fine. Look, we faced the Serpent of Transhoon together. I think we can handle keeping a little secret among—"

"Hello, Devis the thief, Thromdurr the barbarian, Vela the paladin, and Albiorix the wizard!" called June, from behind the party. "Wait up!"

The adventurers stopped and stared at her, dumb-founded. June grinned. They turned to look at Albiorix.

"Okay, yes, I may have, uh, told her everything," said Albiorix.

"He sure did. Are you guys, like, doing a quest right now?" said June. "Are you on your way to go beat up Zaz—"

"Nope!" said Albiorix, shooting her a look. "We're just headed to class at the moment. That's all. Class."

June squinted but, to Albiorix's relief, made no further mention of the warlock.

"Well, June, since you apparently know our true iden-tities," said Thromdurr, "do you have any questions for a battle-hardened berserker of the Sky Bear clan?"

"I do," said June. "How do you get your hair so shiny?"

"Ah! I brush it daily with rare oils from the Floating Isle of Ulvaria," said Thromdurr. "Thank you for asking, June. None in my party have ever complimented its alluring sheen."

"No problem," said June.

"So," said Devis, "some crazy election results back there, huh?"

June laughed. "Yeah. You guys *clearly* pulled something."

"What?" said Devis. "Well, I never—"

"Is it that obvious we had something to do with it?" said Albiorix.

"Oh, yes," said June. "You four are basically the only people who wanted Olivia to win and then Albiorix gave that weird speech and then she received a hundred percent of the vote. That's more than third-world dictators get."

"Ugh," said Albiorix. "How do we fix this mess?"

"Why don't you ask your paladin," said June, "which is 'a knight renowned for heroism and chivalry'? Yep, I looked it up."

The adventurers turned to Vela, who had thus far remained silent.

"As an oath breaker, I can only say that dishonor breeds dishonor," said the paladin. "Lies beget lies. There is no way out of the web. We are doomed."

"Yikes," said June.

"Eh, I guess somebody has to be the Sorrowshade," said Devis.

"Vela's been like this for a little while," said Albiorix, "ever since she told a very, *very* minor fib."

"I am utterly disgraced," said Vela.

"Really?" said June. "'Cause I also looked up chivalry, and it seems like there's more to it than just not lying. Isn't there a bunch of other stuff about standing up for the weak and fighting injustice and all that?"

Vela stared at June. "Yes. There is."

"Well, just 'cause you messed up one part of it, you're going to toss the rest of it out?" said June. "That'd be like throwing out your whole breakfast just because you burned the toast."

Vela said nothing.

"Besides, making mistakes is the only way we learn anything, right?" said June. "And if I'm being honest, sometimes I just eat the burned toast anyway. I'm not proud."

They had arrived at room 106. As Vela, Thromdurr, and Devis made their way to their desks, June held Albiorix back.

"Hey, what's going on?" whispered June. "I thought you were going to tell them about the evil ghost guy."

"I was going to," said Albiorix. "Only . . . Flanagan seems to be fine. I don't think he's possessed at all."

"Really?" said June.

"Yeah, I hid in his rosebushes and secretly watched him for a long time," said Albiorix. "He's completely normal."

"Okay, but that story definitely makes it sound like

you aren't," said June. "Anyway, I still think you should tell them. Right?"

"I will," said Albiorix. "I will."

The last of the stragglers took their seats. Ms. Chapman cleared her throat and addressed the class. "Well, instead of learning about the power of democracy, it appears that we're getting an object lesson in electoral fraud. Needless to say, I am extremely unhappy with this outcome. It makes me reconsider the value of class elections at all."

Olivia, who had been quietly sobbing the whole time, now started to wail loudly.

"Oh, suck it up, Olivia," snapped Ms. Chapman.

Nicole Davenport raised her hand. "Ms. Chapman, personally I think it's sick and unfair what she did," said Nicole. "We *all* know who the real winner was. Hashtag stolen."

A chorus of sympathetic popular kids, including Sorrowshade, seconded her.

"But I didn't do it," blubbered Olivia. "I have no idea how I got all those votes."

"Uh-huh," said Ms. Chapman. "And why don't I believe you?"

"Please. I'm innocent," said Olivia, putting her head down on her desk and continuing to sob.

"There will be a full investigation of this incident, and I have no doubt the truth will come out," said Ms. Chapman.

"For now, it's past time we get back to those essays—"

Suddenly Vela leaped to her feet. "Ms. Chapman, I broke an oath, and to redeem myself, I must right a greater wrong through great personal sacrifice."

"Hmm," said Ms. Chapman. "Okay?"

"Olivia speaks the truth," said Vela. "She is innocent of this crime."

"Oh, no," said Devis.

"She is?" said Ms. Chapman.

"Yes," said Vela.

"And how are you sure of that, Valerie?" said Ms. Chapman.

"Because I know the identity of the true culprit," said Vela.

"Then who was it?" said Ms. Chapman. "Who threw the election—very unconvincingly, I might add—to Olivia?"

"I think it was Evan Cunningham," said Devis. "Yeah, probably Evan," he said in a different, high-pitched voice.

"Shut *up*!" said Evan.

"It was not Evan Cunningham," said Vela. "It was I, Valerie Stumpf-Turner, who committed this grave misdeed!"

Ms. Chapman blinked. "Valerie, that doesn't sound like you at all. Is this some misguided attempt to be noble and spare someone else from punishment?"

"It is not misguided," said Vela. "Olivia has been falsely

231

accused. Even if I am an oath breaker, I have a duty to reverse this injustice."

"Okay," said Ms. Chapman. "Fair enough, Valerie."

"Also, I owe an apology to Brent Sydlowski," said Vela, turning toward Brent.

"What? Nah," said Brent, with a nervous laugh. "That's okay. I don't know what you're—"

"Brent, I am sorry I said your sister told me you secretly sleep with a stuffed bee named Mr. Buzzybottom," said Vela. "That was a lie."

"Wait . . . it was a lie that he does it, or it was a lie that that's how you found out?" said Evan.

"A lie that that's how I found out," said Vela.

Brent buried his face in his palms as Evan and several other students started to laugh.

"Quiet! Everyone be quiet!" said Ms. Chapman. "Valerie, after hearing this I can only say that I am extremely disappointed in you."

"Not half so disappointed as I am in myself," said Vela. "Now, I await your judgment, Ms. Chapman."

The paladin dropped to one knee.

Ms. Chapman sighed. "Get up," she said. "Two weeks' detention. And you are barred from participating in the makeup election next Monday."

"A fair punishment. Thank you, Ms. Chapman!" said Vela, and she sat down, beaming.

After such a dramatic start, the rest of the class period passed uneventfully. When the bell rang, the adventurers and June caught up to one another in the hall.

"Wow, Vela," said Albiorix. "You really stuck your neck out there. Two weeks' detention is bad, but the punishment could have been much worse."

"Yeah. Um, thanks," said Devis, who stared at the ground. "For what it's worth, I'm . . . uh . . . sorry I screwed up."

"Wait," said Albiorix. "Did Devis just apologize for something?"

"Ha!" said Thromdurr. "You owe me a silver piece!"

Albiorix produced a shiny coin from the barbarian's ear and handed it to him.

"Hang on. Did you guys seriously have a wager about whether or not I'm capable of apologizing?" said Devis. "Because I would have wanted in on a bet like that!"

Vela put a hand on the thief's shoulder. "You are who you are. And I understand the rest of you might have a more flexible relationship with the truth than I do. I cannot expect you to follow my code. But you are my friends, and perhaps I can be honest enough for all of us. I believe it is a burden I can shoulder."

"Wow," said Devis. "So does that mean you also want to confess for the locker thefts and the shoelaces thing?"

"I cannot take responsibility for *all* your transgressions, Devis," said Vela. "After all, making mistakes is how we learn." The paladin turned to June. "Thank you, June Westray, for reminding me of that."

"I knew that was a good toast metaphor!" said June.

"Ugh! I cannot believe you people!"

The group turned to see Olivia Gorman standing behind them. She looked furious.

"Er," said Albiorix. "Hi, Olivia."

"You made me into a laughingstock," said Olivia. "You ruined my reputation with Ms. Chapman. You nearly got me detention, which would have gone on my permanent record!"

"And we do feel bad about all of that," said Albiorix. "But you did *technically* get elected president, which was *technically* what we agreed—"

"Nope," said Olivia. "Nuh-uh. No more tutoring from me. So good luck passing math without my help, morons!"

She stomped off down the hall.

"She is right to be upset," said Vela.

"Still," said Albiorix. "What are we going to do? The big algebra test is tomorrow."

Devis shook his head. "It truly pains me to say this, but . . . I think we're going to have to study really hard."

And so the heroes of Bríandalör made plans for an epic cram session, the likes of which they had never known.

Chapter

19

Homerooms & Hall Passes characters periodically face epic academic challenges known as "tests," which are weighted far more heavily than mere quizzes or homework when determining a student's final grade (see pages 76–122 for more information on calculating grade point averages). For each hour a player character spends studying for a test, add a +1 to their final skill check roll for the test. Once the test has begun, roll once on Table 178r: Random Classroom Distractions to determine if anything breaks their focus. . . .

—Excerpt from The Hall Master's Guide

❧

"Ugh," said Sophie Sorrentino. "It's New Kid."

"C'mon, I have a name," said Albiorix.

Albiorix stood at the popular girls' table. Sophie and Madison rolled their eyes. Sorrowshade glared. Nicole

Davenport studiously ignored him while favoriting dozens of social media posts on her phone.

"Look, I just want to talk to Melissa privately for a second," said Albiorix.

"Um. Maybe Melissa doesn't want to talk to you?" said Madison.

"How about you let her answer that question?" said Albiorix.

Sorrowshade narrowed her eyes, but before she could respond, Nicole spoke up.

"New Kid, weren't you, like, the one who gave that weird pro-Olivia speech?" said Nicole.

"Yes, that was me," said Albiorix.

"So you didn't want me to be class president?" said Nicole.

"I mean, I wouldn't say that," said Albiorix. "I had very complicated personal reasons for—"

"It's fine," said Nicole. "But I am going to, like, ruin you or whatever."

"Can I just talk to Melissa?" said Albiorix.

"Go ahead," said Nicole, who was already looking at her phone again. "Melissa, just get this doofus away from our table. People are starting to stare."

Sorrowshade and Albiorix found a relatively deserted corner of the cafeteria where they could speak privately. The gloom elf crossed her arms.

"What do you want, Albiorix?" said Sorrowshade. "To yell at me more?"

"Look," said Albiorix, "I know we've had our differences recently. I'm sorry I got angry. I should leave the raging to Thromdurr."

"And?" said Sorrowshade.

"And the rest of us are getting together tonight to study for the Algebra I test tomorrow. You should be there too."

"Why?" said Sorrowshade.

"Because we don't want you to fail the class," said Albiorix.

"Is that all?" said Sorrowshade.

"Yeah," said Albiorix. "I—I guess that's all."

Albiorix looked at his feet, and when he looked up again, the gloom elf had somehow vanished.

After school, Albiorix, Devis, Thromdurr, and Vela once again convened at June Westray's house to prepare as best they could for the algebra test the next day. Building on what Olivia had taught them, they began a thorough review of the material. And to the surprise of three of the four adventurers, they largely understood it. Yet the fourth still floundered helplessly in a sea of variables and coefficients.

As the hours wore on, Thromdurr became more and more despondent. Each answer he got wrong, every concept he misunderstood, seemed to weaken the barbarian's resolve. Around eight fifteen, after what was supposed to be a restorative milk-and-cookie break, Thromdurr gave up.

"I . . . cannot do it," said Thromdurr.

"You can do it, Thromdurr," said Vela. "And you will!"

"No," said Thromdurr. "Growing up on the Steppes of Ursk, I was always the strongest, the bravest, the cleverest child in the Sky Bear clan."

"Really?" said Devis. "The cleverest?"

"The elders said I was destined for great deeds," said the barbarian. "But alas, I have met my doom. Thromdurr, son of Heimdurr, berserker of the Sky Bear clan, is defeated."

He let out a dying animal wail and dramatically slumped to his knees.

"Maybe another cookie would help?" said June.

"Come on, big guy," said Devis, trying (and failing) to pull him to his feet. "Get up and let's get back to those equations."

"You keep saying that word, but I don't even understand what an equation is!" said Thromdurr. "I am past the limits of my comprehension. Algebra is anathema to a warrior from the Steppes of Ursk."

Thromdurr would not move. And so the rest of the

group left him on the floor and convened in the hall, where they spoke in hushed tones.

"This is bad," said Albiorix.

"I've never seen him like this," said Vela. "Like the lion brought down by a thorn in the paw."

"It's extremely depressing," said Devis.

"What can we do?" said June. "I feel like we're so close, but there's just no more fight left in him."

Albiorix blinked. "Wait, what did you just say?"

June cocked her head. "I said there's no fight—"

"That's it," said Albiorix. "We've been going about this all wrong. It's a fight. That's how he sees it. It's always been a fight!"

The wizard returned to Thromdurr, who still moaned pitifully on the Westrays' living-room floor.

"Hey, Thromdurr, old buddy," said Albiorix. "The rest of us were talking, and we were wondering: what's the key to victory?"

Thromdurr stopped wailing and eyed his companions. "I will cease my powerful lamentations for a moment to answer you, for it is an interesting question and a welcome relief from the agony of math."

"Great," said Albiorix. "We'd really appreciate it."

"Some would say superior strength is the key to victory. Others would argue ruthlessness," said Thromdurr. "But the real answer is this: you must know your enemy."

"Hmm. Interesting," said Albiorix. "Please elaborate."

"You must understand the true nature of what it is you are fighting," said Thromdurr. "What is the size, and strength, and capability of your opponent? A clever foe will always try to conceal these things."

"Ah, right," said Albiorix, "Just like x is doing in this equation."

"Eh?" said Thromdurr.

"Well, we have $2x + 3x - 8 = 37$," said Albiorix. "But we don't know anything about x."

"I follow not," said Thromdurr. "I see two x's written there."

"Nope," said Albiorix, "Just one x making it look like there are more."

"Ah! A clever ruse, common in battle," said Thromdurr. "Make your force appear greater than it really is."

"Sure, so to get to the true nature or our enemy, x, we need to cut through the deception and simplify this equation," said Albiorix. "We can add the $2x$ and $3x$ to get $5x$. Then we add eight to both sides, so $5x$ equals 45. That's a bit simpler. "

"Yet x still hides," cried Thromdurr, leaping to his feet. "We divide both sides by five to see that x equals nine!"

"That's exactly right," said Albiorix. "Congratulations,

Thromdurr, son of Heimdurr, you just did your first algebra."

"Why, that was no challenge at all! Cowardly x shall elude me no longer," said Thromdurr. "EVERY EQUATION SHALL FALL!"

"Honey? Is everything okay in there with the studying?" called June's mom from down the hall.

"Yeah, Mom!" June called back. "Going great!"

And so June Westray and the adventurers studied onward into the night, with Thromdurr leading the way. As his companions managed to reframe each concept in barbarian terms—factoring, the order of operations, writing equations in slope-intercept form, and more—his enthusiasm grew, and so did his algebraic prowess.

It was nearing eleven when Ms. Westray politely informed the bold young heroes that it was a school night and definitely time for them to go home. Thromdurr did not want the algebra to stop, but his companions persuaded him a good night's sleep would be invaluable before the big test.

And so four weary Bríandalörians called their parents and ate more cookies as they waited for them to arrive, while Albiorix prepared to return to JADMS on foot. And as the wizard gathered his things, something caught his eye: out the living-room window, in the darkness beyond, he thought he saw the silhouette of someone close enough to have been listening in the whole time. Yet when he checked, there was no one to be found.

"Okay, pencils down," said Mr. Botello.

Albiorix was in the midst of furiously factoring the polynomial $3h^3 - 6h^2$.

"Ahem," said Mr. Botello. "Pencils down, Mr. Boort."

"Okay, sorry," said the wizard. He stopped writing, blew the stray eraser bits off his test, and passed it toward the front. Well, that was one question he was certain he had missed. The lunch bell rang, and the Bríandalörians converged on their way to the cafeteria.

"So how did my little math heroes do?" said June.

"I am not confident in my answers to questions nine and seven," said Vela. "Yet I feel cautiously optimistic."

"I think this about sums it up for me," said Devis. He held up his phone to show a picture of a baby hedgehog wearing sunglasses with the words "MY BRAIN IS OWEE GIVE ME CHOCOLATE."

June pulled a half-eaten candy bar out of her pocket and tossed it to him. "How about you, Albiorix?" she said. "You're the smart one, right?"

"Well, there wasn't anything I didn't understand but . . . I couldn't quite finish that last question," said Albiorix. "Very annoying."

"Oh. So you did not arrive at $3h^2 (h - 2)$?" Thromdurr asked.

"No, I didn't!" said Albiorix, frowning. "But, for what it's worth . . . I think I may have passed the test?"

"Me too," said Devis.

"I'm starting to believe we can really do this, comrades!" said Vela, smiling.

"Yeah, you guys definitely aren't the dumbest kids in class anymore," said June. "I'd say you're only, like, slightly below average at this point."

"SLIGHTLY BELOW AVERAGE!" cried Thromdurr. "PRAISE THE GREAT SKY BEAR, WE ARE SLIGHTLY BELOW AVERAGE!"

The barbarian grabbed his four companions in a mighty hug.

"Excuse me, Armando," said Ms. Roland, who stood up ahead in the hallway.

"Yes?" said Albiorix.

"Can you come with me, please?"

Albiorix split off from his friends, and Ms. Roland led the wizard into the school office, past the Inspire Leadership poster, and down the short hallway toward Vice Principal Flanagan's office.

"You wanted to see me, sir?" said Albiorix as he sat down.

"Armando," said Flanagan, "it appears we have some irregularities with your paperwork after all."

"Irregularities?" said Albiorix. The wizard's blood ran cold.

"How do I put this?" said Flanagan. "You're not who you say you are."

Albiorix gave a reedy, unconvincing laugh. "What?" said the wizard. "What makes you say that?"

"Because your birth certificate looks exactly like this one," said Flanagan. He turned his laptop screen to face Albiorix. The web browser showed the same image that June had used as the basis for Armando Boort's.

The wizard swallowed. "Well, of course it looks similar. It's the same template—"

"Actually, I checked, and this template hasn't been in use since the early 1960s," said Flanagan. "So then I spoke with our IT guy and took a look at the computer logs. Imagine my surprise when I found someone else had recently visited this exact same web page. You used this image to forge the one you gave me. Is that about right?"

Albiorix blinked. He'd been caught. The jig was up.

He opened his mouth and closed it again. The wizard said nothing.

"No implausible explanation? No snappy comeback?" said Flanagan, who was smiling now for the first time since Albiorix had arrived. "Well, the good news is, I think there is a way we can work this out,"

"There is?" said Albiorix.

"Give me the Malonomicon," hissed Flanagan.

Chapter

20

In the real world, violence is the best solution to many (if not most) of life's problems. If a band of angry orcs is waylaying travelers, you slay them. If giant rats have made a lair in the basement of the local brewery, you slay them. Yet in the fictional world of Homerooms & Hall Passes, violence is frowned upon. Part of the fun of the game is thinking up creative solutions to problems that can't merely be solved by brute force. After all, there is no quicker way to Blow It than attacking a nonplayer character and suffering the disciplinary consequences.

—*Excerpt from* The Hall Master's Guide

❧

ALBIORIX LEAPED TO HIS FEET.

"I guess you didn't already get that message about us killing you . . . once!" said Albiorix. "I mean, the message didn't get to you about it, or . . ."

"Huh?" said Flanagan.

"Trust me! It sounded really good the way I said it before!" said Albiorix. "Anyway, I don't have the Malonomicon!" The wizard scrambled back, knocking over his chair as he prepared to . . . what? He had no offensive spells to cast. He had no weapon. He didn't even have his umbrella.

"You know where it is," hissed Flanagan. "Do not trifle with me, fool. I am an immortal mage of untold power."

"Then . . . why do you need your spellbook so badly?" said Albiorix.

"Because . . . just give it to me," said Flanagan.

"Oh, I get it," said Albiorix. "We're in the same boat. You can't cast any of the good stuff without it, can you?"

"I will destroy you!" cried Flanagan, pounding his desk. The warlock had finally lost his cool.

"Will you?" said Albiorix. "Because whatever we were back in Bríandalör, right now I'm a middle-school student and you're my vice principal. If you destroy me, I mean, talk about a lawsuit against the district."

"Lawsuits do not concern one such as I!" said Flanagan. His eyes burned with unholy green fire.

"Yeah, that's spooky and all," said Albiorix, who was starting to feel more confident. "But I'm still not going to give you your book."

Flanagan grimaced and settled back down into his office

chair. "Perhaps you are right. In this body I am just a lowly academic administrator," he said. "So allow me to repeat my first offer: give me the Malonomicon, or I shall expel you from this school. That, I believe, is well within my powers as vice principal."

Albiorix was speechless.

"And such a punishment will mean your final end," said Flanagan. "Those are the rules of this idiotic game. In Homerooms & Hall Passes, if you get expelled, you've Blown It, yes?"

Albiorix's eyes narrowed. "The game's not idiotic. It's a great way to socialize and build imagination and have fun with your friends!"

"Pshaw. It's for geeks and weirdoes," said Flanagan. "Now, you have until I complete this disciplinary action form to make peace with your gods." Flanagan pulled a photocopied form out of his desk drawer and started to fill it in.

Albiorix crossed his arms. "So do your worst, old man."

"Playing the martyr? How tiresome," said Flanagan. "If that is not enough to persuade you to bargain, then perhaps I shall expel all of your companions as well?"

"On what grounds?" said Albiorix. "They didn't do anything! I'm the one who summoned you. This is between you and me, Zazirak."

Flanagan put down his pen and steepled his fingers as a

ghastly grin spread across his face. "Mmm. And while we're discussing disciplinary action, there is a *very* troublesome student I've had my eye on—a recent transfer; not a good fit for JADMS. I believe her name is June Annabelle Westray."

"Hey!" said Albiorix, who felt himself starting to panic. "You leave her out of this!"

"After all, it was June's computer station at which your counterfeit documents were forged," said Flanagan. "A grave academic transgression. Perhaps a crime—"

"She's not even an adventurer!" cried Albiorix, losing all composure. "She's a nonplayer character!"

"Then spare her and give me my book," said Flanagan.

Albiorix's heart was beating fast. He thought about leaping across the desk and attacking the monster with his bare hands. But as he'd said, he was a middle-school student and Zazirak was his vice principal. Fighting the man would only get him expelled so much quicker. What was the right answer? What was a real hero supposed to do?

"Zazirak," said Albiorix, "if I do what you ask, do you swear by whatever dark powers you hold dear that you will leave June Westray alone?"

Flanagan grinned. "In the name of great Azathor the Devourer, I swear it."

"Then wait here," said Albiorix.

And so the wizard trudged down the now-empty

hallway of JADMS and into the school library. There, on a shelf between an instructional manual for making kites and a field guide to North American birds, Albiorix found the ancient spellbook, exactly where he'd hidden it.

Chapter 21

Conflict is the key to making your game of Homerooms & Hall Passes interesting. But the antagonists of the game are quite different than the dastardly villains of the real world. Instead of an ancient dragon that lays waste to the surrounding countryside or a bloodthirsty orc warlord hoping to usher in an eon of fire and chaos, the typical middle-school villain might be a cranky teacher who habitually calls on students exactly when they aren't paying attention, or a kid who relentlessly makes fun of one of the characters for wearing glasses.

—Excerpt from The Hall Master's Guide

THE SKY OUTSIDE HAD darkened ominously by the time Albiorix entered the cafeteria. He found Devis, Vela, and Thromdurr sitting with June at the wobbly table near the flagpole.

"Guys, we have a problem," said the wizard.

"Indeed," said Vela, "there is something gravely wrong with the baked ziti." The paladin pointed at the grayish lump sitting on her tray.

"Please. It's fine," said Devis. "Just put a little yellow sauce on it. I mean, at least it's not soup, right?" The thief squirted a line of mustard onto his pasta and started to chow down.

"No, thank you," said Vela. "I shall fast."

"Is the food really that much better where you guys come from?" said June. "I imagine it being all stale bread and giant hunks of blackened meat?"

"Mmm. Blackened meat," said Thromdurr, licking his lips.

"Zazirak the warlock is here," said Albiorix.

Silence fell over the table. The other three Bríandalöri-ans stared at Albiorix. Devis's fork fell out of his mouth.

"In the cafeteria?" said Thromdurr, glancing around, ready to spring into action.

"In Vice Principal Flanagan," said Albiorix.

"How can you be sure?" said Vela.

"Because, well . . . I brought him here," said Albiorix.

And Albiorix recounted the story of performing the ritual of the Returning and, instead of transporting them home, conjuring the evil ghost. When he had finished, his adventuring companions had grave looks upon their faces.

"And you guys were on my back for breaking into a few lockers?" said Devis with a whistle. "Somebody owes me an apology."

"You are not the smart one, Albiorix," said Thromdurr, shaking his head. "This is clear now."

"I thought you were going to destroy that evil book?" said Vela.

"I was," said Albiorix. "I should have. But it's too late now."

"Guys, I think Albiorix was just trying to do his best. He wanted to help you all get home," said June, "even if he should have told you earlier."

"Wait," said Devis. "June already knew about Zazirak? You told her before us?"

"Yeah," said Albiorix. "Sorry."

"But she's not even an adventurer!" said Thromdurr.

"Excuse me. I have *plenty* of adventures," said June. "The other day my mom and I had to go to three different stores looking for the right dry food for my cat."

"Well," said Vela, folding her napkin, "we cannot change the past, only the future. Our course is clear. We must banish Zazirak back to the underworld as quickly as possible, or this entire realm is in danger."

Devis scrunched up his face. "Fine. I'll be the one to say

it. Do we actually care about that?"

"Hey!" said June. "This might be a game to you guys, but some of us have to live here!"

"June is right," said Albiorix. "I'm not sure exactly what this place is, but . . . it certainly seems like it may be as real as Bríandalör."

"Besides, we're stuck here," said Vela. "Until we find a way home, our fate and the fate of this world are intertwined. But take heart. We defeated Zazirak before. I am sure we can defeat him again."

"That's exactly what I said," said June. "It's clear I already think like an adventurer."

"Hmm," said Thromdurr. "When last we faced the warlock, it was the elf who finished him off."

"Yes," said Vela. "I hope Sorrowshade is not too far gone to help us in this fight."

They gazed out across the cafeteria to see the gloom elf at her usual place, whispering and giggling by Nicole Davenport's side.

"I'll go talk to her," said Albiorix. "She deserves to hear the truth from me."

"If there's any of the Sorrowshade we know left," said Devis, "she'll definitely want to point out what an idiot you are."

"That's what I'm hoping," said Albiorix.

The wizard stood and crossed the lunchroom to Nicole's table.

"Did you guys know that Evelyn Roy secretly bites her toenails?" said Nicole to her three besties.

"OMG, really?" said Madison.

"Yuck," said Sophie.

"That's dis-*gust*-ing," said Sorrowshade in the perfect singsong inflection of the popular girls.

"And that's, like, not even the worst part," said Nicole, lowering her voice. "After she bites the toenails, *she eats them*."

The besties groaned.

"How do you even know that, Nicole?" asked Madison.

"I, like, have my sources," said Nicole with a smirk. "Anyway, did you guys know that C. J. Meier is terrified of pigeons—"

Albiorix cleared his throat. He'd been standing beside the table silently for several seconds, while the girls studiously ignored him.

"Ugh," said Sophie. "I think New Kid is sick. He keeps coughing."

"Shoo, New Kid," said Madison. "Go make phlegm noises somewhere else."

"Hello, Sophie. Hello, Madison. Hello, Nicole," said Albiorix. "I hope you're all having a wonderful day here at

J. A. Dewar Middle School. I'd like to talk to Melissa, please."

"Anything you have to say to Melissa you can, like, say to all of us," said Nicole. "We're besties."

"Fine," said Albiorix. "I accidentally raised the warlock Zazirak from the dead and now his spirit has possessed Vice Principal Flanagan. I know you like it here at this school. You've found acceptance among this group of popular girls. And I get it. You have something at JADMS you never had back in Bríandalör. Maybe I do too? But the truth is, we need your help—we need Sorrowshade's help—to defeat Zazirak, or everyone here could perish."

There was a long moment of silence. Sophie and Madison stared at Albiorix like his head had just fallen off his shoulders. Nicole eyed him with an unreadable expression. Sorrowshade stood.

"Listen up," said Sorrowshade. "I don't know you, New Kid. And I don't want to know you. I have no idea what any of that gibberish means. But what I do know is that you have five seconds to get lost. I don't want you anywhere near this table because, frankly, I'm worried you *are* sick. *And that loser is contagious!*"

An "Oooooh!" erupted from the kids at the nearby tables as Albiorix realized the cafeteria had gone quiet to listen. Practically all of JADMS had heard the gloom elf dress him down.

"Is there, like, anything else, New Kid?" said Nicole.

Albiorix shook his head and slowly returned to his table, as the collective eyes of the student body followed him.

"Well, that went well," said Devis.

"The elf has become ensorcelled by the enticements of this strange land," said Thromdurr. "A pity. She was quite a fighter."

"Eh, don't be too hard on her," said Albiorix.

"Really?" said Devis. "Because, in case you forgot, forty seconds ago she just roasted you in front of the whole school."

"Sorrowshade is just doing what she thinks she should," said Albiorix.

"A shame," said Vela. "Yet we must not tarry. The four of us need to vanquish Zazirak without delay."

"Hey, there are five of us," said June. "Quest time, baby! Let's go!"

The Bríandalörians gave each other an awkward look. Albiorix cleared his throat.

"June," said the wizard, "it's probably for the best if you, ah, don't accompany us."

"What?" said June. "Why?"

"Zazirak is incredibly dangerous," said Vela. "We are talking about the Blight of the Shield Coast, the Slayer of Hotus the Good. In a confrontation, we could not guarantee your safety."

"Who's asking you to?" said June.

"Look, June, we're professionals," said Devis. "What we do takes a lifetime of training."

"You have mustard all over your shirt," said June.

Devis started frantically trying to blot out the yellow splotch on his chest.

"June, you are very skilled in graphic design and *Oink Pop*," said Thromdurr. "But I killed an ice tiger with my bare hands when I was nine. Do you see the difference there?"

"This is not fair," said June. "It's my world that Zazzmatazz wants to blow up!"

"Zazirak," said Albiorix. "And June, I say this as someone who is barely an adventurer himself: you have to sit this one out."

June frowned at the heroes as, one by one, they discreetly left the table and made their way out into the hall. The party reconvened in an empty alcove near the language lab.

"All right, what's the plan?" said Devis. "I'm thinking Thromdurr could, like, throw me at him!"

"Yes!" cried Thromdurr.

"Perhaps, but first we must head to the prop closet and reclaim our weapons," said Vela. "I need my sword and shield to face this evil."

"Ah, how I long to feel Boneshatter's heft within my

mighty grip!" said Thromdurr. "It has been an eternity since I smashed something!"

"As you know, I don't have any weapons," said Albiorix, "but I'm very excited for you guys! Anyway, after that, I think we should go to the office and see if we can draw Zazirak out somehow. Battling him on school grounds seems inadvisable."

"Agreed," said Vela. "Then let us away—"

"Wait."

They turned to see a shadowy figure step out from behind a nearby trophy case.

"You're all going to die without me," said Sorrowshade. "I mean, in the long run, we're all going to die. But . . . still."

"Sorrowshade," said Albiorix. "We thought we'd lost you to the popular girls for good."

"Not quite," said Sorrowshade. "I just had to put on a convincing performance for Nicole in there. She really doesn't like you, Albiorix."

"That I gathered," said Albiorix.

"Also, for the record," said Sorrowshade, "you're an idiot for accidentally summoning an evil warlock."

"Sorrowshade is back, baby!" said Devis.

The party stealthily made their way to the auditorium prop closet. Vela threw open the door and turned on the lights. Then the paladin gasped. No longer the cluttered space they'd seen before, the prop closet was now clean and orderly. Everything was stacked in neat piles, with ample space to move between them. It contained maybe a fifth of the random junk it previously had.

"I don't understand," said Vela. "Where are our weapons?"

The heroes began to frantically dig through the few remaining props. After several minutes of searching, they came up empty. There was no sign of Vela's sword and shield, Devis's daggers, Sorrowshade's bow, or the war hammer Boneshatter.

A few minutes later, they found Mr. Driscoll on his way to restock the toilet paper in the first-floor bathrooms.

"Mr. Driscoll, sorry to bother you," said Albiorix, "but do you know what happened to the prop closet?"

"Huh? Oh, I cleaned it out last week," said Mr. Driscoll. "Took me all day. That place was a rat's nest."

"But what about all the weapons?" said Devis. *All the high-quality prop weapons?*"

"Tossed them in the recycling," said Mr. Driscoll.

The party groaned.

"Well, I did keep the plastic Tommy gun and the rubber butcher knife that squirts fake blood," said Mr. Driscoll. "I figured that would suffice for most middle-school dramatic productions."

"You threw Boneshatter in the trash," whispered

261

Thromdurr, who looked like he might cry. "It belonged to my father and his father before him."

"Sorry," said Mr. Driscoll. "For what it's worth, I *did* keep the horse costume." He shrugged and continued on his way.

"Well, what do we do now?" said Sorrowshade. "Fight Zazirak with pencils and loose-leaf paper?"

"No," said Vela. "But we still need to figure out what the warlock's vile plans are, before we decide what must be done."

The party cautiously made their way toward the school office.

"Ooh, you just missed him," said Ms. Roland, when they asked if the vice principal was in.

"We did?" said Vela.

"Yep. He went home for the day," said Ms. Roland. "He said he had something very important to take care of."

"Did he say what it was?" said Vela.

Ms. Roland shook her head. "Nope, when I asked he just kind of laughed."

"And would you describe that laugh as *maniacal*?" said Sorrowshade.

Ms. Roland looked around. Then she discreetly made the "little bit" sign with her fingers. The bell rang.

☙

262

"Well, at least whatever evil stuff Zazirak's doing, it's not happening at school," said Albiorix as the adventurers made their way toward Ms. Levy's social studies class.

"He obviously wanted the Malonomicon for something specific," said Vela. "We must find him before it's too late."

"I do know where he lives," said Albiorix.

"Good," said Vela. "Then that's where we'll start."

"My. Ancestral. War hammer. Got . . . *recycled*," said Thromdurr, still reeling.

"Aw. Don't worry about it, big guy," said Devis. "Boneshatter will live on. Maybe as a wok? Or a soda can?"

The barbarian moaned in despair.

Chapter 22

In lieu of being driven by their parents—or enduring the humiliation of begging an older sibling for a ride—middle schoolers must rely on bicycles, skateboards, or scooters to get where they want to go. If none of these modes of transportation are available, walking is the only option left. Distances in Suburbia are measured in blocks, and a nonadventuring party, walking at average speed, can travel up to forty-five blocks per hour.

—Excerpt from The Hall Master's Guide

B LACK CLOUDS ROILED IN the afternoon sky. From the flower garden, the adventurers peered through the window into the house at 1120 San Antonio Way. The lights were off. Sorrowshade listened intently with her heightened elven senses.

"I can hear the upstairs toilet running," said Sorrowshade.

"But there's nobody in this house."

"Hmm. I do also know Flanagan's favorite pizza place," said Albiorix.

"Should we check it out?" said Devis. "I could definitely go for a slice with yellow sauce."

"It feels like a long shot," said Albiorix. "I'm pretty sure Zazirak is in the driver's seat now."

"Where could the foul wight be?" said Thromdurr, gazing out over the town of Hibbettsfield behind them.

"I wish we had Homerooms & Hall Passes sourcebooks to help us figure it out," said Vela.

"Yep," said Albiorix. "If only *the person who stole them* would give them back." The wizard turned to Devis and crossed his arms.

"This again?" said Devis. "I told you before: I did not steal your books! You know me. Do I strike you as a prolific reader?"

"Devis, you are only belaboring this," said Vela. "Unburden your soul. Confess and be forgiven."

"What did I ever do to you people to deserve such suspicion?" said Devis.

"Everything?" said Thromdurr. "You probably already traded the books for magic beans or some such."

"I didn't!" said Devis. "Although that does sound like a good offer. Wait, do you know somebody who has magic beans? Because I would potentially be interested in—"

"Devis didn't take your books," said Sorrowshade. "I did."

"Why?" said Albiorix.

"I'm not proud of it," said Sorrowshade, "but I thought it would impress Nicole. She's been using them to learn the darkest secrets of everyone in the school and consolidate popular-girl power."

"Well, that certainly sounds terrifying," said Albiorix. "Can you get them back?"

"Of course," said Sorrowshade. "Nicole is my friend. I'll just ask her."

Though as the gloom elf said it, Albiorix thought he heard a slight hitch in her voice.

Soon after, the party arrived at a beautiful gabled house on Kenmare Street. The other Bríandalörians waited down the block as Sorrowshade approached the door. The gloom elf steeled herself and rang the bell. Nicole answered.

"Nicole, hiiiii-eee," said Sorrowshade in perfect popular girl dialect.

"Melissa, hiiiii-eee," said Nicole.

The girls exchanged air kisses as Sorrowshade stepped inside.

"This is going to sound crazy," said Sorrowshade, "but you know all those books I gave you? I kind of need them back. Please don't hate me!"

"Mmm," said Nicole. "Wish I could. But I'm still, like, mining them for juicy stuff. Did you know Dave Pittman sometimes just eats a whole stick of butter right out of the fridge?"

"Dis-*gust*-ing," said Sorrowshade. "Still, I . . . I actually really need the books back."

Nicole's expression hardened. "Um, yeah, no. Not going to happen, Melissa."

"It's an emergency," said Sorrowshade, her popular-girl voice dropping a little. "We are besties, right?"

Nicole snickered. "Look, it was funny to have a spooky weird girl around for a while, but, like, right now we're all getting super tired of it."

"Funny?" said Sorrowshade. "Weird girl? Are you talking about me?"

"Duh," said Nicole. "Madison and Sophie thought it would be hilarious if we all acted like we were your friends. But let's face it: you dress weird. You talk weird. And even though you do that thing with your hair, we've *all* seen your weird ears. They are dis-*gust*-ing."

Sorrowshade's hand instinctively moved toward the side of her head. The assassin blinked at something she hadn't felt in years: tears starting to well in her eyes.

"Face it," said Nicole. "You can't be something you're

not. And you're, like, not one of us."

"But—but I thought—"

"You thought wrong." Nicole raised her phone and snapped a picture of Sorrowshade's face with her phone. "Perfect. Just need to caption this with 'Hate . . . fake . . . people.' And . . . posted. Yay!"

Sorrowshade swallowed and wiped the tears away with the back of her sleeve. "I guess—I guess you're right. I am not one of you. I never will be. It was stupid for me to think that I could be."

"Wow. You're *finally* catching on. Kudos or whatever," said Nicole. "Now it's really time for you to go—"

"I am a gloom elf assassin of Bríandalör, doomed to tread alone, followed only by darkness and misery," said Sorrowshade. *"Now give me what I came for."* Her voice rose in an unearthly whisper, as the shadows of the foyer seemed to grow and to gather around her.

Nicole laughed. "Do you have any idea who you're talking to? I'm the most popular girl in J. A. Dew—"

"I am talking to a petty, spoiled brat who is terrified no one actually likes her," said Sorrowshade. *"Now give me the books or I will reveal to everyone what you did at the Hibbettsfield Fall Festival last year."*

Nicole blinked, and the color drained from her face. She stared at Sorrowshade for a long moment, then swallowed.

"You know about that?"

Sorrowshade gave a joyless grin. "*Of course. Haven't you read your own entry in the* The Cyclopedia of Students? *Very, very juicy stuff.*"

"Look, about what happened at the festival," said Nicole, panic rising in her voice. "I—I honestly thought it was a candy bar, okay?"

The Bríandalörians turned as Sorrowshade stepped out from a mailbox behind them.

"Ha! Very surprising!" said Thromdurr. "I have truly missed your dramatic entrances, elf."

"Thanks. I'm sure I missed something about you too," said Sorrowshade. "Don't worry. It will come to me."

The gloom elf held out her arms, now full of Homerooms & Hall Passes sourcebooks. Albiorix took them.

"Great," said the wizard. "So Nicole gave them up without any trouble?"

"Perhaps she's not so bad after all," said Vela.

"No," said Sorrowshade. "She is."

Devis squinted at Sorrowshade's face. "Hang on," he said. "Have you been . . . crying?"

Sorrowshade leaned in close to the thief. "*Ask me that again and see what happens.*"

Devis gulped. "Probably just allergies. We did just spend

half an hour sitting in a flower bed—"

"That's right," said Sorrowshade. "Allergies."

Evening fell on the town of Hibbettsfield. Black thunderheads still hung in the sky, and there was an eerie charge in the air, as though just before a storm. Still the rain did not come. At the public library, the party pored through every one of Albiorix's H&H sourcebooks and searched online for any clue as to where their enemy might be hiding. Though they were initially hopeful, their energy waned as the darkness outside deepened.

Thromdurr flipped through *The Hibbettsfield Handbook* for the ninth time.

"Perhaps Zazirak is hiding in . . . Cedar Point Plumbing Supply?"

Devis shrugged and dialed the number on his phone. "Hello, Cedar Point Plumbing Supply? Yes, hi. I'm just wondering if anything strange has been happening in your store lately? . . . Specifically? Well, are there any, um, evil warlocks hanging around?" The thief put his hand over the phone and whispered, "He's checking."

"Really?" said Vela.

"No. He definitely hung up," said Devis. "That makes forty-three places we've called so far. Still no sign of Zazirak."

"In our world, such a warlock would make his lair in a

270

dungeon or a ruined castle or perhaps an active volcano," said Vela.

"There are no dungeons or castles or volcanoes here," said Albiorix, who was lying on the floor with his feet up on a chair. "That's what I've been trying to tell you guys."

"Then by the Great Sky Bear," cried Thromdurr, leaping to his feet. "ALL THESE HOMEROOMS & HALL PASSES BOOKS ARE USELESS!" The barbarian reared back as though he meant to fling *The Hibbettsfield Handbook* across the room.

"Ah. That's what I missed about you," said Sorrowshade, rubbing her temples. "The yelling for no reason."

"THE REASON," cried Thromdurr, "IS THAT I'M ANGRY—"

Three other library patrons loudly shushed him.

"No battle-raging in the library," whispered Vela.

Thromdurr snorted and plopped back down into his chair.

"Guys, we have to be able to figure this out," said Albiorix. "Villains back home live in dungeons because they're dark and grim and creepy."

"So what, then, is the Homerooms & Hall Passes equivalent?" said Vela.

"A forgotten place," said Sorrowshade.

"That mortals shun," said Thromdurr.

"Full of ghosts and sadness," said Devis

It suddenly became obvious to the five of them.

"The Old Mall," said Albiorix.

Chapter 23

*Characters may occasionally wish to obtain a new piece
of equipment to aid them in their nonadventures—a pair
of stylish sneakers, a faster bicycle, a top-of-the-line
three-hole punch. Yet if they lack the necessary money
saved from birthdays, holidays, or part-time jobs, they
generally must persuade a parent to purchase the item
for them. Have the player roll a Likability or Cunning
check contested by the parent's Willpower. Add +2 to the
difficulty of the roll for each $50 of the item's price. . . .*

—Excerpt from The Hall Master's Guide

❧

FIVE BOLD HEROES STOOD before the West End Shopping
Center on Cleveland Street. There, between Ronnie's
Sporting Goods and an Aeon Wireless mobile phone store,
was the familiar storefront of Pan-Galactic Comics and Collectibles. Through the window, the adventurers could see

Waldo Franks carrying on what appeared to be a very spirited debate with his two pet turtles. The man looked happy.

"Why are we here, Albiorix?" said Sorrowshade. "You need to pick up a few misprinted toys before our big climactic battle?"

"We're not going to the comic book shop," said Albiorix. "We're going to Ronnie's Sporting Goods."

"Why?" said Vela. "I'm all for fun and games—"

"No, you're not," said Devis,

"—but we must arm ourselves for a clash with evil!"

"Exactly," said Albiorix.

He pulled *The Great Grimoire of Games* out of his pack and opened the book to show the others. His companions all smiled, as they understood what the wizard had in mind.

The adventuring party entered Ronnie's Sporting Goods and split up. It did not take long to find what they were looking for. Sorrowshade the assassin returned to the counter holding an archery set. Vela the Valiant carried a regulation fencing épée in one hand and a pentagonal home plate that almost looked like her old shield in the other. Devis had a handful of figure-skating blades, sharp as daggers. And Albiorix, not usually one for weapons or armor, carried a hockey stick and enough goalie pads to make Armando Boort's fictional Canadian sports career seem plausible.

"Wow, Magic Man," said Devis. "Usually you hide in the back and zap them with spells. Are you really planning to get in there and mix it up with the rest of us?"

"I want to do my part," said Albiorix, "but none of the magic at my disposal will be very useful."

"Good thinking," said Vela. "In those heavy pads, you can get out front and distract Zazirak as a sort of human punching bag."

"That's, uh, not really what I had in—"

"While the warlock is pummeling you," said Vela, "the rest of us will close in and take him down."

"Er. Hmm," said Albiorix.

"Don't worry," said Sorrowshade, placing a hand on Albiorix's shoulder. "Death comes to us all."

"Great. Thank you. I feel so much better," said Albiorix.

"Glad to help," said Sorrowshade. "What's taking Thromdurr so long?"

"Behold!" said the barbarian. "I have found it at last!" With a huge grin he held up his chosen weapon: a wooden croquet mallet. "I call it . . . Boneshatter II!"

And so the brave heroes placed their pile of Ronnie's Sporting Goods merchandise on the counter and waited for the cashier to ring them up.

"And your total comes to . . . $670.11," she said.

The adventurers gasped. They hadn't reckoned that

arming themselves against darkness might carry such a hefty price tag.

"Okay, uh, one moment, please," said Albiorix.

The wizard whispered an arcane word of power and pulled a coin out of the pocket dimension. He handed it to the cashier. She examined the coin, which was covered in strange Bríandalörian runes and had the bearded profile of King Brammus the Benevolent in bas-relief.

"And there's more where that came from," said Albiorix, reaching toward his other ear.

"Yeah, no, I can't take this," said the cashier. She handed the coin back.

"Perfect," said Sorrowshade. "Now what?"

"Allow me," said Devis. "Hey, lady! Look over there!" The thief pointed and the cashier turned. Devis grabbed his ice skates and prepared to bolt out of the store.

"Devis, no!" said Vela, catching him by the arm and holding him fast. "Not like that."

The thief gave a long sigh. "Okay, fine. I *really* didn't want to do this, but . . ."

Ever so slowly, Devis reached down into his sock and rummaged around. At last he pulled out a massive bloodred gemstone.

"The ruby from the Temple of Azathor!" said Vela.

"Yep," said Devis. "I could've used this rock to buy a

castle back home. Instead I guess I'll purchase six hundred and seventy dollars' worth of sporting goods." He plunked the ruby down on the counter. "Do you guys take priceless jewels?"

The cashier's eyes lit up. "Absolutely."

And so the adventurers exited Ronnie's Sporting Goods armed for battle, yet still they had one more stop to make.

❧

It was well after dinner when the doorbell rang. June answered it clutching her orange tabby, Cheese, in her arms. Outside in the darkness, she saw the five Bríandalörians, decked out in their new athletic gear. There was purpose in their eyes.

"Hi," said Albiorix.

"Hi," said June, "You guys look like you're ready to . . . play several sports."

"Just one for me," said Sorrowshade. "Pin the arrow on the warlock."

"So you're off to fight Zazzma—er, Vice Principal Flanagan?" said June.

"That's right," said Albiorix. "We think we finally figured out where he's hiding."

"And I'm guessing I still can't come with you?" said June.

"We commend your bravery. Truly," said Vela. "But it would be best if you did not."

June started to protest again, but Albiorix stopped her.

"June, you know she's right," said Albiorix. "Anyway, I just wanted to thank you for everything you've done for me. For us."

June blinked. "That sounds like you think you might not come back."

"Ha! Not likely, June Westray," said Thromdurr, thumping his chest. "We shall crush the puny warlock and see you at school bright and early tomorrow, ready for English class!"

"Still," said Albiorix.

June dropped her cat and gave the wizard a hug.

"Be safe out there, guys," said June.

"Safe?" said Devis with a roguish grin. "That's not really our style."

"Is there anything you need before you go do your quest?" said June.

"Well," said Albiorix, "there is one thing."

"What?" said June.

"You wouldn't happen to have any torches, would you?" said Vela.

And so June Westray descended into the basement to obtain several mosquito-repellent citronella torches, which had somehow made the move with them from the big city.

❧

The Old Mall squatted in the empty parking lot like some massive gray toad. The adventurers approached the glass double doors that marked the north entrance. Closed. Sorrowshade peered inside.

"It's completely dark," said Sorrowshade, throwing her hood up. "Kind of like life."

"Devis, the door?" said Albiorix.

"Okay, so *now* me being a thief is good thing again?" said Devis as he pulled out his lockpicks and got to work. "Got it."

"When last we faced Zazirak, I called upon the Powers of Light to rebuke him," said Vela, clutching her sunburst pendant. "Yet here in this world, the Powers cannot heed my call."

"Bah! You give yourself too much credit, paladin. Boneshatter II will make short work of this ghoul," said Thromdurr, raising his mallet. "WITH SMASHING!"

"I don't know," said Albiorix. "This time he knows we're coming and he has his spellbook. I've looked through the Malonomicon and it's pretty nasty."

"What a coincidence," said Sorrowshade. "So am I." The gloom elf went for her hood but realized it was already up. She attempted to play off the awkward gesture like she was trying to scratch her back with both hands.

"Onward, then, comrades," said Vela, drawing her épée. "Evil awaits."

Devis popped open the lock, and the adventurers slipped inside the Hibbettsfield Galleria. Albiorix murmured a quiet incantation and his light spell bathed the way ahead in silver moonglow. The wary party trudged forward through the deserted mall. They glanced around as they walked, scanning the flickering shadows for any sign of their foe. They passed the Chicken Hut and LA Jewelers and Trundlebee's Toys with no sign of any warlocks.

"Stop," said Sorrowshade, holding up a fist. "I think I saw someone." The party froze as the gloom elf gazed out into the darkness toward a clothing store called Style Shack. Albiorix's luminous orb drifted over to reveal rows of dead-eyed mannequins, sporting stylish winter outfits and accessories, standing motionless in the window.

"Whew," said Vela. "Not to worry. They are just—"

The window shattered as ten mannequins charged toward them.

"Well, that's . . . unexpected," said Devis.

"There is a spell in the Malonomicon for turning inanimate objects evil," said Albiorix.

"Then we have found Zazirak's lair for certain," said Vela.

The charging line of mannequins clashed with the

280

heroes. Thromdurr roared as he exploded one's head with a mighty downward swing of Boneshatter II. Two of Sorrowshade's arrows took out the feet of another, sending it toppling to the floor. Devis scrambled between the legs of a third and popped up to plunge an ice skate into its back. Meanwhile, Vela fended off three more mannequins with her makeshift shield.

True to habit, Albiorix found himself hanging near the back of the fray, away from the main action. He swatted at an errant mannequin (decked out in full ski gear) with his hockey stick, and missed. The thing turned and lunged at him, tackling him to the floor.

"Unhand our wizard, fashion golem!" cried Vela, running the mannequin through with her épée, before it could tear Albiorix's hockey mask off.

"Whew! Thanks," said Albiorix, panting as the paladin helped him to his feet. "Respect to you guys. Fighting is . . . difficult."

"Hardly!" cried Thromdurr, pounding the last of the mannequins into smaller and smaller bits. "To feel an opponent's plastic skull smash beneath my hammer is almost as thrilling as passing an Algebra I test!"

With their final enemy defeated, the adventurers now stood in a field of scarves and sweaters and disembodied arms and legs. The Old Mall was eerily quiet once more.

"Was that it?" said Devis, glancing around. "Amateur hour, Zazirak."

"Likely a test," said Vela. "A greater challenge is surely ahead."

The party pressed onward toward the escalators. In the darkness, they found the moving staircases still and silent.

"Huh," said Devis, as he started to ascend. "When it's turned off, it's just a simple set of—"

The escalator groaned and shifted beneath his feet, causing the thief to stumble. A horrendous ripping crunch followed. Devis clung on for dear life as the up escalator violently pulled itself free of the mechanical track and reared up like a gigantic metal serpent, ready to strike.

Chapter 24

As a Hall Master, it's easy to get overwhelmed when running a game of Homerooms & Hall Passes. You are expected not only to know the rules, but to portray every nonplayer character and make sure the nonadventure is running smoothly. At times, you may wonder, "Am I doing it wrong?" The answer to that question is no, as long as you and your players are enjoying yourselves.

—Excerpt from The Hall Master's Guide

"**G**UYS?" CRIED DEVIS, WHO desperately clung to the up escalator as it swayed in the air like some gargantuan metallic cobra. "I think this might be the greater challenge!"

"Not good," said Albiorix, backing away.

There was another metal-tearing crunch as the down escalator pulled itself free as well. The pair of escalators now loomed menacingly over the heads of the adventurers.

"Double not good," said Albiorix. He doubted a hockey mask would protect him from an angry moving staircase.

"I KNEW ESCALATORS COULD NOT BE TRUSTED!" bellowed Thromdurr.

The barbarian swung Boneshatter II at the up escalator, but his blow glanced off harmlessly. An instant later, the escalator struck down at the barbarian like an angry snake. Somehow Thromdurr managed to somersault out of the way as the force of its attack pulverized the floor where he had been standing. The escalator reared again. Miraculously, Devis still managed to cling to it. Three of Sorrowshade's arrows plinked off it in quick succession.

"These things are made of steel," said Sorrowshade. "So unfair."

The gloom elf dodged a strike from the down escalator, but its sweeping tail whipped around and smashed into her. The assassin went sliding across the mall floor. Vela saw an opening and charged in to stab at it, but as she did her épée bent nearly in half.

"None of our weapons are effective," cried Vela. "What can we do?"

"PURE BRUTE STRENGH MUST BE THE ANSWER!" cried Thromdurr.

The barbarian wrapped his mighty arms around the up escalator and attempted to wrestle it. Yet with a shrug, the moving staircase threw him off. Thromdurr pinwheeled through the air and painfully smacked against a concrete column.

"Or perhaps we need a plan," cried Vela.

"Hang on, I think one just came to me," cried Devis, who still clung to the up escalator's writhing form, like a spider on a garden hose.

"Hey, stupid!" Devis yelled over at the down escalator.

The down escalator recoiled from its fight with Vela and slowly turned toward the thief.

"Oooh, look at me, I'm an escalator! I'm for people who are too lazy to take a flight of stairs!" cried Devis in a ridiculous voice. "Yep. I'm pretty much a glorified conveyor belt!"

The down escalator lunged at Devis, who nimbly flipped out of the way. The down escalator smashed into the up escalator, knocking them both into a nearby photo booth. The up escalator rose—now apparently enraged at its twin—and rammed the down escalator, knocking three steps loose.

And with that, the pair was locked in mortal combat. Their huge snakelike forms coiled over and over, dislodging more steps as they battled. The heroes watched until the fight ended with both escalators immobile—badly damaged and inextricably tangled with each other on the floor in front of Shoe Cave.

"Nice work, Devis," said Thromdurr, cuffing the thief on the back. "How did you know they would turn on each other?"

Devis shrugged. "Up escalator, down escalator; I figured there had to be a little tension there."

Vela hooked her grappling hook onto the railing above, and the party used a nearby sunglasses kiosk to climb up to the second floor. The five adventurers strode with purpose now. Somehow they knew where they were going.

"There, up ahead," said Sorrowshade.

Standing before the fountain near the Cheesecakery, they saw a figure clad in dark robes. Myron Flanagan turned to face them. He looked ghoulish now; his flesh was taut and sallow, with dark circles around glowing green eyes.

"Welcome, adventurers, to the Hibbettsfield Galleria," said Zazirak, who chewed as he talked. "You really *must* try the soft pretzel. It almost makes me regret that this world will be destroyed." He took another bite of pretzel.

"Destroyed?" said Albiorix. "What are you talking about, Zazirak?"

At this Zazirak merely cackled again.

"Next question," said Sorrowshade. "What are you wearing?"

Zazirak stopped laughing and looked at himself. "What?"

"Is that . . . a bathrobe?" said Sorrowshade.

"It is!" said Devis. "Oh, man. Look, it's still got the Maximo's tags on it."

Sorrowshade snickered.

"Do NOT mock my unholy vestments!" cried Zazirak. With a flash of light, a blast of sickly green energy leaped from the warlock's fingertips toward the gloom elf, who dove behind a bench. The spell left a smoking notch in the wood.

"Enough!" said Vela. "We have defeated your mannequins. We have beaten your escalators. Surrender now, warlock."

"Okay?" said Zazirak. "And then what?"

"Return to the underworld as a restless spirit," said Vela. "Leave this realm in peace."

"Or," said Thromdurr, "and honestly this would be my preference: I could pound you into the linoleum with this croquet mallet first. The choice is yours, ghost man."

"Hmm," said Zazirak, taking another bite of his soft pretzel and thoughtfully chewing. "No, I think I shall take the third option. I will slay you all and then watch this realm—"

"Burn?" said Sorrowshade as she darted out from behind a palm-tree planter. The gloom elf lunged at Zazirak with a lit citronella torch.

But the warlock whirled and raised a small fire extinguisher from beneath his bathrobe. With a chemical whoosh, Sorrowshade's flame was instantly snuffed.

"Ha! I remembered that little maneuver from last time and planned accordingly: Top Alert kitchen fire extinguisher, only $31.99 at Maximo's," said Zazirak. "And I wasn't going to say 'burn,' I was going to say—"

A mighty blow from Boneshatter II cut Zazirak off and sent him flying.

"I SUPPOSE WE SHALL NEVER KNOW!" roared Thromdurr.

Zazirak's limp body tumbled to a stop ten feet away. After a long moment, the warlock slowly sat up.

"Owee," said Zazirak, massaging his jaw. "This has been delightful, but . . . that *really* hurt. Prepare to face my dark magicks, mortals."

"Yeah, that's going to be tough without your spellbook, Zazzmatazz," said Devis. The thief held up the Malonomicon and flashed a grin.

"Good point. I need it back." The warlock yanked a shiny chain that originated from his pocket, and the book jumped from Devis's grasp.

"Men's chrome steel wallet chain with trigger snap hook, only $7.99 at Maximo's," said the warlock as he caught the Malonomicon. "Not just for wallets, though. Works for tomes of ancient evil too! And now to end this pathetic fight."

"Stop him!" cried Vela. The paladin charged forward.

Zazirak opened the spellbook and began to wave his hand as he incanted. *"Ars raz ilai si'arras nau. Giurr zi'as? Yai'su zi'asi'asilus!"*

A nova of mystical power exploded from the warlock. Vela fell first. Then Devis. They were followed by Sorrowshade and Thromdurr. Albiorix felt himself go limp and slump to the floor. His arms didn't work. Neither did his legs. He couldn't move at all. The only part of his body that would obey him were his eyes. He fixed them on Zazirak.

The warlock cackled wildly as he balled up his soft pretzel wrapper and tossed it into a nearby trash can.

"For those who don't speak fluent Shadownese," said Zazirak, with a wink at Albiorix, "that spell was a little ditty I like to call 'mass paralysis.'"

He strolled past each of the helpless adventurers, chuckling and occasionally prodding one or the other of them with his toe. None of them moved. Albiorix tried to reassert control of his body: his arm, his hand, even his finger. He strained with all his might. Nothing. He was frozen.

So this was how it would end. Not with a failing grade or a disciplinary expulsion from JADMS, but killed by an evil undead mage. So normal. So predictable. He never should have tried to be an adventurer in the first place.

"And now," said Zazirak, "you all get to watch as I perform the ritual to summon Azathor the Devourer, the demon who will feast upon this world!"

Suddenly there came a crackle of energy, and a blue light shone somewhere to Albiorix's left. Zazirak's eyes grew wide. Albiorix couldn't turn to see what the warlock was staring at.

"No! NO!" cried Zazirak, raising his hand to cast another spell. "Begone, you—

A familiar voice spoke a word of arcane power. A radiant blue bolt blasted Zazirak off his feet and sent him flying. Then came another incantation. Albiorix watched as, one by one, his limp companions begin to levitate, slowly rising off the floor. Last of all, Albiorix floated up off the ground himself. As he spun in the air, he saw that he was drifting toward a glowing dimensional portal. Beyond it, there was another world, a world he knew well.

"Albiorix," said the Archmage Velaxis, who stood beside the portal in all her terrible magnificence, "I've been looking everywhere for you!"

Chapter

25

Table 419d: School Punishments

Whenever player characters run afoul of a teacher or an administrator, roll one to five times on the following table, depending on the severity of the infraction.

1 to 4: Stern talking-to

5 to 6: Pointless, unpleasant homework assignment

7: Visit to the vice principal's office

8 to 10: Formal letter of apology

11 to 14: After-school detention for 1 to 4 weeks

15 to 16: Saturday detention for 1 to 4 weeks

17: Visit to the principal's office . . .

—*Excerpt from* The Hall Master's Guide

$\sim$

ALBIORIX STOOD IN THE Archmage's study on the top floor of her floating tower in Bríandalör. He stared at the carpet—an ornate design comprised of interlocking phoenixes, all the way from Far Draïz. His companions, now free of Zazirak's mass paralysis spell, stood behind him rubbing their limbs and stretching their necks. All were quiet as the Archmage addressed them.

"I have scoured the myriad planes of the multiverse looking for any sign of you, Albiorix," said Velaxis. "My time is precious, and this was a needless waste of it."

"Sorry, ma'am," said Albiorix.

"You're lucky I am a skilled enough sorceress to traverse countless worlds, and compassionate enough to save the life of a mere *apprentice*," said Velaxis. "I've had dozens of apprentices, you know. And believe me, you are *hardly* the most remarkable. Except in the amount of vexation you seem to cause."

"I understand, ma'am," said Albiorix. "Thank you, ma'am."

"You do realize you nearly died in that place, which, as far as I can tell, was some sort of mystical manifestation of the ridiculous game you play with your friends."

"Archmage," said Albiorix, "I think it might actually be real. Another world we discov—"

"Silence!" boomed the Archmage. "I have told you over and over again that you spend far too much time playing that foolish game!"

"Yes, ma'am," said Albiorix, staring at the floor again. "You have said that."

"It is useless frippery that constantly distracts you—not only from your magical studies, but from exploring the ancient dungeons of this land to uncover forgotten lore, as is a wizard's duty."

"It can be a time-consuming hobby," said Albiorix.

"Well, no longer," said Velaxis. "You are hereby forbidden to ever play Homerooms & Hall Passes again."

Albiorix blinked.

"If you disobey me in this, you may consider your apprenticeship with me over," said Velaxis. "Oh, and if you ever get yourself into another situation like that again, *I will not be there to save you*. Are we clear?"

"Yes, ma'am," said Albiorix.

"Now begone," said the Archmage. "I expect you here bright and early tomorrow to work on minor charms. We will be hypnotizing tadpoles."

Albiorix nodded and turned to go.

"Archmage," said Vela. "If I may, on behalf of all of us, I would just like to—"

"Begone!" thundered Velaxis.

The adventurers made a quiet procession down the spiral staircase toward the "ground" floor of the tower (which was actually still twenty feet in the air). Along the way, Albiorix stopped to grab his own spellbook. When they reached the bottom, the party secured a rope and climbed down.

At long last, their feet again stood on Bríandalörian soil. The world spread out around them, vibrant and green. The hills were dotted with mysterious ruins, every one of them promising adventure. In the far distance, a range of impossibly tall mountains climbed toward the heavens. Devis let out a hoot.

"We made it back!" cried Devis. "We're home!"

Sorrowshade looked around and shuddered. "Worse than I remember."

"C'mon," said Devis. "We beat the curse. We didn't die. We even had a few laughs along the way. Things are looking pretty— Aw, man!"

Devis had reflexively checked his phone and realized he wasn't getting any service.

"Devis is right," said Vela, gazing toward the horizon. "We can once more resume our adventuring career. Fighting evil!"

"Finding treasure," said Devis.

"Feasting upon blackened meats," said Thromdurr.

"And getting revenge on those stupid minotaurs," said Sorrowshade.

The party turned to Albiorix, perhaps hoping he would add something. He didn't.

"Though I will concede it is a shame we did not get to defeat Zazirak," said Thromdurr. "I sense the empty feeling coming on. . . ."

"Then let us find a new quest to test our mettle," said Vela. "To the Wyvern's Wrist! Plenty of quests there!"

It wasn't until the first gnome they passed along the road burst out laughing that the heroes remembered they were still wearing the strange garb of Suburbia. As soon as they reached the hamlet of Pighaven, the group made for the town tailor, then the blacksmith. Soon they had ditched their hoodies and sneakers and attired themselves in the clothing and equipment of Bríandalör, including proper weapons.

"Well, well, well, I ain't seen you young folks in here for a spell," said the owner of the Wyvern's Wrist as they entered.

"We were magically trapped inside a game," said Vela.

"The one you play on Thursdays? With them wee little figurines?" said the innkeeper as she polished her flagons. "That's too bad, innit?"

"What can you do?" said Vela with a shrug. "Anyway, might I have a simple plate of bread and cheese?"

"Certainly," said the innkeeper. "And for the rest of you?"

"Sheep," said Thromdurr. "Well done."

"The whole sheep?" said the innkeeper.

"Not the hooves," said Thromdurr.

The innkeeper nodded and turned to Devis. Devis studied the menu.

"What is your soup of the day?" said Devis.

"Turnip," said the innkeeper. "Also the soup of tomorrow. And the soup every day thereafter till the end of the Age of Man."

"Hmm. Is there any chance you could do something with egg and cheese, like a nice stracciatella?" said Devis.

The innkeeper stared at him.

"Okay. No problem. How about a white borscht?"

The innkeeper stared at him.

"Fine," said Devis. "Turnip soup it is."

"And for you, O wondrous child of the forest?" said the innkeeper to Sorrowshade.

"Doesn't matter. Human food is gross," said Sorrowshade. "Surprise me."

"Two orders of turnip soup, then." The innkeeper turned to Albiorix.

The wizard shook his head. The innkeeper rolled her eyes. The party sat down at a corner table, and a few seconds later, a mysterious man with an eye patch approached.

"Hail, travelers," said the man, with a courtly bow, "I could not help but notice you have the dangerous and worldly look of adventu—"

"So nobody took you up on the map yet, huh?" said Sorrowshade.

"Er, no," said the man. "Which is really too bad. The Caves of Thunderbeard are filled with riches untold, and it—"

A woman in an elaborate headdress elbowed her way past the man with the eye patch. "I offer a handsome reward to any who can rid the Manglewood of giant spiders!"

"Hey, back off, lady," said the eye patch man.

"What?" said the headdress woman with a shrug. "Free kingdom."

"Yeah, sorry," said Devis. "I think we might already be doing Caves of Thunderbeard."

"You are!" said the man with the eye patch, clapping his hands together.

"We are?" said Sorrowshade.

"Hmm," said Vela. "Might we have a moment to confer among ourselves?"

"Certainly," said the man. "If you need me, I shall be by the fire. Brooding." And with a ruffle of his dark cloak, he withdrew.

"Maybe you could do the giant spider thing on the way

back from that other dungeon?" said the headdress woman. "Just a thought." She also turned to go.

"So . . . Caves of Thunderbeard?" said Vela. "Yea or nay?"

"Untold riches sounds pretty good," said Devis. "As of now, I'm a soft yes."

"I am in as well," said Thromdurr. "No use tarrying. 'Tis better to delve into some horrible dungeon than sit around with our thoughts as company."

"Yeah, why not?" said Sorrowshade. "Though eye patch over there is *definitely* going to betray us."

The rest of the party nodded in assent, and they began to discuss their strategy for the inevitable double cross.

"I don't know, guys," said Albiorix, breaking in. "What's the point?"

The group fell silent. Vela cleared her throat.

"Well, this is an adventure," said the paladin. "We *are* adventurers."

"Was it all just some make-believe fantasy?" said Albiorix. "Mr. Gulazarian and morning announcements and Nicole Davenport and . . . and June?"

"'Twas an ancient curse, friend," said Thromdurr. "Nothing more."

"The food was pretty good, though," said Devis.

"No, it wasn't," said Sorrowshade. "You complained about soup nonstop!"

"What? I never! How dare you?" said Devis. "I would *kill* for a piping-hot mug of Dad Stinky's Cullen skink right now!"

"I don't think I can do this adventure with you," said Albiorix. "I'm . . . I'm sorry."

And without another word, the wizard stood and walked out the door of the Wyvern's Wrist.

And so Albiorix the wizard left the hamlet of Pighaven and struck out into the wilderness alone. He faced many perils along the way, and by cunning and bravery and, yes, sorcery, he survived them all. And at last he found himself standing before a lonely cliffside and a weathered portico that resembled the jaws of a great beast.

With a simple incantation, he lit the way forward and descended into the depths of the Temple of Azathor. And down in the darkness he fought his way past a tribe of reluctant and traumatized goblins (who were only just starting to rebuild after their last tragic encounter with adventurers). And he blithely passed a disarmed poison dart trap without even noticing it and walked right though an open magical door, though he would have easily guessed the answer to its riddle was "Love." And at last he came to a grand hall of fallen columns and piled bones. He saw a doorway with an inscription in Old Dragonian. The wizard stopped.

"Well, I'm here," said Albiorix to himself. "Now what?"

But there was no one around to answer. He peeked inside the vault. It was empty now. Someone had thoroughly looted it in the interim. They'd even taken the throne. Albiorix sat down on a toppled statue to think. And soon sleep overtook him.

Chapter 26

Table 224h: Random Hallway Encounters

Whenever characters travel between school locations, roll three times on the following table to determine who/what they encounter along the way.

1 to 3: Two bullies, spoiling for a fight

4 to 5: One to six students loudly rehearsing lines for the school play

6 to 9: A discarded note (roll once on Table 601d: Passed Notes to determine its contents)

10 to 13: One to four popular kids, gossiping about one of the characters

14 to 15: The custodian, mopping up a particularly disgusting spill (roll once on Table 336v: Disgusting Spills to determine what it is)

16: The district superintendent making a surprise school visit . . .

—*Excerpt from* The Hall Master's Guide

THE WIZARD AWOKE TO a sound coming from the tunnels behind him. He scrambled behind a pile of rubble. Soon faint torchlight flickered on the stonework, and he saw four figures enter the chamber.

"Albiorix?" called Vela.

"You here, Magic Man?" said Devis.

"Curses!" said Thromdurr. "We are too late!"

"No," said Sorrowshade. "He's over there. I can hear him breathing."

Albiorix stood up. "Don't try to stop me. I know Homerooms & Hall Passes is just a game, but Zazirak is still in there. I cannot allow him to just destroy Suburbia. I'm not going to let that happen to June, even if she is a nonplayer character. I'm going back!"

"We are not here to stop you, sorcerous friend," said Thromdurr.

"What?" said Albiorix.

"We want to come with you," said Vela.

"I can't ask you to do that," said Albiorix.

"You do not have to ask," said Vela. "I stand against evil. The innocents of Suburbia must be saved."

The paladin stepped forward.

"It will be my pleasure to smash the warlock yet again," said Thromdurr, brandishing his newly forged war hammer. "'Tis a rare joy to kill a foe twice."

The barbarian stepped forward.

"And if we go back, I can finally charge my phone again," said Devis. "I'm at like eight percent."

The thief stepped forward.

"But you all heard the Archmage Velaxis," said Albiorix. "If we return, we're on our own."

"Story of my life," said Sorrowshade. "So let's be on our own *together*."

The assassin stepped forward.

"All right," said Albiorix. "So . . . how do we do this?"

"Well, perhaps our best hope is to re-create the series of events that brought the curse upon us in the first place," said Vela. "First, Devis stole something from that hidden chamber."

"Too bad it's empty," said Albiorix.

"Not quite," said Devis, who was already inside the room and using his dagger to pry something from between the floor stones. "Whoever cleaned out this place was a complete amateur." He held up a single tarnished copper piece that had somehow been left behind.

"You know we split that five ways," said Sorrowshade.

"Split what?" said Devis, who showed the gloom elf both sides of his now-empty hands. He'd already pocketed the coin.

"That's step one," said Sorrowshade. "Then we played Homerooms & Hall Passes."

"Right! Our 'respite,'" said Albiorix. "But we've got to do this quick!"

The wizard blew a thick layer of dust off a nearby sarcophagus and dumped out all his gaming gear—maps, miniatures, dice, and books. The other adventurers gathered around.

"Okay, you're all at school. It's"—Albiorix rolled a handful of dice and consulted *The Hall Master's Guide*—"seven twenty-seven Wednesday morning, at J. A. Dewar Middle School. You have three minutes to first bell. What do you do?"

"Valerie the Overacheiver steels her spirit for a final clash against evil," said Vela. "She turns to the others and says, 'Time to overachieve our destiny.'"

"Great," said Albiorix.

"Douglas the Nerd calls upon his nerdly ancestors to bring him strength," said Thromdurr.

"You feel the Schillers of old watching over you," said Albiorix.

"Melissa the Loner pulls up her hood," said Sorrowshade.

"Her eyes are inky pools of blackness now, filled with other-worldly purpose. She is ready."

"Ooh," said Albiorix. "Evocative."

"And Stinky the Class Clown will use his phone to find a hedgehog meme that is perfect for this occasion," said Devis.

"Ah," said Albiorix. "Roll your Computer skill."

Devis scooped up the dice and rolled them. "That's a 22!"

"Success," said Albiorix. "After careful searching, you find a picture of a tough-looking hedgehog in a little cowboy hat. It says, 'MESS WITH THE HOG YOU GET THE PRICKLES.'"

"Nice!" said Devis. "So do you guys think that's enough H&H-ing?"

"Let us hope so," said Vela. "The final step was when Albiorix proclaimed the curse aloud."

The wizard nodded and took a deep breath. Then he gazed up at the inscription chiseled into the stone.

"Woe to thee who loots this room. . . . Let thy respite be thy doom."

His words echoed through the empty chambers and mazy tunnels of the underground temple. The adventurers stared at each other. And then they were gone.

The five Bríandalörians suddenly found themselves standing in the crowded hallway of J. A. Dewar Middle School.

The cacophony of kid noises was a jarring contrast with the eerie silence of the Temple of Azathor.

"Ha! Here we go with the costumes again," said Evan Cunningham. "Spirit Week is over, losers. Go back to Ye Olde Renaissance Faire!"

"So great to be back," said Devis. "Should we save the world now?"

The party walked down the hall. Up ahead, Nicole Davenport, Madison Gray, and Sophie Sorrentino stood in a tight cluster by the water fountain. They whispered and giggled, then went conspicuously silent as the party passed.

"Melissa, hiiiii-eee," said Nicole with a smirk. "I was just telling Sophie and Madison what *you* did at Fall Festival last year. I don't care if you thought it was a candy bar, that was dis-*gust*-ing."

Sorrowshade smiled and put her hand on Nicole's shoulder. "Pity is not an emotion an assassin often feels, but . . . I do pity you."

Nicole's smile faltered. "What? You don't pity me! I'm amazing! My life is amazing! Just look online! You're the weirdo with the freaky ears!"

"Exactly," said Sorrowshade. "And one day I hope you have some real friends. Like I do." She waved to Albiorix, Devis, Vela, and Thromdurr.

"Um, excuse me?" said Sophie. "She has real friends. We're her besties!"

"Yeah, we're her besties!" said Madison.

"Oh, shut *up*, Madison," said Nicole. "All you ever do is repeat what other people say! It's incredibly annoy—"

"Don't tell her to shut up," said Sophie, furrowing her brow.

Nicole blinked, apparently speechless. "But I alw—"

"Yeah, Nicole," said Madison. "You're not our, like, boss or whatever."

Before Nicole could respond, the first bell rang. The party left the popular girls behind and approached a cluster of students staring out the windows to the parking lot.

"Dude, that is not normal," said Dave Pittman.

Outside, it was immediately clear that something about the weather was . . . *off*. Strange winds blew through the empty streets of Hibbettsfield, whipping the trees and kicking up little whirlwinds of trash. The sky was all thunderheads that seemed to converge in a swirling vortex in the distance. Green lightning flashed.

"Not good," said Albiorix. "I'm ninety-nine percent sure that storm is Zazirak related. From what I remember of the Malonomicon, the ritual to conjure forth a greater demon is long and complicated, but we may not have much time left."

"Guys!"

The heroes turned to see June, who looked terrified. "I've been looking everywhere for you! What is even happening out there?"

"The warlock Zazirak is summoning a demon to end the world," said Sorrowshade. "Cool jacket."

"Thanks," said June. "So I take it you *didn't* beat him?"

"Quite the opposite," said Devis.

"We are lucky to be alive," said Vela. "Praise the Powers of Light."

"Bah!" said Thromdurr. "The battle was cut short before we could claim victory!"

"We were all magically paralyzed," said Albiorix.

"Indeed," said Thromdurr, "the perfect way to lure our enemy into a false sense of security!"

"So is there any way to stop him?" said June. "Or should I go home and say goodbye to my cat?"

"Honestly, I don't know," said Albiorix. "But we're going to try. And we need you to come with us."

"I thought it was too dangerous," said June.

"Oh, it most certainly is," said Albiorix. "But Zazirak beat us last time. It's clear we could use every bit of help we can get."

"Really?" said June.

Vela put a hand on June's arm. "Congratulations, June

Westray. You are an adventurer now."

"All right!" said June, pumping her fist.

"So," said Sorrowshade, throwing her hood up, "are you ready to march into the gaping jaws of certain doom?"

"Sure, yeah," said June. "Let me just grab my phone."

June jogged off toward her locker. Despite the clearly supernatural weather, the other JADMS students had begun to pull themselves away from the window and head to their homerooms to avoid being marked tardy.

"We should go," said Albiorix.

"Yes," said Vela. "But there is one thing I must do first."

The paladin strode off in the direction of room 311. The tardy bell rang. Devis plugged his phone into a nearby outlet, and on the wall-mounted TV nearby, the title sequence of morning announcements began to play.

"Gooooood morning, Titans. I'm Olivia Gorman, and this is the J. A. Dewar morning bulletin," said Olivia. "Today is Wednesday, October fourteenth. For lunch we will have chicken sandwich or hot dog. Don't forget: Today is the last day to sign up for auditions for the school play. Please use the clipboard outside room 206. And now Valerie Stumpf-Turner will lead us in the Pledge of Allegiance even though she's an election thief."

Olivia crossed her arms. The Bríandalörians braced themselves.

"Oh, no," said June, who had returned from her locker. "Her one thing was doing the school announcements?"

"I guess?" said Albiorix, who almost couldn't bear to watch.

Devis clucked his tongue. "And you thought the end of the world was going to be painful."

Yet Vela spoke confidently in a clear and commanding voice: "Thank you, Olivia. Regretfully, I must skip the Pledge of Allegiance today, for my time is short. At this moment, your school, your town, your very world faces grave peril—an ancient evil beyond all comprehension. I warn you, do not venture outside, do not unlock your doors, and if you see anything unusual, do not engage. Instead, flee as fast as you can. The last thing you must not do is despair. For I, and my brave companions, are on our way to confront this evil right now. Though this is not our world, we have come to love it as our own, and we will fight to the last breath to protect it. I have no doubt that light will triumph over darkness. Thank you, and be safe. Farewell."

And with that, Vela the Valiant stood and left the video lab.

"So . . . I guess I'll do the Pledge of Allegiance, then?" said Olivia.

A few moments later, Vela rejoined the party in the hallway.

"Vela, you did not freeze!" said Thromdurr, cuffing her on the back.

"No time for that," said Vela. "To the Old Mall."

The party strode out the double doors of J. A. Dewar Middle School. As they crossed the school parking lot, there came a clattering sound from the bushes.

"Guys," said June, "what is that?"

A skeleton, clad in tattered rags, barreled out of the underbrush toward the group. June shrieked. Thromdurr swung his new war hammer and missed. The other Bríandalörians paused for a moment, confused. They weren't used to seeing the mighty berserker whiff.

"Bah! The weight feels all wrong," cried the barbarian. "The haft length is off!" He fumbled in his belt and produced the wooden head of Boneshatter II, which he started to screw into the croquet mallet's shaft. Yet before he could finish, the skeleton tackled him to the ground. With a hiss, it opened its bony jaws wide to take a bite out of Thromdurr's neck.

"Na lya'a'n ha'oi zaeny e phaesima'rn koih!" read Albiorix from his spellbook, while he focused his will and traced the secret sigil for flame with his right hand. A ball of fire erupted from his fingertips and hit the skeleton, exploding it in a hail of charred bones.

"Whoa!" said June. "Albiorix, that was awesome! And terrifying! And awesome!"

"Thanks," said Albiorix, waving the smoke off his hand. "No time to celebrate. Look!"

Five more skeletons shambled down the sidewalk toward them.

"The whole town is crawling with Zazirak's vile minions," said Vela, drawing her sword.

Sorrowshade nocked two arrows at once, and let fly— the lead pair of skeletons fell before they reached the heroes. Vela blocked a bony swipe with her shield and replied by chopping off a skeletal arm. Albiorix froze a fourth with an ice spell, giving Devis an opening to dart in and shatter it with his dagger. As the one-armed skeleton swung at Vela with its other fist, a blow from Boneshatter II sent its head clattering down the street like the world's most macabre croquet ball.

"You guys don't mess around," said June.

Yet no sooner had they finished off the last of the undead band, than they realized that a dozen more were converging on them from every direction.

Sorrowshade sighted one and felled it at a hundred yards with a well-placed arrow to the eye socket.

"They just keep coming," said the gloom elf, drawing another arrow from her quiver.

"THEN BY THE GREAT SKY BEAR, I WILL

SMASH THEM ALL!" roared Thromdurr, holding Bone-shatter II aloft.

"No!" cried Albiorix. "This is just a distraction to slow us down so Zazirak can finish the summoning ritual."

"We must stop him!" cried Vela. "Onward, friends!"

And the heroes started to run toward the Hibbettsfield Galleria.

Chapter 27

As Hall Master, it is your duty to present fresh challenges to your players! Pop quizzes, lazy lab partners, and malicious gossip all represent unexpected difficulties in the lives of middle schoolers. No need to go easy on your group. The threat of losing a beloved character is actually what keeps the game interesting. . . .

—*Excerpt from* The Hall Master's Guide

ARK CLOUDS SPUN IN a churning cyclone over the Old Mall. Green lightning crackled in the sky, and the six heroes slipped inside. As they made their way toward the second-floor fountain (near the Cheesecakery), the air grew thick and sulfurous, and soon it was impossible to see more than a few paces ahead. Through the greenish haze, it was June who somehow spotted him first.

"Look, it's Vice Principal Flanagan!" she whispered.

The warlock Zazirak hunched over a glowing sigil inscribed on the floor of the mall with the Malonomicon spread open before him. He read a continuous stream of sorcery in Fiendish, the unholy language of demons: *"Orek Crovsar ek umrae kur Eqer, kur vesr sra Saekburk raraem va com coks Svarrk, omd vurd aqarae demd uk Eqer—"*

"Zazirak!" cried Vela. "Cease this madness at once!"

"Huh?" cried Zazirak, apparently startled. "You lot again? But I thought you all left!"

"We just couldn't stay away," said Devis. "We had to come back and try that soft pretzel."

"And pummel you to within an inch of your life, you naughty necromancer!" said Thromdurr.

"Ah, well. I guess you got me," said Zazirak with a shrug. "I know when I'm beaten. Okay, I surr— *Ars raz ilai si'arras nau. Giurr zi'as? Yai'su zi'asi'asilus!*"

"Tsag'h mog toimt go dop!" cried Albiorix, instantly countering the mass paralysis hex with a ward of protection from his own spellbook.

Zazirak's curse fizzled out.

"Huh," said Zazirak. "Not quite as weak as I thought. Well, it's a good thing I don't need spells. When Azathor the Devourer arrives, you will be consumed like everything else."

"But why?" said Albiorix.

"Why?" said Zazirak, now utterly confused.

"Why are you doing this?" said Albiorix. "Why are you summoning a demon lord to destroy this world? Why?"

Zazirak paused, then frowned. He started to say something, but instead chewed his lip for a while. He chuckled. "You know, to be honest, I've never really thought much about *why*. I mean, I *am* an evil warlock, right? So it makes sense that I *would* want to do something like this. But that's sort of a chicken-egg thing, isn't it? Truly, I don't know. But I'm pretty sure it's too late to get introspective about it now. Instead I think I'll finish this dark ritual while you battle my skeletal hordes."

"Skeletal hordes?" said Vela.

And from out of the greenish haze, the party was set upon by a legion of undead warriors. The arrows of Sorrowshade the gloom elf flew fast, and every one of them found its mark. Vela the Valiant, Knight of the Golden Sun, struck down many with her sword while fending off others with her shield. Heedless of danger, Thromdurr, son of Heimdurr, berserker of the Sky Bear clan, waded into the thick of the battle, wielding Boneshatter II like a force of nature; while Devis, the wily thief, fought with trickery and cunning to dispatch his enemies. And Albiorix the wizard hurled fireballs and lightning bolts across the field of battle at his foes. Even June Westray, untrained in combat, managed to choose a lucky moment to shove a distracted skeleton, so that its head got stuck in the balcony railing and it was effectively taken out of the fight.

Yet all the while Zazirak incanted double time, hoping to finish the infernal ritual to summon Azathor the Devourer before the last of his minions fell. At last, roaring as he shrugged off four skeletal foes, Thromdurr charged the warlock and delivered a crushing downward swing of his mallet to the top of Zazirak's skull. The hammer blow was so powerful that it instantly knocked Myron Flanagan's body unconscious. And Zazirak's glowing eyes dimmed as he slumped to the ground. But the coup de grâce had come a moment too late. For the final words of the spell had been spoken.

There was a boom like a thunderclap, so loud it seemed the whole world had torn itself asunder. Then the arcane sigil started to open.

"What's happening?" cried June.

"Get back!" cried Vela.

The fissure in the floor widened, and a plume of black smoke issued forth. And then a clawed hand the size of a couch gripped the edge. A colossal creature began to pull itself out of the hole.

"Azathor the Devourer," whispered Albiorix.

It was a horrid, vaguely human-shaped *thing* with great

black wings, hairy hoofed feet, a long spiked tail, and burning red eyes set in the head of a gigantic rodent. And as the heroes backed away, they had to admit that Zazirak had been right right: a mole-headed demon was scary. Terrifying, in fact.

Azathor pulled himself out of the smoldering crack and stood to full height. The huge mole head nearly touched the mall ceiling twenty feet above them. The demon stretched its leathery wings and let out an unearthly bellow.

"BACK TO THE THIRTEEN HELLS WITH YOU, MOLE DEVIL!" cried Thromdurr, who flew at the fiend, swinging Boneshatter II.

Yet with a flick of his great clawed hand, Azathor—almost lazily—swatted the barbarian aside like an inconvenient insect.

"May the Powers of Light guide my hand!" cried Vela as she charged.

Azathor whirled and exhaled a blast of searing flame, stopping the paladin short. Vela was forced to dive behind her shield or be incinerated.

There came the quiet twangs of Sorrowshade's bowstring—*thwip, thwip, thwip*—yet lightning-quick Azathor somehow caught the three arrows in his fingertips. With a horrid smile, he snapped them like twigs.

"Tyael ael e raekyntaetk ma'rn na' phsh ha'oi!" incanted

Albiorix from his spellbook, and a bolt of lightning leaped from his hand.

But the demon lord raised his palm, and the wizard's spell dissipated on contact with his flesh. An instant later, the same lighting bolt jumped back from Azathor's hand at Albiorix. The wizard felt every muscle in his body seize an instant before he was racked with agonizing pain as the electricity coursed through him. His body jerked uselessly, and he could smell his own hair burning. At last Azathor dropped the spell, and Albiorix crumpled to the ground.

"ANYONE ELSE?" said Azathor in a voice that sounded like ten thousand bones being snapped at once. The demon fixed his horrible gaze upon Devis, who crouched behind an information kiosk, dagger in hand.

"HOW ABOUT THEE?"

"Nah, I'm . . . I'm good," sputtered the thief, lowering his blade.

"THEN YOUR PATHETIC RESISTANCE HAS FAILED!" bellowed Azathor. "AND I SHALL SAVOR YOUR TERROR AS YE WITNESS ME DEVOUR THIS WORLD!"

With his massive hand, Azathor ripped up a nearby coin-operated massage chair and shoved it into his mouth, whole. And as he chewed and swallowed, the demon's great bulk swelled, and his head now touched the ceiling. He turned and and picked up a decorative palm tree—planter and all—and stuck it into his maw. Again, he ate it and grew larger.

As Albiorix watched from the ground, his ears still ringing from the lightning bolt, he had a terrible vision: Azathor the Devourer, a demon the size of a mountain, impervious to any attack, striding across the landscape and consuming *everything* in his path—cars, trees, houses, people—and growing larger still. . . .

Suddenly the wizard remembered something he'd read in the Malonomicon.

"Wait!" cried Albiorix.

Azathor paused. He dangled Myron Flanagan's limp body like an hors d'oeuvre over his open mouth.

"Great Azathor the Devourer, Lord of Hunger, Jaws of Destruction, we invoke the ancient custom of the infernal bargain," said Albiorix, pulling himself to his feet. "We ask a boon of thee."

"A BOON?" Azathor dropped Flanagan and laughed, an awful rumbling sound. "FOR A BOON YE MUST BEST ME IN A CONTEST. AND IF YE LOSE, YOUR SOULS ARE MINE."

"We accept the terms, O evil one," said Albiorix with a bow.

"THEN WHAT SHALL BE THE NAME OF THE

CONTEST?" said Azathor. "AND WHO SHALL BE YOUR CHAMPION?"

"Uh," said Albiorix. He hadn't thought that far ahead. "Hmm. Yep. Okay. I'm going to have to get back to you on that one. Just give me a moment to confer with my companions—"

"TRY NOT MY PATIENCE, MORTAL!" roared Azathor.

"Two minutes," said Albiorix.

Azathor crossed his arms. That party regrouped and spoke in hushed voices. June had been stunned speechless. Perhaps this was not how she had imagined her first adventure?

"Albiorix," said Vela, "you've offered up our souls to a demon, a fate worse than death. I hope you know what you're doing."

"I have a plan," said Albiorix, "I mean, sort of. I have twenty percent of a plan. Let's say fifteen percent. Look, one of us just has to, uh, beat him at something. That's all."

His companions stared at him, wide-eyed.

"Beat him?" said Devis. "He's twenty-five feet tall. He's invulnerable. *He can literally catch lightning bolts!*"

"I know, but it's our only shot," said Albiorix. "So, who wants to, uh, be the champion?"

Thromdurr shook his head. "Though I am perhaps the

obvious choice, I cannot hope to win a contest of might against that . . . *thing*."

"And if he can snatch my arrows right out of the air," said Sorrowshade, "his reflexes are superior to mine."

"Personally, I don't think there's any tricking him," said Devis. "Not confident he'd fall for the kobold in a knapsack."

"And in a battle of wills," said Vela, "I'm afraid mine would break first."

Albiorix nodded. "Indeed, it is also clear to me that in any sort of magical duel, I would be defeated."

"So it's hopeless, then?" said Sorrowshade. "Well, at least a lifetime of pessimism *finally* paid off."

"No," said Albiorix. "There's got to be something. Something that one of us is the best at. Something that—"

"YOUR TWO MINUTES ARE UP," said Azathor. "NAME YOUR CHAMPION!"

"Uh . . . ," said Albiorix.

This whole thing was his fault. He knew that, of course. He'd messed around with the Malonomicon and brought Zazirak back from the dead, and this was the final result: the end of all things. The wizard looked into the battle-stained faces of each of his companions: a barbarian, a thief, a paladin, an assassin, and a girl who had somehow decided he was worth helping, even though she didn't know him.

These were his best friends in the world, in *two* worlds, and he'd just wagered their souls. How could the party possibly hope to beat a demon lord from the pits of the abyss? Yet at that moment an idea came to him. And a smile spread across the wizard's face as he turned to address the demon.

"Our champion," said Albiorix, "shall be June Westray."

"It shall?" said June, suddenly jolted out of her stupor.

"It shall?" said Vela.

"It shall," said Albiorix.

"SO BE IT," said Azathor. "AND WHAT SHALL BE THE NAME OF THE CONTEST?"

"The name of the contest," said Albiorix, "shall be *Oink Pop*."

Chapter

28

Like any good heroic tapestry or bard's song, all Home-rooms & Hall Passes campaigns must eventually come to an end. But the good news is that the next non-adventure is only as far away as your imagination. If you're looking for more inspiration, check out the dozens of published scenarios—such as The Term of Tedium, The Field Trip of Disappointment, *and* The Sameness of Summer Vacation—*available from your friendly local book merchant.*

—*Excerpt from* The Hall Master's Guide

❧

"*OINK POP?*" SAID AZATHOR. "WHAT IS *OINK POP?*"

"It's just this game on my phone," said June in a barely audible voice.

"SO BE IT," said Azathor. "THE NAME OF THE

CONTEST SHALL BE *OINK POP*. NOW BRING ME A 'PHONE'!"

The heroes looked at each other. Devis crept forward and handed Azathor his smartphone.

"It's the icon that looks like a little pig," whispered Devis.

"The terms of the contest are this," said Albiorix. "Whoever holds the high score after one round shall be the victor. If it be Azathor the Devourer, then our souls are forfeit. But if it be June Westray, then our boon shall be granted. Do you accept the terms?"

"Um," said June. "Okay."

There came a horrible sound, low and rumbling. It was Azathor laughing. "AGREED!" said the mole-headed demon. "YET KNOW THIS: IN TEN THOUSAND YEARS, NONE HAVE EVER BESTED ME. I ATE THEIR VERY SOULS!"

The adventurers all looked at each other. June pulled out her phone and rolled her shoulders and stretched her fingertips.

"Competitors, are you ready?" said Albiorix.

"I AM READY!" said Azathor.

"Sure. I guess," said June.

"Then let the contest begin!"

The game's zany theme song started to play. June swallowed and selected "New Game" from the menu. The Bríandalörians crowded around their champion to watch her play.

A grid of multicolored, adorably round pigs bounced onto the screen and a sixty-second countdown timer appeared. And quicker than the eye could follow, June tickled three of the pigs in a row, causing them to laugh-burst away. The words "TRIPLE TICKLE!" ricocheted across the screen. And they had barely faded before she got a PORCINE POWER POPPER! bonus worth 9,000 points, quickly followed by a RIGHTEOUS RAINBOW! for an additional 6,000. June was in the zone now, popping virtual pigs with the ease of a master, sometimes using three or four fingers at once. Her score climbed ever higher. There were ten seconds left now, and she somehow cleared the entire board in a single tickling motion, earning a rare OINKOCALYPSE! for 80,000 points. Eight . . . seven . . . six . . .

"WAIT. HANG ON," said Azathor. "I'M SUPPOSED TO . . . TICKLE THEM?"

The timer buzzed. The round was up. Final score: June Westray, 480,925; Azathor the Devourer: 950.

The heroes burst out in a cheer. Albiorix clapped. Thromdurr cuffed June on the back. Devis turned a somersault. Vela did a little dance. Even Sorrowshade beamed.

"NOOOOO!" roared Azathor, punching his fist

through a nearby column. "YOU FAILED TO EXPLAIN THE RULES OF THIS STUPID GAME TO ME!"

"Um," said June. "You didn't ask?"

"SILENCE!" said Azathor. The demon turned and exhaled a jet of fire that completely destroyed the Cheese-cakery. "THAT WAS A PRACTICE ROUND."

"Hey, come on," said Albiorix. "You know that wasn't the de—

"PRACTICE ROOOOOOUND!"

"It's okay, Albiorix," said June. She turned to the demon. "Sure. That was a practice round."

"THEN LET THE REAL CONTEST BEGIN!" said Azathor.

A minute later, another round of *Oink Pop* had finished. Final score: June Westray, 521,300; Azathor the Devourer, 726.

"HOW DID I SOMEHOW DO *WORSE*?" said Azathor.

"You're overthinking it," said June.

"MY BIG CLAWS MAKE IT HARD FOR ME TO USE THE TOUCH SCREEN," said Azathor.

June shrugged. "Want to go one more time?"

"Hey, June, come on," said Albiorix, as the other heroes tried to wave her off.

June merely smiled and shrugged.

"YES, ONE MORE TIME!" said Azathor. "I WILL

DEFEAT YOU AND CLAIM YOUR SOULS!"

"Sure you will," said June.

A minute later, another round had finished. It was June Westray, 601,870 (a personal best); Azathor the Devourer, 3,072.

"WELL, AT LEAST I'M GETTING BETTER," said Azathor.

"Yeah, you landed a Triple Tickle," said June. "Not bad."

"SO YOU GET MORE POINTS FOR DOING THE DIFFERENT COLORS?" said Azathor.

"Yep," said June.

"GOOD TO KNOW," said Azathor.

"So we're done here, right?" said Albiorix.

"UGH. FINE," said Azathor, who had already started up another game. "THOUGH THE NEXT MORTAL TO CHALLENGE ME TO A GAME OF *OINK POP* WILL NOT BE SO LUCKY."

The party regrouped nearby. June grinned as she stuck her phone back in her pocket.

"Wow," said Devis.

"No big deal," said June.

"Your bravery and skill are unrivaled!" said Thromdurr.

"Thanks," said June.

"It wasn't hopeless," said Sorrowshade, blinking. "If I can't believe in hopelessness . . . then what hope is there?"

"That's a tough one to figure out," said June. "Not sure I have the answer there."

"I invoke the Powers of Light," said Vela, "and hereby dub you an honorary Knight of the Golden Sun!" She touched her sword to June's shoulders.

"Neat," said June. "My mom is always harping on me for more extracurriculars."

Albiorix smiled and shook June's hand. "I never had any doubt you could do it!"

"Yeah, you did," said June.

"Okay, but I was ninety percent sure," said Albiorix. "No . . . ninety-five percent."

"So what's our boon?" said June. "We tell ol' mole head over there to get his spiky tail back to the flaming pits and never come back?"

Azathor was too engrossed in his game of Oink Pop to notice the insult. Albiorix's smile turned bittersweet.

"Yes, Azathor must go," said Albiorix. "But . . . he's not the only one."

"What do you mean?" said June.

Albiorix looked around. "You know, I've been obsessed with Homerooms & Hall Passes for as long as I can remember. This game—this world—is awesome. In fact, sometimes I think I prefer it to my own, but that's just it . . . it isn't mine. It's not any of ours. Not really."

The other Bríandalörians nodded solemnly.

"Wait," said June. "Come on. You guys are just hitting your stride. You stopped stealing everything and you passed the algebra test and Vela got through the announcements without going into a coma—"

"I know," said Albiorix. "But as long as we're here, we put everyone at risk. Magic spells and walking skeletons? That's not what Homerooms & Hall Passes is about. We have to go too. It's the only way you'll be safe."

June started to say something, but then she stopped herself. She merely nodded.

"Azathor the Devourer," said Albiorix, with tears glinting in his eyes, "the boon we ask is this: all who are not of this place—be they demon, warlock, or adventurer—shall return from whence they came."

"SO BE IT," said Azathor.

"Hey, uh, can I also have my phone back?" said Devis.

"NO," said Azathor. "AND SO SHALL AZATHOR THE DEVOURER, LORD OF HUNGER, JAWS OF DESTRUCTION, GRANT YOUR BOON!" The demon began to incant a spell in Fiendish.

"Goodbye, June," said Albiorix. "I won't soon forget you."

"Goodbye," said June.

And in a puff of impressively colored magical smoke, the adventurers were gone.

Chapter 29

*Sure, you cut your teeth on Homerooms & Hall Passes,
but as a veteran Hall Master, you're ready for something
more: more class options, more complex social dynam-
ics, more high-stakes standardized testing. It's time to
take your players to the next level: high school! Next fall,
the greatest fantasy nonadventure role-playing game of
all time is about to advance with . . . Advanced Homerooms & Hall Passes!*

—Advertisement from the back of
The Hall Master's Guide

❧

"AND NOW I MUST bid you farewell, heroes!" cackled
the man with the eye patch, as he dropped the rusty
portcullis between himself and the party with a clang. "The
Jewel of Krenqôthoor will be my prize, and the Caves of
Thunderbeard will be your tomb!"

"Oh, you betrayed us," said Sorrowshade, rolling her eyes. "How unexpected."

Vela shook her head. "'Tis a shame. I really wanted to see the good in you . . . eye patch . . . man?"

His laughter stopped abruptly. "Eye patch man? *Eye patch man!* You know I have a name, right?"

The party was silent.

"We've traveled together for days! You must have heard it a hundred times!" said the man. "Are you all so self-absorbed that you can't even remember my name?"

"Hey! Easy on the guilt trips, buddy," said Sorrowshade. "You're right in the middle of stabbing us in the back."

"Wait!" said Thromdurr, slapping his forehead. "Of course! I *do* remember your name! It is . . . Thunderbeard!"

"What? Seriously?" said the man. "The Caves of *Thunderbeard* is the name of the dungeon!"

"Hmm," said Thromdurr. "Perhaps your name is Krenqôthoor?"

"No, you oaf! It's the Jewel of—" Suddenly the man froze and began to frantically pat his pockets and pouches as a look of horror spread across his face.

"Oh, hey," said Devis. "Looking for this?" The thief held up a yellow sapphire that glimmered in the torchlight.

"That's right," said Sorrowshade, "preemptive reverse betrayal. Life's tough, huh? I think so, anyway."

Instantly the man's frown turned into a wheedling smile. "Ha ha ha. Well, I hope you enjoyed this joke, friends, because that's what it was: a hilarious joke. A bit of dungeon humor to lighten the mood after that harrowing troll fight! You must know by now that your old friend Mirt would never turn on you!"

"Who's Mirt?" said Devis.

"Farewell, traitor," said Vela. "Perhaps being abandoned in these nightmarish caves will lead to some necessary personal growth." The paladin unrolled a parchment map and studied it for a moment. "This way, comrades."

One by one, the party members disappeared down a dark corridor.

"Wait, you took my map too?" said Mirt, as he helplessly rattled the bars of the portcullis. "That's stealing! You did that before you knew a hundred percent for sure that I was going to betray you. So let's admit we were both wrong and put this behind us. Please! These caves are crawling with monsters! I don't even have any torches!"

Sorrowshade shook her head. "Always bring torches." And with that, the gloom elf followed her companions into the shadows.

The sun was setting as Albiorix made it to Pighaven, winded and dripping with sweat. In addition to his usual twenty-seven Homerooms & Hall Passes sourcebooks, he was also carrying all his worldly possessions in his over-stuffed backpack. He stepped into the common room of the Wyvern's Wrist tavern to find it empty.

"Well met, er, how's it going?" said Albiorix to the inn-keeper.

"Mmm," said the innkeeper. "Yesterday a tree fell on my brother."

"Whoa," said Albiorix. "Sorry to hear that."

"Don't be. It were a magic tree," said the innkeeper. "Granted him a wish, it did."

"Oh, nice," said Albiorix. "What did he wish for?"

The innkeeper cocked her head. "That's a very personal question."

"Sorry," said Albiorix. "Anyway, I'd like a room for the night." The wizard plunked a small stack of silver on the bar.

"Your friends are already here, you know," said the inn-keeper.

"They are?" said Albiorix.

"It's Thursday game night, innit?" said the innkeeper.

"I suppose it is," said Albiorix.

In the small back room that was reserved for them, Albiorix found the party rehashing their latest adventure.

"Thromdurr, I cannot believe you struck down three trolls with one swing of your croquet mallet," said Vela.

"Boneshatter II is mightier than its namesake!" said Thromdurr.

"The fact that we didn't solve that puzzle still bugs me," said Devis. "The troubadour statue clearly unlocked some sort of secret door."

"We should have smashed it," said Thromdurr.

"Please," said Vela. "Smashing is literally *never* the solution to a dungeon puzzle."

"Still," said Thromdurr, crossing his arms. "It would have been most satisfying."

"Seconded," said Sorrowshade. "That statue had a smug face."

"Hi, guys," said Albiorix. "Just a guess, but maybe you should have checked beneath the statue."

"Why?" said Vela.

"Well, you were exploring the Caves of Thunderbeard, right?" said Albiorix. "If you rearrange the letters in 'Thunderbeard,' you get 'Under the Bard.'"

The other heroes all threw up their hands or face-palmed as they heard the obvious solution to a puzzle that they'd spent the better part of an hour failing to solve.

"Okay, fine," said Sorrowshade. "You're the smart one again."

"You're also the sweaty one," said Devis. "How did your backpack get even heavier?"

"Well, I put everything I own into it," said Albiorix.

"Oh, no," said Vela, "The Archmage didn't . . ."

"She did," said Albiorix. "True to her word, Velaxis ended my training. As of today, I am no longer an apprentice wizard."

"I am sorry, friend," said Vela.

Sorrowshade put a friendly hand on Albiorix's shoulder. "You know, sometimes life can seem like an unending series of disappointments and pain."

"But?" said Albiorix.

"But what?" said Sorrowshade, confused.

"Well, for what it's worth, I'm not too broken up about it," said Albiorix. "I actually feel pretty good."

"Yeah, no more boring magic practice," said Devis, "Now you've got the time to focus exclusively on dungeon delving!"

"Speaking of which," said Thromdurr, "on our journey back from the Caves of Thunderbeard, we encountered a mysterious traveler all the way from Far Draïz. She told us a story of an ancient tomb beneath the shifting sands that is filled with gold. And presumably monsters to wallop!"

"There is a ship departing from Cloudport in the morning," said Vela. "If we set out tonight, we should be able to make it."

"So what do you say, Magic Man?" said Devis. "You in?"

"I think I'll skip this one," said Albiorix. "Honestly, I don't know if I'm an adventurer either. I'm not sure I feel it in my bones, like the rest of you do."

"Not an adventurer, not a wizard," said Thromdurr. "What then shall you be, Albiorix?"

"I think I'll just be . . . me," said Albiorix.

A momentary hush fell over the group as they stared back at their friend, unsure of how to respond.

"Lame," said Devis.

Everyone burst out laughing, and Albiorix laughed even harder than the rest. And so five brave Bríandalörians (four of them adventurers) spent a warm and companionable evening in the Wyvern's Wrist tavern, reminiscing about their old adventures and even more about their time at J. A. Dewar Middle School. And as the darkness fell on the land and the moon rose high in the sky, Vela the paladin, Thromdurr the barbarian, Devis the thief, and Sorrowshade the assassin bade their friend Albiorix farewell, and set out on the road toward their next adventure.

And Albiorix found himself alone, sitting by a cozy fire in the Wyvern's Wrist tavern. And with a smile he reached into his pack and pulled out his Homerooms & Hall Passes *Hall Master's Guide* and started to read.

acknowledgments

This book would not have been possible without the love and support of so many people.

First and foremost, thank you to my wife, Colleen Duffy, who has always believed in me, no matter what. I'm grateful that my scattershot, borderline illogical approach to a writing career has always made perfect sense to her. Without Colleen, I would not be doing this.

I'd like to thank my agent, Noah Ballard, who first reached out to me years ago after he read something I wrote online about cannibalism and thought, "I'd like to take a chance on this guy." And many thanks, as well, to Holly Frederick and the rest of the team at Curtis Brown.

I'd also like to thank everyone at Balzer + Bray, especially Donna Bray, who was excited about this idea from the jump and worked so hard to make it much better. Thanks to Barry Blankenship for an awesome jacket illustration, Stephen Gilpin for amazing character art, Jordan Saia for his wonderful map designs, Renée Cafiero for topnotch copyediting, and Dana Fritts for a beautiful layout.

A lot of folks rolled a lot of twenty-sided dice with me over the last couple of years, and without returning to the world's greatest role-playing game after a long hiatus, I never would have written this book. A big thank-you to Guy Molinary, Eric Moore, Josh Moore, Eric Hamilton, Bryan Yeary, Matt Pritchard, Chris Mischaikow, Katie Mischaikow, Julian Graham, Nina Ippolito, Hanlon Smith-Dorsey, Ted Rounsaville, Lars Casteen, Geordie Broadwater, Scott Hoffer, Kevin Roe, Will McCutcheon, and Liba Vaynberg.

Thank you to my father, Hugh O'Donnell, and my mother, Suzanna O'Donnell, who taught me that books are important and have always been happy for me, no matter what path I chose. Thanks to my sister, Caitlin O'Donnell—a real-life school-based hero—for her unwavering support. My in-laws, Gary and Anne Duffy, have never hesitated to pitch in whenever I needed help with anything, and I'm so grateful to them for it. And thanks to my stepmother, Teresa O'Donnell, who literally taught me algebra (it finally came in handy, sort of!).

Last of all, I'd like to thank my son, Rudy, and my daughter, Suzanna, for bringing immeasurable joy to my life every single day. Sleep is a fine price to pay for that.

Turn the page for a sneak peek at

Chapter 1

So you think you know Homerooms & Hall Passes, huh? Well, think again, pal, because you don't know diddly-squat about the new and improved Advanced Homerooms & Hall Passes! Think you're ready to kick the greatest fantasy nonadventure game of all time up a notch? Welcome to high school.

—*Excerpt from* The Advanced Hall Master's Guide

❧

FOUR YOUNG ADVENTURERS TRUDGED across a torrid wasteland. The scorching sun seemed to fill the sky above them. All around, shimmering dunes stretched out as far as the eye could see. The only landmarks here were the quickly fading tracks they left in the sand behind them.

"Onward, comrades," said Vela the Valiant, paladin and leader of the band. "We must not lose hope."

"Can't lose what you don't have," said Sorrowshade, the

gloom elf assassin, mopping her brow with a corner of her cloak. "I can admit wearing all black on this quest was a mistake, but Vela, how can you can have on armor in this heat?"

"It is not for a Knight of the Golden Sun to complain," said Vela. "But I will admit, there are some, ah, chafing issues."

"I just sneezed and nothing but dust came out," said Devis, the party's wily thief. "We better find this dungeon soon, because we're completely out of water." He dangled an empty waterskin upside down.

"Bah!" said Thromdurr, the mighty barbarian. "Water is for the weak! If I grow thirsty, I shall slurp the blood of my enemies!"

"Gross," said Sorrowshade as she surveyed the empty horizon. "Also, what enemies? There's nobody here. There's nothing but sand, sand, and more sand."

"We are not lost," said Vela, perhaps a tad too quickly. "Though it took us many months of adventuring, we collected all of the nine Sacred Keys, and we have journeyed to the very heart of the Blazing Barrens. The Sanctum of the Shifting Sands shall reveal itself soon."

"Before or after we die of thirst?" said Devis, plopping down on the hot ground to rest or possibly expire.

"You shall not perish, little friend!" cried Thromdurr. "For I see an enemy full of thirst-quenching blood out yonder!"

"Nope," said Sorrowshade, whose eyes were far keener than those of her human companions. "That's just a pile of sand."

"Ah," said Thromdurr, continuing to search the landscape. "Well, is *that* a fearsome foe, mayhap?"

"No," said Sorrowshade. "That's different sand."

"Curses!" said Thromdurr. "But, wait, surely that dark speck, there, must be an adversary."

"Just a rock," said Sorrowshade. "I truly cannot imagine what it must be like to barely be able to see what's a mile in front of your face—

"Did you say a rock?" asked Vela. "Legend tells of a rock, average in size and ordinary in appearance, that marks the hidden entrance to the sanctum!"

The paladin began to stride, then run, toward the distant speck, and the rest of the party quickly followed. Once Vela reached it—truly as unremarkable a rock as any the adventurers had ever encountered—she counted out forty steps due west and plunged her hand into a tall dune. At first she found nothing. Then a smile spread across her face as she brushed away the sand to reveal a heavy door made of bronze. Sure enough, it had nine keyholes.

"Behold," said Vela. "The Sanctum of the Shifting Sands."

"Well done, paladin!" said Thromdurr, cuffing her on the back. "You have truly—"

"Hold that thought," said Vela. "I just need to jot this down in my Journal of Deeds before I forget." Vela produced a small leather-bound book and a quill pen from her pack. "Located . . . long-lost . . . mythical . . . dungeon," she said as she wrote. Then she signed and dated the entry and got a witness (Sorrowshade) to initial beside it.

"Now then," said Vela. "What were you about to say, Thromdurr?"

"—outdone yourself this time!" said Thromdurr.

"Thank you, comrade," said Vela. "I only hope the Order of the Golden Sun is as impressed."

"Didn't you just earn a new rank from them?" said Sorrowshade. "Do you think another meaningless promotion will somehow distract you from the long, boring slog toward the grave?"

"Hopefully!" said Vela. "And I didn't *just* earn the rank. It's been nine whole weeks since I made Justiciar of Honor and Virtue. I cannot rest on my laurels."

"Bah!" said Thromdurr. "Climbing some imaginary ladder does not a hero make. 'Tis the glory of your exploits themselves that make them worth doing!"

"Personally, I prefer monetary compensation," said Devis. "Speaking of which, let's hit this temple that's supposedly filled with treasure beyond all imagining?" Despite his advanced dehydration, the thief was somehow drooling at the thought of so much gold. "I need to get my hands on that sweet, sweet loot. I hereby officially call dibs on any enchanted daggers, flasks of fleetness, cloaks of covertness, sandals of levitation, rat-summoning flutes, magic war hammers, and/or genie lamps we find."

"Wait," said Thromdurr. "Why should *you* get magic war hammers?"

Devis shrugged. "I dunno. I'm thinking using a war hammer could be my new thing."

"But it is already my old thing!" said Thromdurr. "None can deny that I am the war hammerer of this group!"

"Look," said Devis, "as the bard in my old party always used to say, 'There are no original ideas—'"

"Fine, then!" roared Thromdurr. "I hereby call dibs on all gold we find herein. How does that sound, thief?"

"You can't call dibs on gold," said Devis, shaking his head. "That's absurd. Totally against the spirit of dibs."

"You are inventing the rules of dibs as you go along!" said Thromdurr. "'Tis trickery meant to deceive a simple warrior like me!"

"You're so right," said Devis. "You *are* simple."

"Foolish mortals," said Sorrowshade, "arguing over riches you don't yet possess. Money can't buy happiness. Though, if this dungeon is as loaded as they say, I have always wanted to own my own castle. Somewhere dark,

5

crumbling, preferably haunted. A nice, quiet place to just *brood*."

"I am sure we will find rewards aplenty," said Vela, "But do not forget the true reason we came here: to destroy the ancient evil that resides within."

"Sure, yep, uh-huh, the evil. Hate the evil," said Devis, still daydreaming about mounds of loot. "Ooh, just remembered I also need a cap of invisibility. Somebody write that down."

No one did. Instead, the heroes made their final preparations for the adventure ahead.

"Are we ready, comrades?" said Vela. "Torches?"

"Obviously," said Sorrowshade.

"Rations?" said Vela.

"We're really counting rations?" said Devis, rolling his eyes as he checked his pack. "Ugh. Okay, fine. Yes, we have enough rations."

"And is anyone currently afflicted with any persistent conditions such as temporary blindness, petrification, or magically induced fear?" said Vela.

The others shook their heads.

"Well then," said Vela, "may the Powers of Light guide our way." The paladin turned toward the dungeon entrance.

"Wait," said Thromdurr. "Before we enter in, can you tell us anything of the evil we will face? The elders of the

Sky Bear clan have a saying: 'Knowledge is the deadliest weapon (apart from swords, war hammers, axes, spears, morning stars, and ballistae).'"

Vela shrugged. "No one knows for sure the nature of that which haunts this dungeon. Only that it guards an item of immense power."

"Cha-ching," said Devis.

Sorrowshade dramatically threw up the hood of her cloak. "Perhaps the true evil is the greed that lurks within each of our hearts."

The heroes all looked at one another.

Vela cleared her throat. "No, I suspect it is more likely some sort of extra-large monster that will be difficult for us to defeat."

"Well, we will either vanquish the beast and emerge victorious or die the death of heroes and our names will live on in legend," said Thromdurr. "So I call it a win-win!"

"Into darkness then?" said Sorrowshade.

And so the party of adventurers inserted the Nine Sacred Keys into their Nine Sacred Keyholes to open the great bronze door. And they descended into the fabled Sanctum of the Shifting Sands, a labyrinthine temple of sandstone and glittering lapis lazuli. And there they did face many dangers. They were ambushed by a pack of magically animated jackal-headed statues, and they triggered a devilish trap that filled the room with sand, which was quite thematic. To disarm it, they were forced to decode a tile puzzle written in the hieroglyphics of a long-lost civilization (the solution was "Owl," "Owl," "Viper," "Eyeball," "Owl"). And indeed, they did accumulate much treasure along the way, filling their packs and pockets with coins and gemstones and fine jewelry.

Yet still they pressed on, till they came to a great stone doorway that was guarded by an evil sphinx, who posed a fiendish riddle to any who would pass. And when the party could not solve the riddle (the answer was "Sand"), they were at a bit of an impasse and it was slightly awkward. Even the sphinx seemed a little annoyed with them and gave them a few extra hints, to no avail. So at last they shrugged and simply attacked the creature (who, again, was quite evil!) and defeated it after a harrowing fight.

And here on the threshold, the heroes took a short rest to recuperate from their injuries before exploring further. While Devis power napped and Thromdurr quietly sang an ode to the great Sky Bear while he slathered on more muscle oil, Sorrowshade silently crept toward Vela as the paladin prayed to the Powers of Light.

"Look at this," said Sorrowshade, holding out a scrap of parchment.

"What is it?" said Vela. "A map?"

"No," said Sorrowshade, nodding toward the other two, "and keep your voice down."

Vela held the parchment close to the light of her sputtering torch. It read:

Warm and soft; they love to bound.
Puppies make the world go round.
Little noses, cold and wet—
Puppies are my favorite pet.

"What is this?" said Vela.

"A poem. Some pathetic, starry-eyed naïf must have written it," said Sorrowshade. "It sickens me. Do you like it?"

"I cannot lie," said Vela. "It is a *tad* saccharine. Even for me—"

"*I wrote it!*" hissed Sorrowshade.

The paladin was shocked. "Sorrowshade, I had no idea you had poetical aspirations. Nor a favorite pet. If you had pressed me, I suppose I would have guessed some sort of blind, venomous eel."

"I know," said Sorrowshade. "It's not like me at all. I've been feeling strange lately. Like I don't totally *hate* everything? It's awful."

"Perhaps," said Vela, "you are feeling . . . happy?"

"Ugh," said Sorrowshade. "Like you?"

9

Vela nodded.

"Is there a way to get rid of it?" said Sorrowshade.

"We cannot always control our feelings," said Vela. "Sometimes the best we can do is try to understand them."

"Okay, what you said did irritate me a little," said Sorrowshade. "It's a start."

And the gloom elf spoke no more of the matter. Though Vela did catch her out of the corner of her eye setting the scrap of parchment alight with her torch.

Rested and re-oiled, the adventuring party continued through the great stone doorway to the very heart of the subterranean complex. They came to a sheer ledge with a perilous rope bridge crossing a fathomless pit. Carefully they traversed the chasm, and on the other side they found a semicircular chamber lined with hundreds of sarcophagi—the final resting place of the forgotten paraohs and queens who had built the place.

And there, upon a stone pedestal ahead, stood the prize of the Sanctum of the Shifting Sands: a splendid battle axe, illuminated by a slanting shaft of sunlight from somewhere far above.

Vela's eyes widened. "I *know* this weapon," said the paladin. "It is the Axe of Destiny!"

"Pure mithril with gold inlay and an emerald the size of a goose egg stuck in the pommel," said Devis. "I'd have to consult my magic item price guide, but I'd say it's the Axe of Early Retirement."

"I call dibs on axes!" cried Thromdurr.

"Aw, come *on*," said Devis, throwing his hands up.

But the barbarian was already striding toward the weapon.

"It's clearly an ancient relic of incredible power," said Devis, trotting after him. "So we need to sell it to the highest bidder and split the money!"

"Comrades, we simply cannot barter away such a remarkable weapon," said Vela, who hurried after the other two. "The Axe of Destiny has a higher purpose. According to legend, its wielder can turn the tide of one unwinnable battle. At a critical moment it could stanch the onslaught of evil!"

"Or, and hear me out on this one," said Devis, "each of us could buy a boat."

"As usual, you mortals ignore the obvious," said Sorrowshade, whose keen eyes darted around the chamber as she drew her bow.

"What is that, elf?" said Thromdurr as he grabbed the handle of the axe and pulled.

"Do you truly think we can just waltz in here, grab the priceless artifact, and be on our merry way without facing the ancient evil of the temple?" said Sorrowshade.

11

"Huh?" said Thromdurr, straining with all his might. "Was not the sphinx the evil?"

"It was certainly rude," said Devis. "I mean, if four professional adventurers can't guess your dungeon riddle, maybe it's not their fault. Maybe it's *yours* and you need to rethink—oh." The thief slapped his forehead. "Guys, the answer was 'Sand.'"

"Sand!" said Vela and Thromdurr in unison, slapping their foreheads as well.

And at this moment the Axe of Destiny came free from the pedestal with an audible click.

"Still, all is well that ends well," said Thromdurr. "The axe is ours."

And the barbarian held the battle axe above his head. The weapon gleamed in the shaft of improbable sunlight, and none who saw it could deny that it looked extremely heroic. But Sorrowshade's eyes were elsewhere.

"It's not the end," said the gloom elf, nocking an arrow. "We're just getting started."

The other heroes turned to see that all the sarcophagi lining the walls of the chamber had opened. Each contained a desiccated figure, clad in rotting bandages and royal garb. Their sunken eyes glowed red with hatred for the living. The corpses began to lurch toward the adventurers.

"Mummies!" said Vela. "Don't look them directly in

the eyes. That's how they use their curse power, which they can each do three times a day. To destroy a mummy, you must strike for the heart. Now, Sorrowshade, you strafe left. Devis, you strafe right. I'll press down the middle and attempt to rebuke them with my holy symbol to create an opening for—"

"DIE AGAIN, DUSTY GHOULS!" roared Thromdurr, swinging the Axe of Destiny with both hands and charging forward.

"Thomdurr, no!" cried Vela. "If the Axe of Destiny is wielded in a battle that is *not* unwinnable, it will curse its wielder with certain defeat!"

"Kind of a lot of rules for an axe," said Devis.

"BAH! I COULD BEAT THEM WITH MY BARE HANDS!" bellowed Thromdurr, dropping the axe and unslinging his mighty croquet mallet. "BUT BONESHATTER II WILL BE FASTER!"

And so the four heroes fought a desperate battle against the ancient queens and pharaohs of the Sanctum of the Shifting Sands. Sorrowshade's arrows flew fast, pincushioning their undead foes, while Thromdurr's mallet swatted them down in twos and threes. Devis the thief fought with guile and finesse, while Vela the Valiant called upon the Powers of Light to sear the vile creatures with luminous power from her holy symbol. Yet each time a mummy was defeated, it was only a moment until it rose again to attack with renewed vigor. And as the battle raged on, the heroes found themselves on the defensive, guzzling healing potions, forced to fight enemies they had already beaten.

It was only then that Vela put together that the horrid creatures didn't carry their hearts within their bodies. And while the others kept up the fight, Devis snuck from sarcophagus to sarcophagus, smashing clay jars until he found the particular vessel that held each monarch's dried-out heart. And in this way, one by one, were the mummies truly defeated.

The party was victorious, but the battle had taken its toll. Vela's sword had been broken in the fight, and Sorrowshade had used all but four of her arrows. Thromdurr bled from a dozen wounds, and Devis's pockets were so filled with gold and jewels plundered from the sarcophagi that he could barely move.

"Okay," said the paladin, exhausted from the fighting. "Those mummies must have been the true evil of the Sanctum of the Shifting Sands."

And that was when the giant scorpion appeared.

"Seriously?" said Devis.

A colossal arthropod the size of a horse cart scuttled up from the dark pit they had crossed. In front it had two pincers, big enough to shear a person in half. In the back, it had

a stinger full of deadly poison that could strike at its enemies lightning quick. Worst of all, the monster had blocked
the heroes' only exit from the chamber, back across the rope
bridge.

Vela charged in, wielding her broken sword. A slashing
strike from the scorpion's pincer tore a wicked gash across
her chest, while she barely managed to raise her shield in
time to avoid the deadly stinger. Thromdurr swung his mallet, yet the creature's chitinous shell was as tough as plate
armor and the haft of Boneshatter II snapped. The scorpion
barely seemed to notice. As Devis watched Sorrowshade's
last four arrows ricochet off the monster's hide, he knew his
own daggers would be of little use.

The scorpion danced back, surprisingly agile for a creature its size, still blocking the bridge. In its crude intelligence
it knew the weary heroes' attacks were ineffective and was
content to bide its time and pick them off one by one.

"I am sorry to have led you here," said Vela as she
regrouped with the others. "We cannot win. Nor can we
hope to escape."

"Sounds pretty unwinnable to me," said Devis. "Would
now be a good time to break out the good old Axe of Destiny, or what?"

Vela sighed, uncertain, and picked up the enchanted
weapon, but Thromdurr stopped her.

"Nay," said Thromdurr. "We cannot risk the axe's curse. There is a way to win this fight. Though the price will be great." The barbarian threw down his broken croquet mallet. "Know that I have valued my time with you more than gold or precious salves. Truly, in your own way, each of you has the spirit of a warrior. Tell the same to the wizard Albiorix, if you ever see him again."

"Thromdurr, what are you saying?" cried Vela.

"FOR THE SKY BEAR!" bellowed Thromdurr.

Before anyone could stop him, the barbarian charged toward the giant scorpion. Instantly it snapped a pincher around his chest, pinning him tight. Thromdurr winced as the barbs bit into his flesh, but somehow he kept pressing forward. Though caught in the monster's iron grasp, he used his incredible strength to force the creature backward a single step. Then, two steps. Then three . . .

"Look!" cried Devis. "He's unblocked the bridge."

"The fool is sacrificing himself to save the rest of us," said Sorrowshade.

Tears welled in Vela's eyes. "I cannot leave him here to die!"

"We have to!" cried Devis, who was already emptying his pockets of their burden of treasure as he darted toward the bridge. "Or the rest of us will die too!"